# The
# Maid's Tale

## Book One

# Anne

### by
### Liz Orwin

The cover image is taken from a manuscript of
Boccaccio's Teseida: *Arcita and Palemone Admire Emilia
in Her Garden*. The illustration is c1460

With thanks to J and L for their help and guidance.

_To Jan_

_best wishes_

_Liz_

*Also by Liz Orwin:*

Changes of Apparel Part One: The King's Niece

Changes of Apparel Part Two: The King's Wife

The Painted Man Book One: Edge of the Circle

The Painted Man Book Two: In the White Room

The Painted Man Book Three: Willow Song (Part One)

# Chapter One – Rising Stars

*The City of London – 1461*

'Papa!' Skirts flying, shoes abandoned where they fell from my feet, I shot from the shadows and ran towards the man as fast as my short legs would go.

He turned with the speed and skill of a soldier on alert, squinting into the bright sun. The brown eyes narrowed, swiftly assessing the threat at hand until they focused upon my wild form almost flying across the cobblestones. A smile spread across his rugged, handsome face, while the arms opened wide as he stepped closer. The strong arms caught me, and he swung my little body high into the air. I squealed with delight, my skirts flying higher still. Then down I fell, so fast I feared plummeting to the ground. But no, I was pulled into his chest and held firmly in place.

'Sweeting,' he whispered into the wildness of my hair. 'My littlest sweeting, I am returned at last.'

Though other, fleeting images have lingered in my mind, this is by far the strongest and most revealing one from my formative years. Each time the memory resurfaced, I relived the overwhelming sense of relief as Papa clutched me tight, believing all would be right in the world now my dearest father has returned. There was relief he was not dead, relief I was not alone, and hope that Mama would smile once more.

I snuggled down, the fur of his travelling cloak tickling my cheek. 'Stay, Papa, don' go away.'

He halted in the centre of the stable yard, still holding me close. No thoughts of reprimand were reflected upon his face, despite the dangers I had risked running headlong between armed men and their great horses. Though his men carried out their business around us, my dearest Papa had eyes for no-one but me and his smile was warm as one finger traced a tear on my cheek.

'Alas sweeting, I may have to leave again shortly.' As a sob escaped from my lips, Papa kissed the tip of my nose. 'You know we have a new king, do you not?'

I nodded and he laughed, saying how solemn was my little face so I buried it back in the fur.

'My little Anne.' He stroked my hair with such gentleness, I could scarce feel his hand. 'As you already know, both His Grace's father and mine are dead. These days, I am the king's right-hand man, the one he looks to for guidance and support, so my counsel will be needed for some time to come. He could be a great king, but he is still young and there is much he does not yet know. I hope to be the man to teach him, but that means I must attend the court.'

Though only a small child, I understood Papa was one of England's greatest men. An earl, Richard Neville was a rich and powerful man with wealth beyond many, even perhaps the young king. I was continually reminded how our line was of old blood - noble and royal blood. We were one of the foremost families in England, something I must never forget.

Papa still held me close, his beard scratching my cheek. 'You recall King Edward is Duchess Cecily's son, of course.'

I nodded yet again. Though I could picture almost nothing of this promising young man not yet twenty years old, I recalled his mother with clarity. We had stayed with her while Papa was away fighting with her husband, the great Duke of York. In her magnificent London house upon the shores of the surging river Thames, the duchess cast a terrifying figure, even though she was family. To one so young, her eyes seemed cold and uncaring, her countenance unmoved by anything other than news of her eldest son, though I was oft reminded she had recently been widowed and was still deep in mourning.

Papa was fond of Cecily, declaring her the grandest lady of the land. Yet Mama seemed oblivious to this grandeur, speaking to the duchess as her equal and oft incurring dark looks from the great lady. Isobel whispered it was because Mama did not like to be reminded Cecily had wed a duke and so out-ranked her, even allowing for Mama's proud and ancient origins from the Beauchamp Earls of Warwick. As our stay with the duchess had lengthened, the ice in Mama's eyes became more obvious each time the Lady Cecily spoke. When Mama reminded us to mind our manners, Isobel always whispered how our mother ought to take note of such good advice. I could not agree. The duchess was not unkind, leastways to me; she was simply economical with her words and emotions, a trait I later discovered her youngest son had inherited.

After a terrible battle at Towton in the north, Cecily's son Edward, my father, and a great many Yorkist lords finally triumphed over the Lancastrians. 'Twas a victory long desired after battles and violent disagreements spanning many years and as Papa was wont to remind me, a dissatisfaction that began long before I was even a thought in the angels' minds. Glorious in his triumph, Edward returned to London to claim the throne. Papa stayed in the north for a time, why I know not, though Mama came expressly to tell my sister and me that he had been injured. At the time, I did not understand all that occurred over those months, aware only Mama was constantly on edge and Papa gone from us but, finally, he returned and I forgot all else, consumed with the joy of his smiling face. As he carried me across the ward, I did not notice Mama and Isobel. Only as I was placed upon the ground behind the silken cascade of Mama's skirts, did I notice how far we had walked.

'Richard.' Mama's arms stretched out to Papa.

'Ann.' He smiled, all thought of me vanishing into the blue of the day.

'I feared the worst, Richard, as always.' Mama's voice faltered as her fingers caressed an ugly gash on his cheek that was barely healed.

Papa's fingers touched her lips. 'No tears now, I am returned and the thigh wound is fully recovered. There is no lasting damage and I am quite able to ride as before.'

Only in later years did it occur to me how Papa might have died, alongside so many others on that wintery Palm Sunday. I learned the wound most likely saved his life, for unable to stay in the saddle for long, he was not in the thick of the fighting. Mama could not speak, so glad was she to have him home. I watched from behind her skirts as trembling hands reached out again towards Papa. He clasped them, and pulled her forward into an embrace. So wrapped up in each other were they, it was as though Isobel and I did not exist.

'Weep not, my Lady of Warwick.' Papa's voice was low but his tone was that of a command, even as a child I understood that much. 'All is well, for our star rises higher than ever. It rises into the heavens and will shine bright alongside the sun we have set upon the throne of England.'

The stars cannot be seen when the sun shines. Any fool knew that, even a girl-child as young as I was upon that day. Papa was clever and learned so it surprised me he should say such an ignorant thing. I pulled on his tunic, trying to attract his attention and tell of the error, but Papa did not look down.

Wheedling her way between us, Isobel soon craved Papa's attention, loudly demanding tales of bravery and chivalry, and of battlefield heroes. As Mama took Papa's hand, Isobel the other, I was all but forgotten. At first, I thought it because I had openly defied Mama, racing from her side to surprise my father. She was sorely displeased by my escape, her terse tones demanding my return to her side that instant. I had not done so, side-stepping the horses' great hooves in desperate need to reach my father before his attentions were caught elsewhere. Such open defiance must be paid for, though at the time I prayed Papa's arrival would be enough to gainsay Mama's constant disapproval. But my beloved father had no thought for me, distracted so easily by my mother and sister. It was with great difficulty I suppressed the sobs, causing a pain in my chest but an outburst before so many eyes would secure nothing more than the flat of Mama's hand. Her sharp lessons were well remembered, for I had endured enough in my short life already. Silent and grave, I trailed behind, eyes only for the father I adored. Then, in a heartbeat, Papa turned and his gaze fell upon me. In that moment, the world was made right once more as he smiled upon me. Blinded by the brightness of a father's love, I made no mind of Mama's frown, squealing as I was scooped up into the air for a second time. Before I could blink, I was placed astride my father's shoulders, skirts askew and crumpled, but I cared not. Nor did I care he clasped their hands, for I sat above them all; a queen for the day. I was the smallest and least significant of our family but, in those precious moments, I was a queen nonetheless.

One afternoon, shortly after Papa's return, I stood before my sister as she studied my stained and dishevelled gown. I cannot recall the exact colour of that gown but it was pale, most likely a soft shade of gold, chosen to bring out the coppery highlights of my brown hair. What I do recall was the softness of the cloth, how it floated as I walked and how the calf slippers dyed to match were so finely made it seemed I trod on clouds that day.

Isobel scowled at what she saw. My sister thought as Mama did, that I was wild and untamed and inherently ungrateful. I was nothing of the sort, simply liking to run. I did not just like to run; I loved to run, the wind in my face, grass between my toes and hair trailing out behind like a great cloak. I almost believed I could fly, wanting only that last breath of wind beneath my skirts to lift me high into the blue above. I was a swallow or a swift; small and quick I darted and swooped, no thought for anything or anyone and no need for manners or etiquette. The beautiful gown gave me wings of pale silk. With a chemise of the finest linen beneath, the gown's sheer panels caught the merest breath of air, billowing out from my sides, urging me to run faster still. The lightness of the slippers added to my joy though I soon abandoned them to free my toes as I twirled and leapt, whirled and skipped away under The Lord's bluest of skies.

Still fixated by the blemishes marking my new gown, Isobel truly believed she had the right to scold me. As the flat of her hand stung my cheek, I squealed, protesting loudly and indignantly at such a despicable act. A heartbeat later, I felt the heat of Mama's hand also. She was wroth indeed; having sent servants to

6

scour the gardens and yards only to find me curled up asleep inside a hayloft above the stables. Though often disapproving of my desire to play outdoors, she was not usually so hysterical, berating my actions as though I was a common felon. For reasons unfathomable to a child, that day she was more on edge than usual.

Out of the stables I was dragged, across the yard and up the steps to the house. I hung like a ragdoll between the unforgiving grasp of my mother and sister, sobbing at the unfairness of it all. I did not understand why I could not play on or why they admonished me in so violent a fashion. No one had said I should not go out in my new gown, no one had said I must not play. I only wanted to feel how the fine silk would fly in the breeze. I meant no harm but they did not listen.

'Be still, Anne,' Isobel chided, as our nurse tried to untangle my hair. 'You are in such a state, poor Bessie cannot do her work while you struggle so.'

The nursemaid scraped the comb so close to my scalp I was certain the skin would break open, scored deep by its unforgiving teeth. Isobel watched the nursemaid's every move, a look of approval on her young face. Though I cried and protested at the top of my small voice, it was all to no avail.

'If you did not resist so violently, it might hurt less.' Isobel's tone was so sugar-sweet it served no other purpose than to inflame my sense of injustice. But then, I doubt my perfect sister had ever been subjected to such brutish force from a comb.

Though Bessie nodded at my sister's words, she continued to apply the same force to her task. Wriggling and writhing, most likely I made it worse, but my poor scalp was so sore, I could bear it no longer.

'Oh, be quiet, Anne,' Isobe snapped. 'I am weary of your noise.'

This rebuke was all the more hurtful for the fact my sister was not yet nine years' old, and until the previous summer, had loved nothing more than to shed shoes and stockings and run with me. I sobbed still, unable to understand why my behaviour had caused such concern. Though Bessie had combed out my hair to her satisfaction at long last, I could not still my mouth, screaming as much as my four-and-a-half years would allow. At that moment, Mama appeared in the nursery. At sight of her, I held my arms out for rescue from the pain and unfairness inflicted upon me but, instead, I was bundled up by Bessie and taken through the far doorway. Tears still streaming down my face, I was deposited inside my bedchamber, the door locked and barred from without.

As I cried for a comforting embrace, Mama's voice called though the door. I recall its tone still. It was cold and utterly without feeling. She declared that as I was unable to behave like the lady she expected, I was to not be treated as such and must therefore stay from the feast. I could not watch the salt cellar arrive, see the king wash his hands before all the guests. I could not watch the carvers' magnificent display as they presented dishes to the high table. I could not dine upon swan, nor peacock, nor hot custards or cakes, nor could I see fine ladies dance. I could not see Papa and most certainly could not be presented to our new and glorious king in the rags of my gown. So I remained behind to consider the error of my ways, to pray for my sins while suffering the plain, nursery supper Mama had ordered to be served instead. Alone, without company or refinement of any kind, I was to stay in the duchess' great house till they were all returned from Westminster.

'Twas no matter I could not eat swan, no matter I could not eat peacock. Nor did it matter I would miss the fine ladies' dancing. I cared for none of them. I cared only how Papa would think poorly of me and that I would not see Dickon.

In my heart, I knew Dickon would not care about a ruined gown. He would not care I had lost my fine shoes or ran through rainwater in the yards. He would only laugh and ruffle my hair in the manner of an elder brother. He would call me 'small trouble' and laugh some more. Though not my brother, he was a cousin of sorts, for his mother and my Papa were cousins. In our world, so many were kin to one degree or another it mattered not, leastways until those who arrange such things began to consider where we should wed. But such thoughts did not enter my head, for I was not yet out of the nursery. I had grown up with Dickon, youngest of Duchess Cecily's children and brother to our king. Yet I did not think of him in such a grand manner, for he was my friend and companion oft as our families had gathered together, save for a terrible few weeks after the sacking of Ludlow when the duchess sent her youngest sons away while Edward fought on with my father. My playmate both in joy and in loneliness, Dickon later confided how he had missed Edward quite as much as I missed Papa.

Thanks be to God, he was safely returned also, but I should not see him laugh, shou d not see his kind face light up as he hears tell of my nu sance, all because of a foolish gown. I cared not he was the youngest and least significant brother of the king. I cared only he was kind to me and that I could not see him.

Most likely Papa would not care either. He would frown and look at me sternly, but then his eyebrows would rise and though the words from his mouth might speak severely of decorum and behaviour, his eyes would twinkle. Perhaps he might even lean close and whisper as he is wont to do. 'Sometimes I think you should have been born a boy, Little Sweeting. For certes you have the heart of a boy, the courage of one too.'

I did not respond to Papa's jests of this nature. Something told me there was more than a grain of truth beneath his light-heartedness, especially as Mama had never made a secret of the fact she wished I was a boy. Too often, she declared how different things might have been if I had been born a male-child, too often I saw the disappointment in her eye. Isobel never remarked on the matter either, suggesting she did not care, but I knew she cared. If I had been that boy then she would be of no importance, for as the only son and heir the importance would be all mine. But there were no boys. Two girls only Mama delivered alive, yet more were dead. But not one boy. Blood and pain and heartache in profusion, but not one single baby boy, not even a stillborn. Mama resented that fact. 'Twas always there in her eyes, and especially clear when I behaved like the boy I could never be.

Within my hearing, Papa never mentioned the elusive boys. Yet once, creeping into their private chamber, I overheard him berating Mama for something that had inflamed his displeasure. As he complained, Papa decried the lack of a son. He decried it loudly and unkindly to my mother's face, saying she had failed in the only duty she was charged with on God's earth; providing her husband with an heir. Mama sobbed, saying she could do no more than pray, and perhaps if he remained at home more often a son might be the result. Papa's voice was colder than I have ever heard before as he reminded her they had been wed long enough for many sons to be conceived and born, and what was the point of fighting so hard to keep and add to an inheritance, only for it to be divided between grasping sons-in-law.

The incident of the gown was soon forgotten – at least by Papa. He was always busy, spending much time at Westminster with the young king. Mama oft attended him there, when she was summoned and, occasionally, when she was not. Sometimes, Isobel and I were allowed to accompany her and so I did not miss out on seeing Papa, the finery of court, or thanks be to God, Dickon's company. On occasions, our handsome new king beckoned to Mama and ourselves, to join his table upon the dais. As the adults discussed the business of the country, I often crept away to find a more interesting entertainment. Isobel never joined me, pretending to be a lady grown by making eyes at the king's other brother, George. Though still only a child herself, she thought him as fair and handsome as his older brother. When I said otherwise, she slapped my face and called me a foolish babe. Yet I had no liking for George, the dogs did not trust him so neither did I.

Dickon was different. Quiet and thoughtful, it was as though he knew his voice would never be heard and so did not waste his efforts. Often, he would creep away with me to sit under the longest table, where we would feed the king's hounds treats they ought not to have had. The hounds loved us for it and we laughed together at such mischief, knowing it likely one or another would later regurgitate its gains within the king's chamber, or may God forgive us, upon his great bed.

Like me, Dickon was the younger child. Like me, he had little or no importance in his family and likewise, understood this completely. In silent allegiance we defied our elders and betters, seeking a place in the world where we might be content, and undisturbed by those deciding what was best for us.

Some weeks later, after I had been chastised by Mama for yet another misdemeanour I can no longer recall, we were taken to the court and, before a great many visitors, presented to His Grace, King Edward. As he looked upon me, the king remarked upon my solemn face, asking if I was frightened of him. I said nothing, more frightened of Mama's swift hand than this handsome, smiling man. As the silence stretched on, the king seemed bemused by my reticence and so took me upon his knee. Determined not to be found wanting again that day, I meekly obliged as he fawned and petted me. Once settled upon the royal lap, he whispered in my ear that he knew of my friendship with Dickon and he had a secret only to be revealed if I smiled. As Mama had taught, I did as bidden and gave the king a wide smile, eager to hear of my dearest friend. The king was delighted by my reaction, his blue eyes bright as he announced to all around that when we departed the court, Dickon would accompany us north to be educated in Papa's household. Murmurs filled the great chamber as the court discussed such a reveal.

I slipped from the king's lap, running to Papa to thank him. Papa was smiling, clearly pleased with such an arrangement, though as I thought on it later, he must have known of the scheme beforehand. Bending down to me, he whispered how I ought to thank His Grace for such a kindness. So that is what I did.

Turning back to the dais and with the solemn expression upon my little face once more, I curtseyed to the king, thanking him most graciously for allowing his brother to come into our home. The fair Edward smiled his most beautiful smile, declaring how easily I was pleased, unlike most other noble ladies he had come across. Perhaps he meant no harm, perhaps my childish manners amused him, but as those around laughed long and loud, Edward did not chide them for such disrespect. I curtseyed once more, the lords and fine ladies still tittering amongst themselves, and turned back to Papa. I was proud of my bravery, relishing the king's kindness, but as I resumed my seat at the table, the eyes Mama turned upon me were pure ice.

'He may never speak to you again,' she hissed. 'I saw what you did not, I saw Dickon's face. You have made a fool of him before the court. Indeed, you have made fools of us all.'

I made to speak, protest my innocence and good intentions but all I incurred was the wrath of Mama. The slap of her hand was sharp upon my thigh, her countenance severe.

'Silence, Anne. Your actions were wholly inappropriate, more like a kitchen maid grateful for a coin than a great lady born.'

'But Dickon is pleased he is to come to us,' I protested, braving more censure.

Mama leaned down level with my face. Spittle landed on my cheek as she spat the words. 'And so he should be. Though the king does us a great honour, 'tis no more than we deserve. Remember who we are, child. We do not grovel before the court, displaying gratitude for whatever crumbs are cast our way!'

As I balked at such sharp words, Mama took a deep breath as though she had said more than she ought. 'Dickon understands his position is to do as bid, and says naught of it when elders and betters decide upon his behalf. Be silent child, and behave as you ought.'

She made it sound as though Dickon knew there was no choice about being a ward of the great Earl of Warwick, and though it pleased him not, he had manners enough to stay quiet.

Though I looked around the hall, Dickon was nowhere to be seen. As soon as I could, I made excuses and left the table. Avoiding Mama and Isobel, I searched the great hall but she was right; Dickon had gone. I cried all that night.

Eyes still swollen and my heart heavy, the next morn we prepared to depart the duchess' great house. I had not grasped our departure would be so soon. Frantic, I sobbed and cried that I could not bear to leave awhile. Mama was beyond impatient, too preoccupied ensuring everything was packed and despatched to be bothered with my small troubles. Desperate to see Dickon, I ran from room to room, succeeding only in getting in the way of stewards, servants and Mama. Her patience quite worn out, she ordered I was to be confined to the solar and remain there till it was time to depart. For two long hours I sat in the great window seat, eyes fixed upon the comings and goings in the courtyard below, desperate only to make amends for my faux-pas before the court.

Only when Mama came to fetch me away did Isobel announce she saw Dickon ride out with Papa just after dawn. I was heartbroken to think my friend had ridden away so early without a farewell. That my sister had known and kept the knowledge to herself rubbed salt into an already raw wound. Sullen and unwilling, I had to be dragged into the carriage, incurring yet more disdain from my mother and sister. Huddled in one corner of the carriage clutching a grubby, tear-stained kerchief, I steadfastly refused to look up or speak as we began our journey. Isobel soon gave up trying to coax me to peek out and watch the world go by. Mama said nothing, her disapproval as icy as the silence.

After a long, unhappy day, we arrived at our lodgings. Only as we descended from the carriage did I notice our party included another. Dickon. He had ridden alongside throughout, joining us as we pulled away from the duchess's great house. In my foolishness, I had stubbornly refused to peer out and, in doing so, missed seeing my dearest friend. After such a discovery, I could not cease glancing up in his direction. Each time I dared to peek through my lashes, his dark blue eyes flicked towards me. Once, as our eyes met, he gave a fleeting smile. In that moment all was right in the world and I forgot the miserable company I had been forced to endure, warmed by thoughts this quiet, dark-haired lad was to become part of our family.

# Chapter Two – Secrets

*Middleham Castle - 1462*

Once we had returned to my father's castle, nestled deep in the moorland of Wensleydale in the county of York, our lives settled into a comfortable routine. Many hours were given over to our education and training. Dickon and my father's other wards spent much time in the schoolroom with their tutor, learning Latin and French, practising their script with quill and ink or reading texts selected especially to educate young men of good birth. The priest often joined them to discuss matters of theology, and to widen their knowledge of Scripture far beyond the responses required in chapel and confession. In time, the boys also learned of statecraft, for as sons of noble families they would undoubtedly be required to lead men in keeping the king's peace upon their lands.

Out in the tilt-yard, the boys were placed under the strict supervision of a small number of men-at-arms, carefully selected by my father for their patience and prowess with weapons and horses. All young men learned to fight: to wield a sword, ride and be competent in combat. Out in the yards, the boys worked diligently at these lessons, for the earlier a lad began to train for combat, the more practised and accomplished he became. This was of the utmost importance, for one day his life may depend upon such skills. Whenever time allowed, I crept out to watch the practise, hiding in the shadows or around a secluded corner, wincing and stifling gasps as the swords clashed together, for I was fearful my only true friend in this world would be hurt.

Upon a fine spring day, a few months or so after Dickon joined our family, Isobel discovered my secret. On an errand for Mama, she spied me hiding in a niche beside the stones steps up to the keep. It took her a moment or two to understand why I was there but, once my sweet sister understood, she took great delight in declaring to my friend how I watched over him like an aging nurse-maid. Betraying my confidence further, she revealed before all the boys, how I prayed out loud each night for The Lord to keep Dickon safe from their thrusts and swings. How she laughed at my secrets, indeed, how they all laughed. Isobel especially, revelled in my misery, declaring I was a simpleton for not knowing how they practised with swords of wood. Shamefaced, I fled from the scrutiny, embarrassed to be exposed before the person who mattered most to me. For hours, I hid out in the stables, safe in a private space in the hayloft while my hot cheeks cooled, praying Dickon would not also think me foolish.

'Tis true The Lord works in mysterious ways. When Dickon learned I was missing after Isobel's spite and name-calling, he walked straight from the schoolroom to seek me out, risking the wrath of the tutor as well as my father. Though he said nothing to those frantically scouring the bailey and outer ward, it seemed Dickon knew exactly where I was hid, climbing up into my haven with the stealth of a cat. Appearing beside my forlorn figure, he simply sat, saying nothing for some time.

'You do not need to hide,' he said at last.

I could not face him, could not turn my eyes towards his, so deep was my shame.

'Little friend.' He stroked my matted hair, teasing stands of hay from the unruly plaits. 'I am concerned for your welfare. 'Tis long past dinnertime and you have eaten naught this day.'

My face still hidden in the crook of my arm, I murmured something about never speaking to me again after learning I was a fool.

'Anne,' Dickon's tone changed. 'Sit up and face me.'

I did as bidden, only to see sadness in his dark eyes. As I lowered my gaze, ready to plunge back into the sweetness of the hay, he grasped my arm, keeping me upright.

'Your sister is the fool, not you.' He looked deep into my eyes. 'How little she esteems the virtues of loyalty or friendship.'

I must have frowned at his words, for I do not recall speaking. He gave a soft laugh. 'Ah, little Anne, do not be ashamed. If only there were more in the world with your devotion and steadfastness. I consider the virtue of loyalty one to be especially admired.'

'Are we still friends?' My voice was a whisper.

Dickon gave a lop-sided grin. 'Always.'

Though what I desired most to hear at that moment, his answer troubled me somewhat. He meant well, I am sure, but Dickon had no more control over our futures than I did. No child upon God's earth controlled what their elders might decide was best.

We stayed nestled in the hayloft for some time, oblivious to the passing of the afternoon and the demands of our elders. As the sun traversed the sky, shooting golden beams through breaks in the roof tiles, we discovered the nest of a queen cat. Her kittens were so newly-born their eyes had not yet opened. We watched in awe as they suckled and slept, their perfect but tiny bodies breathing in unison. At last, Dickon turned to me. In that quiet way of his I had grown to know, he expressed gratitude I should be so concerned for his safety, explaining how swords used for the youngest boys, though wooden, were still wielded with great force and could easily bruise or knock a boy out if used incorrectly. I recall how he laughed; not at me, but at those who expected young boys to use real weapons, wryly observing how the nobility would have much to say if their offspring were returned lacking a limb or two. He thanked me again for such deep concern and spoke of how he took pains to ensure he did not suffer the ignominy of bruising by a wooden sword. Most importantly, he declared he did not think me a fool. That night, I thanked God for such a kind and thoughtful friend, though I took care to say the words inside my head, for fear Isobel would hear.

My sister and I were taught by Mama, and a governess. Our lessons encompassed all a lady of good breeding ought to know. From manners and courtesies, reading and scripture, we learned much. We learned to speak fluent French, sing and play an instrument, how to welcome guests and ensure their comfort, select dishes to be served to the lord and his guests, employ household servants and keep discipline therein. We learned to embroider, sew, and a thousand other duties to recommend us to the husbands we would one day have.

Secured in both his father's and mother's inheritances alongside that of Mama's, Papa was now a man of title and great property, and the premier earl of the land both in position and power, eclipsing even his own father's achievements. We were taught of this lineage, to recall it in detail and not forget from whence we came. This was a most important part of our education and preparation for marriage, and we were reminded often how our point and purpose was to continue these noble bloodlines. On top of all this, we were drilled continually in how to behave, in all ways that might please our husbands and recommend us to The Lord above. There was little time left over for frivolity or mischief, but still I found a moment or two to think on my friendship with Dickon, for I could not imagine my world without him.

Though we knew not at the time, these were the best of days. We were young and had no real cares in this world, save to learn our lessons and please our elders. Dickon and I were the least significant of our families and had no burdens or great expectations placed upon us. Though most of the day I saw little of Dickon and his companions, we would all come together to pray, to eat, to read and, on rare occasions, be in company so Papa could show off his family and his wards. Though Dickon and I might not be able to speak, there was always a connection between us, an unseen link. It may have taken the form of a glance, a knowing look, or a single spoken word. Almost always, we seemed to know what the other thought, what the other needed or lacked. At times, we said nothing, simply sharing a space and a moment of solitude, but it was enough, for that link was always there, binding us together in ways no one else understood.

Over the next twelvemonth, Papa was oft away. Despite our return to Middleham, for my father to keep the king's peace in the north, small uprisings still occurred with frightening frequency. Papa and his men dutifully put down these risings on behalf of King Edward, our glorious cousin. Papa revelled in his position, riding off again just a few months later to negotiate a truce with the Scots on behalf of our bright, young king. Mama always worried for Papa's safety, oft times taking to her bed while he was absent, yet our days continued with the same strict routine with no thought given to our concerns. Though Isobel and I might also have worried for Papa's safety, our lessons came above all else. We must be taught, and taught well, for all too soon we would be grown and other demands made of us.

Despite the interruptions, sprinkled with fear of more local disturbances, our world was settled and content. We may have bemoaned the time devoted to study and duty but, in truth, our lives were comfortable and secure. Though we knew our places and did as bidden, there was always the hope adventure might pierce the monotony of everyday life. I recall with clarity the rare, golden moments when Dickon and I pretended we were alone. These moments were when we found ourselves apart from my father's other wards, including Francis, a lad Dickon had taken especial liking to, away from Isobel, away from Mama's watchful eyes and, it seemed to us then, away from the rest of the world. Such times were few indeed, but all the more precious to us for that. Perhaps as we lingered over a single move on the chess board, or rode up onto the moors to hawk, keeping as much distance as we could from the rest of the party. Other times, we tended to our horses in the stables after a ride, nary a word said between us but solace taken in the company of a friend nearby. On rare occasions, we crept up to the hayloft to seek out the newest litter of kittens, or dared furtive glances under the nose of the priest while singing Mass.

As summer waned and autumn chills pervaded, word was received of the deposed queen; Margaret D'Anjou. A party of French troops under her orders had landed farther north, taking Alnwick and Bamburgh castles. Papa was needed again and so he and the men rode to the north-eastern coast, facing a bitter winter and an irate Frenchwoman. Christmas was a dull affair that year, illuminated only by Dickon's brother George coming to join us at Middleham. Isobel was delighted, while Dickon and I accepted George's arrival as one would a sour stomach. We knew how George would dominate our conversations, talk endlessly about the intricacies of court or, how, with witty retorts, he had bested those beside the king. We knew he would strut around the solar, showing off his fine new clothes, while changing the rules of our childish games to ensure he won. He would pay constant and obsequious attention to Mama, pouring nauseating compliments upon her and her household, while a besotted Isobel hung upon his every word. Dickon and I readied ourselves to sit beneath tables once more, the company of the dogs preferable to the attention-seeking peacock George was turning into.

I cannot recall when I first knew I loved Dickon. Perhaps that day he sought me out in the hayloft, perhaps long before that as we had fed the king's hounds beneath the tables of Westminster. It mattered not. Young as I was at that time, just six years of age, I did not truly understand the depths of my feelings, only that Dickon was as dear to me as my own family – and I could not imagine a life without him. Whether Dickon felt anything akin to my emotions, I knew not. Nor would it have occurred to me to ask such a thing, yet the connection between us existed, for we were oft drawn together in solace, but also in comfort and good cheer. Dickon was everything to me and, during that Christmastide, we danced beneath boughs of ivy and holly to the delight of my father returning victorious upon Twelfth Night. I thought such days would never end.

'Come, sweeting.' Papa held out his arms to me. I ran as always, clutching at his torso as though I had not seen him in days. He held me out at arms' length.

'We are to head south.' He smiled, as though this pleased him greatly. I planted a wet kiss upon his cheek, delighted to see him so happy.

'To see the king?' I asked.

He smiled again, lifting me up and into his arms. 'Perhaps, but there is also a task I must undertake. It is something dear to me and so we shall travel south together.'

As his face creased, I sensed it was not a good thing. 'What must you do, Papa? Do not leave us again so soon . . . '

'Ah, sweeting, I shall not leave you unless the king decrees I must.' He looked past me, far into the room. 'Though I shall be parted from you for a day or two while re-interring my family's remains.'

'What is that?'

Isobel's icy laughter sounded behind. 'Still such a simpleton, Anne, do you not know?'

Papa lowered me to the floor, crouching down to look into my face. I tried to ignore the fact he took Isobel's hand as well as mine. 'Your grandfather and uncle died in battle at a place named Wakefield, some three years ago. The country was still at war so they were buried with haste and not in the place they should have been interred.'

I nodded. 'Wakefield was where Dickon's father was also killed.'

Brown eyes looked deep into my face as though he had not expected a child to know such a thing. 'Indeed, the duke was killed there also, God rest his soul, but my concerns lie with my own kin this day, not His Grace's. Long have I desired my father and brother to rest at Bisham Priory, beside our ancestors, and now I shall see it done.'

'Will Dickon's father be re-buried there too?'

Once more, Isobel's laughter rang through the chamber but Papa did not react, his eyes still gazing upon my face. 'Alas no, this place and ceremony is for our family, not Dickon's, though King Edward might decide upon moving his father's remains one day in the future. Indeed, as he now has the means to do so, perhaps my efforts will encourage such a move.'

I was tuned into Papa's moods and expressions even at such a tender age. Having watched him at the chess board so often, I had learned to observe his expression before his move. Perhaps I did this unconsciously but, later, I often watched his eyes for the smallest of clues to his thoughts. At this moment, his expression was one of triumph, arrogance even. It was as though he delighted in a move not considered by others. But all I could understand, all that mattered to me was the fact Dickon would not be staying with us. I would have to endure my mother and sister's company until we returned home.

On a drab February day, Papa duly laid his father and brother to rest with their ancestors. Isobel and I did not attend, left with our governess till the formalities were done. When the winds blew in the month of March, we continued our journey south, travelling the short distance into London so Papa could attend Parliament and, of course, the court and King Edward. I recalled little of that time, miserable without my friend and confidante, sent on to Westminster to stay with his brother, the king. But all too soon our pleasure came to an end. The north rose up in rebellion once more. Sir Ralph Percy, previously pardoned for his involvement in a rebellion, was besieging Norham Castle as we lazed in the south. Furious, my father set off north to resolve the situation, leaving us behind in the city of London – and Dickon at the court.

Papa was much occupied at this time and had not the time to travel back south to join us. Mama insisted our lessons continued without interruption each day and so little intruded upon our world at this time, it seemed life was passing us by. Few came to call, no excursions were arranged and we could not have lived more quietly if we had stayed in a convent. Our only excitement was when a messenger brought word from Papa. Mama would retire to read his words in private, no matter what time of day, nor what instruction her departure interrupted. These letters were always intriguingly long though Mama would only read brief parts out loud to Isobel and me despite our demands for more. Though I understood little or nothing of his business, 'twas enough to learn he was safe, engaging in negotiations with France and Scotland. I did not truly understand what was occurring in the north of the kingdom and perhaps that was just as well. Later, I heard over thirty rebel leaders had been executed as a result of Papa's success retaking the Northumbrian castles. Thirty children or more, no doubt many of ages akin to Isobel and me, had learned their fathers were traitors and would not be returning home.

Mama decided we should not stay in London to suffer the heat of summer. Making our way into the midlands, we halted at the great castle at Warwick, where the ancient seat of her family nestled in a bend of the River Avon. Though we enjoyed the sumptuous comfort of Mama's inheritance, I cared not for its vastness, wanting only to be back in the more intimate arms of Middleham. Day after day I prayed to the Lord above that we should leave, asking also Dickon be returned north. Summer passed slowly in this comfortable loneliness but, at long last, the harvest was brought in and stubble burned in the fields. Swifts darted on the evening air, while the languid river turned golden under the late summer sun, yet the Lord still had not heard my prayers. Isobel and Mama were content enough, the castle providing many cool rooms to while away the hot hours. I could not settle, wandering from tower to hall to chamber all the day, dreaming of a reunion with my dearest friend. Judging by the dark looks she flashed my way, Mama thought me ungrateful or disturbed, her barbed comments souring already miserable days.

As summer waned and trees glowed russet and gold, we took to the road at last, traversing the country before winter rains rendered the roads impassable. Once more confined to a carriage, I kept quiet throughout our journey. Mama declared I must be sickening for something, but I was concealing delight to be returning to the place I regarded as home.

Drawing near at last, Middleham's keep rising high above the grey walls and cluster of cottages, my heart began to pound. Though I had listened with care to Mama reading snippets of letters from Papa, I could not discover if Dickon was returned. He could still be at Westminster for all I knew but I prayed hard he might be in the castle's ward as we entered, the dark head snapping round at the sound of our carriage, a grin spreading across his face. Indeed, I imagined the scene so often over those final yards, I was ill prepared for disappointment.

'Lady Anne?' a voice called, as I whirled around and around, searching for my friend. A sandy-haired lad about eleven years of age stood before me. 'Whatever ails you?'

Dizzy from the sudden stop, I did not answer, my eyes flicking over the face before me. The boy frowned; his kind, open face crumpling more with each passing moment.

'Francis,' I asked. 'Is he not yet returned?'

Francis's eyes lit up with understanding. 'No, my Lady, he is not.'

Tears blurred everything. As laughter pierced the afternoon air, 'twas only then did I realise there was an audience; the other wards of my father, as well as a number of the stable lads. And in these past moments they had been reminded of my devotion to Dickon.

I fled up the steps to the great keep, my little heart pounding after this public unveiling. Francis called after me but I had no desire to speak to anyone. Convinced Dickon would not wish to return once he heard of this incident, I fled to my bedchamber. There I stayed. That night was long indeed, made worse by Isobel's teasing as she lay beside me, relentlessly returning to the subject of my infatuation with Dickon. After such exposure, my misery ran deep.

Next morning, I refused to leave my bedchamber, refused to break my fast and even refused to attend chapel. Mama lost all patience. Taking a slipper to my bare thighs, she hissed that if I wished to be so melancholy and difficult, she would provide sufficient reason. Sending me into the private chapel off the bedchamber in the great keep, I was ordered to stay upon my knees begging forgiveness for my sins until she decreed otherwise.

The candles had burned down so far, their flames came from deep within the holder. Though I did not know exactly how much time that measured, it felt like the best part of a day. My knees burned, cramp seized up my thighs but I tried not to move, certain Mama watched silently from behind. The priest had come and gone a dozen times, humming his approval of my mother's treatment of an errant seven-year-old child. I had hoped he might defy his countess's orders and allow me to rise, but he was my mother's priest and as dedicated to her service as he was to Our Father. So I bowed my head and prayed for forgiveness, prayed for patience, and begged the lord for guidance, but remained before the altar, fearful Mama would consider it not enough. My bladder was fit to burst and my stomach growled with hunger so loudly, I feared chastisement for that alone. As tears streaked my cheeks, a hand came to rest upon my shoulder and a voice spoke low in my ear.

'I asked your lady mother for permission to bring this,' Dickon said. 'After a while, she agreed.'

My poor heart almost stopped beating but I could not run round, could not look up. A sound like a plate scraping the floor tiles grated upon my ears but still I could not look.

'Dickon,' I croaked.

'Here, little friend, I am here.' His hand cradled mine, still clamped tight in prayer. 'Though returned for several weeks now, I had only ridden up onto the moors and am sorry I was not here to greet you. When you did not appear for supper last night, Isobel said you had taken ill, but that does not seem to be the truth of it.'

Perhaps Isobel was right about my being a simpleton for I knew in an instant why Francis called out as I fled. I could not bear to look at Dickon, how thoughtless and ungrateful I must have seemed to him. But then I remembered how I had been unmasked, how they had laughed at my devotion to the boy beside me now. Hiding my face inside my hands, I dare not look up.

'Enough now.' His tone was impatient, or at least as impatient as Dickon ever became. 'You must eat something, Anne.'

I turned. There beside me, kneeling upon the tiles was my one true friend. As our eyes met, he gave a broad grin. Though still disbelieving this was real, life returned to me with such ferocity I burst into laughter. Dickon laughed too, though not quite so raucously.

'Come,' he ordered. 'You ought not to break your fast before the altar. Move out into the chamber.'

'But Mama . . .' I feared her wrath still.

Dickon retrieved the plate. 'She is at last convinced you have spent sufficient time in prayer.'

Though I wondered how much convincing it had taken, I dared not question, happy only to be free of penance. We fled into the chamber, but I could not walk far, collapsing onto a chair at the long table. My poor legs and feet tingled most painfully as the blood rushed back.

While I leaned upon the table, regaining strength enough to visit the garde-robe, my friend's eyes did not leave my face. I was glad to be able to rise and walk the short distance to the corner of the room, drawing the curtain of the garde-robe behind me. Though I had no desire to leave my friend's company, the call of nature was sorely needed. Moreover, his kind attentions had only served to accentuate the faults that had caused me to be in such circumstance in the first place. After, as I resumed the seat beside him, silence hung thick between us but I did not mind it, content to be near my dearest companion. When the quiet became too much, I broke it by protesting at the pile of food set before me. It was to no avail, for Dickon insisted I clear the plate, murmuring how I needed someone to take care of me. How right he was.

'I heard what was said out in the ward.' His voice was low and quiet, the dark blue eyes watching each mouthful I took.

No words came in my mind to answer him, so I stared at the table, wishing I was elsewhere and Dickon did not have to witness my shame.

'I care not what they say of me,' he murmured next, as if fully aware of my discomfort. 'Though it grieves me they think it appropriate to laugh at you.'

As I dared a glance, Dickon grinned. 'It does not matter what they say, Anne, I like that you and I are friends, I like that we share confidences. I even like the way you look for me when you think no one is watching.'

My deepest secrets unveiled. But in that moment I did not care about that, either. The only person who mattered liked my attentions. I breathed in deep and gave a smile.

'That's better, little friend.' He grinned again. 'But we must face your lady mother lest she thinks we are up to no good.'

As we entered the solar, Mama studied me. In her look there was disdain, impatience, even fury, but not one shred of compassion.

'So,' she said. 'You are done at prayer.'

Head bowed, I murmured, 'Yes, Mama.'

'Let us have no more of this nonsense. With your father away so often, I do not have time for disobedience, Anne. Duty to the family and to God is all that is asked of you, why do you find it so difficult to comply?'

In truth, I did not find it difficult. I loved my family and I was as devout and respectful to The Lord above as a seven-year-old could ever be. I glanced up at Mama. Pale blue eyes stared back, reminding me of winter ice. Her words held even less warmth.

'You know what is expected from a child of mine, I should not have to remind you again and again.' She waved a hand in dismissal and I turned to leave, Dickon walking behind me. As we reached the door, Mama's chill tones sounded out once more.

"Tis a poor show when one employs others to plead clemency on their behalf. You are to leave Dickon alone from now on. Indeed, I have instructed him to keep away lest you become a nuisance. Away to your lessons child, for you are sore in need of occupation.'

Lips clamped tight, I left the solar. Tears blurred my eyes, my throat burned with the injustice dished out and my heart was heavy at the thought Dickon had been warned away from my company. At the stairwell, we parted in silence. A hundred words of thanks for his kindness and care filled my mind but after Mama's reproach, I dared not speak them out loud. I stood in the doorway, shadowed by the sun, watching my dear friend make his way back out to the tilt-yard and away from me. About to turn and make for the schoolroom, I stole one last glance at the figure across the yard. At that moment he turned, eyes scanning the doorway for any sign of me. I darted around the door jamb, waving with both hands, my smile wide, yet tears still streaming down my cheeks. He stopped, giving a mock-salute and a grin as wide as the sky.  At that moment I cared not if Mama watched.  I cared not if I must spend the next week upon my knees; Dickon was still my dearest friend in the world.

# Chapter Three – Parting of the Ways

## 1464

'Your move.' Francis had the patience of a saint, repeating it three times over before Dickon acknowledged him.

One hand lingering over the chess-board, Dickon hesitated further before grasping the rook. Through the stillness and heat of a late summer eve, my intake of breath was so loud, Francis scowled. I sent an apologetic look his way but neither boy took any notice. As they lingered over what should have been a simple move, I headed back towards the settle where Isobel complained of boredom. I loved a game of chess, loved it even more when Dickon had the time to play with me but, as always in our world, the menfolk took precedence and while not unwelcome at their table, my advice was not needed in this game.

I yawned. 'Why does Mama not join us tonight?'

Isobel shrugged. 'When Papa's letter arrived earlier, it seems he wrote of something that had made him wroth. She was upset by it and has retired.'

So Mama had taken to her bed. While that in itself was not unusual, I refused to let it worry me, convinced this was a matter between adults.

'I daresay we shall discover what ails Papa in due course.'

Isobel gave a shriek of laughter. 'You may discover it but I shall not. If he is as wroth as I suspect, we had best keep out of his way when he returns.'

It had never occurred to my sister how a kind word might soothe much ill. She preferred to ignore anything that did not suit her mood, and now it seemed that would apply to our father too.

Little notice was taken as a servant entered the solar, our small party engaged in chess or idling beside the open window, awaiting a cooler breeze. Only as Dickon followed the servant out, did I realise this was an unusual occurrence.

'Where does Dickon go?' I called over to Francis.

Francis shrugged, staring at his defeated chess pieces. 'He did not say.'

'Was he summoned?' I could not let the matter drop, despite the sighs from my sister.

'I believe so.' Francis was so reluctant in his response, I suspected he knew full well where Dickon was bound.

Time dragged by and the candles burned low but neither Mama nor Dickon appeared. When at last the door opened, I was so lost in thought its distinctive creak did not distract.

'Anne.' My mother's shrill tones pierced the silence. 'It is long past time for bed. Be gone this instant.'

I rose, studying her face for clues as I passed but her visage was a stone carving.

'Goodnight Mama.'

'Goodnight, child.' Her voice was soft, her mind far away, dwelling on distant thoughts. 'Sleep well and may Our Lady of Heaven watch over you.'

Though I kept walking, the fact Mama had wished such a graceful and polite goodnight had not passed me by. She was much distracted and I feared to learn why. As I stepped on up to my bedchamber, my mind filled with concerns for Papa, something moved a few steps ahead. I had not thought to bring a candle, the night itself clear and moonlit, but now I wished I had.  Fearful what lay in wait, I halted, pressing my small form flat against the cool stones of the wall.  I heard nothing more so dared a peek around the corner. As a shaft of pale moonlight shot through a high window, there sat Dickon, hunched up on the step to my chamber.  I cried out, unable to imagine what had forced him to seek me out in such manner.

As I approached he rose, mottled by shadow and silver from the moonbeam. 'I ought not to be here, Anne, but had to speak with you.'

'Why?' My mind flooded with a hundred terrible reasons why he would deem this necessary.

'I leave at first light.'

'No!'

Dickon's hand flew over my mouth. 'Hush. I risk your mother's wrath if discovered here.'

I fell down onto the step he had occupied but moments before. 'I do not understand.'

'Nor I.' Lowering himself down beside me, Dickon clasped my hand. 'However, your mother thinks it best if I am gone before your father's return.'

I turned to face him, drinking in the weary countenance and troubled expression.  My voice was scarcely more than a whisper. 'What in God's name has happened?'

'My beloved brother.'

'I still do not understand, Dickon . . . '

He stared down at his boots, still dusty from the day's exertions. 'My brother, the king, has done something no one expected.'

I could not answer, seeing the unhappy expression upon my friend's face.  As yet, I was unable to grasp the fact Dickon was leaving.  At that moment, it did not seem real.

'As you already know, your father has been much engaged in negotiations with the French over the last months.' His tone was as dark as the night around us.

I was ignorant of that, but then I did not truly know what Papa did while away from us, only it was upon 'the king's business'. Certainly, the snippets Mama read from his letters gave no clue to my father's employment, only that he missed us and yearned to be home.

'Is there to be a war?' I cried, fearing the worst.

He gave a snort. 'Perhaps, but only between your father and my brother.'

Still I could not grasp the severity of what had occurred. 'What in the name of Our Lady is this about?'

'A marriage,' Dickon spat. 'A marriage that should not be and yet it is. Your father is beyond angry, believing my brother has made a fool of him.'

In whispers, Dickon explained how some months back, while cultivating friendship with the French, my father had taken it upon himself to suggest a marriage between King Edward and Bona of Savoy, daughter of the Duke of Savoy, and sister to the wife of King Louis of France. King Edward, though vague about such matters, had left my father with the impression he was amenable to such an arrangement. Though I knew little of my father's business, I had gleaned enough from Mama's comments to know Papa was conducting far more intimate correspondence with King Louis than many, including His Grace, King Edward, were aware of. Yet it was not so surprising King Edward should need a wife of good family, a wife that would secure alliances and trade agreements, so to learn the lady in question was so close to the throne of France came as no shock. What Dickon revealed next, shook us both.

Upon Mayday of this year, King Edward had taken to wife a certain Elizabeth Grey, widow of a known Lancastrian supporter, Sir John Grey of Groby. Sir John having died at the battle of St Albans early in 1461, Elizabeth was left with two young sons and a husband's family that refused to support her. Throwing herself upon the mercy of the young king as he rode through woods near her home, he was enraptured by her beauty and bravery. After a failed seduction whereby she declared she would rather die than become his whore, Edward wed the widow in secret, only to reveal this marriage at the great council meeting at Reading where my father had so recently gone, brimming with optimism for the future.

I could not respond to Dickon, with little understanding and even fewer words to describe the emotions running through my mind. I oved Papa, loved him with all my heart and could not believe he would do anything to hurt me, yet it seemed Dickon and I were to suffer for the failings of our respective families.

'Your father is wroth indeed.' Dickon did not look at me. 'He wrote to your mother, venting his fury to her alone. However she considered it in my interests to learn of his disappointment and I confess I was less than polite in my responses, believing what unkind words were said of my brother's conduct to be false. At that point I had not opened the letter your father sent to me. When I did, I saw your mother spoke true, and while the letter I received was not quite so angry, it was cold, utterly without the care or consideration he has shown me these last months. I was left in no doubt he believes Edward's faults are mine also.'

The space between us widened at that moment. If I had not known better I should have thought my dearest friend in the world sat yards apart from me. He did not. He sat beside me, our sleeves touching still.

'Your father has rather directly suggested I might like to visit Edward for a time.' Dickon gave a high-pitched laugh. 'I took that to mean he wants me out of the way lest he vents his frustration in ways he might later regret. In this I am in agreement, and so depart on the morrow.'

'When will you return?' I whimpered, scarcely able to breathe.

He stroked my cheek. 'Little friend, I cannot say. Spring perhaps, at the earliest.'

I whimpered again, unable to take in this news. Dickon clasped my small hand between his. 'This is not how I wish it to be, Anne, but I have no choice. My brother has made a decision your father does not agree with and I will not stay here to endure his ill-will on Edward's behalf.'

'What can we do?'

Dickon did not look at me. 'Nothing can be done and therein lies the difficulty for us all. Despite the clandestine circumstances, it appears Edward and Elizabeth were wed before God and will remain so until death do them part.'

There was no consolation to be found and though I tried to say something, the few words I did attempt caught in my throat. Even I understood marriage was a serious business, one all families of the country gave great thought to. For a king to take it upon himself to choose a bride who brought nothing in terms of dowry, lands or trade agreements was exceptional indeed. And though Dickon could not voice it, I sensed he understood my father's anger far more than his brother's recklessness. But it mattered not, for the outcome was still the same. Our fates had been decided by others and we could do nothing to alter that fact. We could only live with the consequences.

I do not recall climbing into bed on that unhappy night. I do not recall falling asleep. All I recall is awaking the next morn with a stone for a heart. Before my sore, swollen eyes had even opened, I felt a great heaviness in my chest, a weight pressing down upon me. As events of the evening before flooded back into my mind, tears flowed once more as I knew Dickon was long gone.

Papa's fury ran deep indeed. Though he said little enough of it to Isobel and me, we were acutely aware of his unhappiness. The whole castle was aware. Everyone still went about their business as before, but they did so upon tip-toes, walking as if the world was made from egg-shells and could shatter at any moment. Though my dear father did not vent his anger out loud, or in violent terms, the threat he might do so hung over us all like a great thunder cloud. Fearful of her husband's silence, Mama spoke in soft, hushed tones and though her words were no less harsh than usual, she delivered them in a tone of ice.

Despite this fragility within the world we knew, our lives continued much as before. Isobel and I still attended our lessons, attended Mass in the chapel, read to Mama and pretended all was well and as it should be. Papa's wards still practised in the tilt-yard, worked at their studies, attended Mass also and occasionally joined us for an evening's entertainment and diversion. But there was now a hole within our family; a deep, dark chasm the departure of my dearest friend had left. Nothing filled that hole and, as time passed, it was as if a ghost stood in the space where Dickon should have been. My young heart ached for my friend, for his company, for his laughter and the confidences I could never exchange with another. I kept my thoughts deep inside, unwilling to allow Mama or Isobel to spy my weakness, but Dickon's absence bored through my soul.

One evening, some while after, Francis glanced my way across the chess board. Boredom affected us all and as we attempted to play, it became clear he still thought of Dickon and the games we had all shared. For the first time, I saw I was not alone in grief. Though Francis could never have filled that hole, could never know the deepest workings of my mind, we drew together in silent comfort, mourning the absence of one we both held dear. Often in those dark days, as Mama read an excerpt from my father's letter, the Priest sang a certain phrase at Mass, or simply over the chess board, Francis and I were united for a brief moment, thinking of the friend whose company we missed.

For months we continued in this strained manner. My Uncle John was a knight of the garter, and had recently been created Earl of Northumberland, a title that had belonged to the now-disgraced Percy family. Here in the north, the power of Nevilles still held sway, and my father continued to conduct the king's business, pretending all was as it should be. Yet his eyes revealed the fury of that secret wedding, still simmering deep below the surface. When he was at home, I watched him as I would when playing tables or chess. It oft seemed as though he was uncertain what move to make next, as though his head was filled with possibilities, but none pleased him enough to commit his hand.

As Christmas came and went and a new year dawned, Dickon remained at court. The pain of his absence had not lessened, indeed, at that time I believe it grew more with each passing day. I could not even write to my friend, could not ask how he fared, or how his lessons progressed. His name was no longer spoken amongst my family and so I heard nothing, learned nothing of his new life - until Twelfth Night. As celebrations continued into the evening, with musicians playing beneath the holly boughs draped around the castle hall, the yuletide log burning in the grate, a magnificent feast with many courses served to our guests, and diverse entertainments presented by minstrels, guisers and players from York brought across the country for our pleasure, Francis sought me out.

'Anne, come with me.'

I did not question, following as though Dickon himself had summoned me. My mother would have scolded me soundly, for I ought to do no such thing, but deep inside I knew Dickon trusted Francis, therefore so would I. Creeping up to the solar, my heart pounding, I still did not question why I followed like a lamb.

Settling into a corner of the darkened room, Francis' voice was soft in the gloom. 'He has written to me.'

No name was spoken but there was little need. Francis would not seek me out unless he had been instructed to. My heart leapt a hundred feet. 'Pray, what did he have to say?'

'That his health is good, and he is content. He attends Edward some of the time, continues with his lessons at others.'

Fearful of the answer, I dared not ask the one question I yearned to ask. Instead, I sought safety in more innocuous enquiries. 'Did he send news from court?'

'He did.' Francis' tone suggested he held back. I struggled to do so too, clamping my lips together. I must wait till the lad offered the news, not jump in like an eager hound at the kill.

After what felt like an hour, Francis whispered, 'He has written of the queen, how he has met her and that she is with child, due to be born in but a few weeks' time.'

'Is she as beautiful as they say?' I had oft heard the way people spoke of Elizabeth Wydville. Yet thereto, had I heard the disdain in Mama's voice as she spoke of this impoverished Lancastrian widow, a woman far older than her husband.

'He does not say.'

'Then what did he say, Francis?'

'He spoke of the grandeur of court, of the high regard in which his brother is held, but he also spoke of growing frustration with his brother George, and how he misses the moors.'

I cared nothing for George. I cared not that Dickon missed the moors, for that I already knew. Anyone living away from this wild, desolate and beautiful place would only ever yearn to be back here. My first and real concern was if there was more he missed.

'Did he say anything else?'

'He did not.' Francis' slow, measured tone ceased and silence hung in the air for several moments. As I clutched at my poor distraught heart, he announced in a brighter tone, 'But he did enclose something for you in his letter.'

I gasped, turning my head towards a lad I could barely see in the dark. Praying with all my might, Dickon had sent a letter for me, I was unprepared for the fingers that sought mine in the night.

'He sent this with the express wish I place it direct inside your hand.'

Inside my palm now sat something small, sharp and warm. I could not ascertain what it might be, despite rolling it over and over in my fingers.

'What is this?' I was confused how Dickon imagined I should like this strange artefact.

Francis shuffled closer, clasping my hand inside his. 'As you know, Dickon was made Duke of Gloucester by the king some time back . . . '

King Edward had invested both his brothers in dukedoms shortly after the victory at Towton. The news had made little impression upon me at the time but the gleam in Papa's eye as he noted the brothers were now the foremost unwed men in the land, I recalled well.

'Dickon has also chosen a device by which his men may be identified. He has sent one to you, saying he understands how much you value loyalty, and hopes you might recall your friendship with him from time to time.'

'I think of him each day.'

Francis' hand enclosed mine once more. 'I am aware, Anne, I see the pain in your face every time we meet.'

So there it was; my soul laid bare before the friend of my friend. I said nothing as his hand tightened around mine.

'I miss him too. There is no one else who shares my trust like Dickon.'

My head dropped onto Francis' shoulder and we sat in this manner for some time, a small metal pin in the shape of a boar clutched in my hand.

For me, the year began with some small measure of hope. Dickon still thought of me, still remembered me. Though the days hung heavy and our lessons became increasingly burdensome, beneath my gown I wore a tiny silvered pin in the shape of a boar, as close to my heart as I could fasten it.

As so often repeated in our lessons, my family were of great renown and heritage and we were ordered never to forget it. While Papa's father had been Earl of Salisbury through his wife, Alice, my grandfather was also descended from the Earl of Westmorland and from the Beauforts through his mother, Joan. Papa's brother, John Neville, had been created Lord Montagu as reward for services to the House of York. George, another of Papa's brothers, made progress worthy of note in the church. My paternal aunts had all married into dukedoms or earldoms or ancient families of great renown. We were the foremost family in the land – save that of the Duchess of York.

My extended family came together later that year when our Uncle George was enthroned in an Archbishopric. As the late summer sun shone warm and golden, we made the short journey across country to Cawood Castle, the ancient palace of the Archbishops of York. Papa had spent many weeks organising the celebration, proud that his brother should be enthroned in such a prominent position. With the naivety of the child I still was, I revelled in his enjoyment, believing all was right in the world and Papa and the king were no longer at odds. Certainly, on the few occasions of late Papa had been at Middleham, his manner and countenance had been all it once was. He stepped out with the brisk pace of a man with much to do but one who did so with goodwill, excitement even. Mama was a little less remote, both in his company and with Isobel and me. Indeed, one day as I sat in a window seat sewing quietly, she came over to inspect my work. Much to my surprise, she expressed astonishment at the fine quality of my stitching as though she had no idea her youngest had become so accomplished. I tucked away that kerchief, vowing never to use it, for I relished a day when I had pleased my mother. That I pleased her in such a small and insignificant way mattered not at all.

As we journeyed to Cawood, my stomach churned so violently, I could scarcely sit still inside our carriage. Mama had unwittingly revealed the name of one of the guests to attend this sumptuous feast. Dickon. My dearest friend in the world was coming and I should see him once again. I had not dared count out the weeks of loneliness endured since his hasty departure, for it would only have caused distress, instead I looked forward to our reunion at such a joyous occasion. Francis joined us also, for he would one day become a part of the illustrious Neville family, betrothed to Papa's niece, Ann, daughter of my paternal aunt, Alice Neville, wife to Baron Fitzhugh. Since discovering Dickon was to attend the feast, I had not had time or opportunity to speak with Francis but I had every intention of doing so. Even if I could not speak directly to Dickon, which was quite likely given the illustrious guest-list, Francis would be more accessible and I needed him to remind Dickon of my enduring affection and loyalty.

The feast at Cawood was like nothing else I had attended in my short life. Even those I had seen at Westminster seemed a homely fire-side supper in comparison. I could not breathe for wonderment upon entering the great hall. Long tables were laid out, each seating more people than I could count as we walked through. Hall and tables were decorated lavishly, banners embossed with the Neville arms dripped from the roof-trusses while as many servants as guests stood by ready to wait upon us, all dressed in the colours of our house. It was with astonishment I learned this was not the only sitting to be waited upon, for so many had been invited, great numbers were forced wait their turn to celebrate my uncle's achievement.

'Anne, look!' Isobel hissed, as we stepped on through the hall.

Though I scanned each side of the lavish room, I had no idea to what she referred. As I murmured as much, she laughed, decrying me for a half-wit. I confessed to a certain pleasure when Mama pinched Isobel's arm to silence her. We stepped on, past yet more carefully laid tables. At the far end of the hall sat one lavishly-dressed table, high upon a dais. For one brief moment, I thought it was there we were bound but, as if she heard my thoughts, Mama noted with a hint of sourness how we were to be seated close to the high table, but were not joining Papa, my uncle and other guests of note.

As I whirled around to ask why, something caught my eye. There he was, standing beside Isobel, his dark eyes gazing at her smiling face as they greeted. I gasped, but could not speak, drinking in the sight of my dearest friend. But this was not the Dickon who had said a sorrowful farewell to me that night in the stairwell; this was a different Dickon, one I no longer knew. He was taller than when we had last been in company, not a great deal taller, for Dickon would never reach Edward's great height, but he had grown nonetheless. Always slender and fine-boned, I noticed how he had broadened across the shoulders, though the finely-cut tunic he wore may have exaggerated his form. But Francis had spoken of how fervently my dearest friend still practised in the tilt-yard, so no doubt such efforts had enhanced his figure. All I could see was how he had changed, grown in far more ways than I had imagined as I pictured him in my mind. More refined in both attire and manners, he barely resembled the lad I had known at Middleham.

My eyes dropped, my breathing became erratic. In my heart I feared he had forgotten me, transfixed by the pretty face of my sister. She was almost the same age as Dickon and owned a body blossoming with womanhood. Attaining the great age of ten was still a long way off for me, while at thirteen and fourteen, Isobel and Dickon were unlikely to acknowledge the child in their midst.

Shown to our places, I sat beside Mama. Answering her enquiries with brevity, I could take no comfort in the splendour for there was none in this place. As Mama bore the indignity of being left off the high table, Isobel kept Dickon engrossed in deep and animated conversation, while I sank deeper into misery.

Later referred to as the 'Great Feast of Cawood', I had no taste for any of its fineries. Many, many dishes were served, each more lavish than the one before, but I cannot recall what I ate, nor what those beside me ate. Every thought I had, every breath I took, was dark and bitter. Dickon had no time for me, could not bring himself to bestow a word of greeting upon an old friend.

'Anne.' Mama's terse tone cut through my melancholy.

I stared at the plate before me, unable to touch another morsel after the countless numbers already served.

'Picking over your food as though it suits you not, what ails you, child?'

I felt her gaze upon me but I did not look up. 'I feel unwell, Mama.'

The sigh she gave, though quiet, was filled with contempt. 'Your father has spent a great deal of time and more money than you can count in honouring your uncle. We have already spoken about how you must taste only a tiny amount of each dish and not fill yourself too soon. I am disappointed, Anne, as will your father be.'

My head hung over the plate as I said nothing. Mama's admonishment continued, till tears escaped, splashing onto the untouched food.

As she saw this, Mama sighed once more. 'Very well, return to our chambers and we shall speak of this later. I will not allow an ungrateful girl to ruin my enjoyment of this splendid day.'

She beckoned to a servant, ordering him to fetch one of our ladies. As she turned back to the table, I lifted my head. Both Isobel and Dickon were staring at me.

'There is no need to delay, Lady Ann,' Dickon's voice was shades deeper than I recalled. 'I shall escort Anne back to your lodgings.'

Mama's eyes blazed. 'And have my husband see one of his most honoured guests depart the feast early? I think not!'

Dickon rose from his seat. ''Tis no inconvenience, Madame, I assure you. I intend returning to the feast directly.'

'That may be so, but I cannot allow an ungrateful, foolish girl to be the cause of you missing the sugared delicacies. They are sure to be served soon and my husband was most insistent they be to your liking, for he remembers you are partial to the subtleties.'

Dickon sat down. He inclined his head to Mama but gave no other response. Mama folded her hands in her lap, clearly pleased with herself. Only now did I dare to look properly upon my friend To my eternal joy, Dickon looked directly at me, the dark blue eyes scanning my unhappy face. Though his features were leaner, the cheekbones more defined and the plumpness of a younger boy long gone, this was still the face I saw as I closed my eyes. The hair was longer, neatly trimmed, and still retaining the hint of auburn I had liked so well. Yet none of this mattered. All that mattered was that Dickon had noticed me, and tried to take care of me despite Mama's efforts.

As I walked from the hall, escorted by one of Mama's ladies, I reached beneath my gown, searching for that small silvered pin, caressing it as though it was a talisman. But lying upon my bed, with only the faint tapping of rain upon the window panes for company, the talisman served as little more than a reminder of what had been so easily abandoned in the great hall. My regret deepened when I learned we were to depart the next morn, leaving Papa behind to continue entertaining the numerous guests. Though I tried, I could not escape Mama or Isobel and it was with a heavy heart I climbed back into the carriage. I had not exchanged a single word with Dickon and nor was I likely to, but I would not cry, would not allow my family to see my unhappiness for I sensed they would relish such misery.

The day after, as we returned to Middleham, my heart was still heavy and wearisome. I had wantonly squandered the only chance to speak to Dickon. Only The Lord knew how long it might be before I had word from him again. We were excused lessons that day, for our governess was ailing after the journey. Mama too, had retired to her chamber with a headache, so Isobel and I were left in idleness.

While my sister lounged upon the settle gorging upon comfits, I sought solace of a different kind. Climbing into the sweet sanctuary of the hayloft, my peace was disturbed as Francis sought me out. Though I protested at the intrusion, he hushed me down, saying how he had tried to speak with me before we left Cawood, but to no avail. At mention of that place, I ceased all contestation, staring open-mouthed at the friend of my friend.

'I was charged with delivering a message.' He twisted strands of hay through his fingers but did not look at me as he spoke. 'I tried, Anne, but you would not come to the window.'

My thoughts drifted away on a sea of regret. 'It did not rain that day did it, Francis?'

''Twas a fine afternoon.' Francis spoke low and quiet. 'Handful after handful of gravel I threw at your window but you did not hear.'

'The message . . .' my voice cracked as I fought the tears.

As Francis took my hand, I was overwhelmed with the sense he was not about to impart good tidings. I braced, aware I should be brave but unable to find strength to do so.

'Dickon sent his good wishes, and hoped you recovered swiftly. I believe he intended to speak with you himself, but events decreed otherwise.'

Though not what I had expected to hear, Francis' words deepened my regrets.

'I should not have left so soon!' I wailed.

'Perhaps it was as well you did.' Francis watched, almost waiting for my head to jerk up. 'Dickon was not happy with what he observed – but be assured his discontent had nothing to do with you, sweet girl.'

'Whatever do you mean?'

He looked away. 'You must speak of this to no one, especially your Mama or sister. Do you understand?'

I did not, but the desperation to learn of Dickon's displeasure ran deeper, urging on my curiosity. So instead, I gave assurances to take the secret to my grave.

Francis grimaced. 'Your father is not recommending himself to the king, it seems. Though deserving of a magnificent celebration, the feast far exceeded your uncle's due. And as it was much remarked upon amongst the guests, no doubt such comments will find their way to the royal ears.'

'Papa said becoming an archbishop deserved a great celebration, he wanted to give Uncle one to remember.' Father's reassuring tones sounded in my head.

'That is not in dispute,' Francis still kept his voice low. 'No one begrudges your uncle a fine celebration, for as Archbishop he is worthy of one, but to display such obvious excess? None but an anointed king should preside over the grandeur shown at Cawood Castle.'

These were hardly the words of a thirteen-year-old boy, even I knew that. 'You make it sound as though Papa has displeased someone.'

Francis twisted a handful of hay around his fist. 'It was mooted how your father was trying to remind Edward how powerful and influential the Nevilles truly are, especially here in the north, so far from Westminster . . . '

Most certainly not the words of Francis – or of the Dickon I knew. Something about this matter did not seem right. By celebrating my uncle's enthronement in outlandish splendour, Papa had reminded the world just how important was our family. Such an obvious and impertinent declaration could only invite trouble.

'Dickon was polite and gracious to my mother and Isobel. Indeed, he seemed genuinely pleased to see them,' I protested. 'Moreover, our friend would never harbour such unkind and suspicious thoughts for it is not in his nature . . . '

'If he was asked to take particular note of the event, he might.' Francis suggested.

I gasped. Though desperate to disagree, everything Francis said made sense, especially regarding the king wanting first-hand reports. And there was no one better to provide such a report than the king's own brother.

'Are . . . are you suggesting Dickon was sent to spy upon Papa?'

Francis did not look up. 'Not exactly. What I am trying to say is Edward wanted an honest view of proceedings by someone who is discreet - and loyal to the crown beyond question.'

Dickon would have relayed exactly what he saw at Cawood. And relayed exactly how it appeared to him, without embellishment or malice, for it was not in him to add such unnecessary ingredients. Always direct, Dickon's words would be few – but well considered. No doubt Edward knew his brother intimately and, with the wisdom of his greater age used to advantage, did not allow Dickon equal knowledge. The king would draw his conclusions from Dickon's report relying upon the fact it was the absolute and unadulterated truth.

It was as though I had been doused with cold water, such was the shiver that ran through my limbs. Though I had not thought nor words to describe my emotions, I was gripped by a fear so strong it was as if the world, at least my world, teetered on edge of a cliff.

'Ah, Anne, do not look so downcast. I did not come to make you unhappy, I came to bring tidings that Dickon hopes you are in good health, and is sorry he was unable to speak with you.'

Forcing a smile, I gave assurances of contentment that Dickon still thought of me with affection, but inside it was as though I had lost something precious, as though something dear had been wrenched from me though I knew not what it was. These dark sentiments stayed with me for some days, to the extent my dear Mama noticed and remarked upon it till I was forced to brighten my visage and feign all was well. But the world was ailing, and my young and unformed mind could not comprehend why this should be.

# Chapter Four – The Lonely Child

## 1466

Our lives continued, uneventful and unfulfilled. To the best of my knowledge, I committed no grave sins before God, save growing resentment for my sister's spite, disdain for my mother's remoteness and worry for my father, much absent from our home.

At this time, I was taught how Papa still served the pleasure of our most gracious king, continuing to do his bidding and keep his peace throughout the land, though often I knew naught of his whereabouts. If Papa kept up his discreet correspondence with the King of France, I knew naught of it. If he found his responsibilities for King Edward irksome and not to his liking, I knew naught of that too. Indeed, what child truly knows the heart and mind of a parent? Strangers to us, we are not destined to know their innermost thoughts, for it is not in our interests to do so, nor indeed, do they think it necessary to consult our opinion. Until the coming of age, we are not allowed to have an opinion. Indeed, there are many wives upon God's earth, grown and delivered of babes a-plenty, who are still not allowed an opinion.

It mattered not what I thought of King Henry's unexpected capture by the Yorkists. It mattered not what I thought of his imprisonment in The Tower, though Papa had the dubious honour of escorting the poor, enfeebled Henry there. It mattered not I listened in to Mama relishing that Henry's queen was now dependent upon the charity and caprice of the French king and in poor circumstance indeed. Nor did it matter Isobel kept Mama's secrets like a miser hoarding coins. The least of our family, it seemed I mattered not at all.

Month after month passed by, another Christmas came, as did another turning of the year. As another winter turned to spring, a maid sat alone, caressing a token she was given once by one dear to her.

'Anne, why do you sit out here? 'Tis not a pleasant place in this bitter wind.' Isobel screwed up her face as she surveyed my seat upon the battlements.

'The day is fine and I find the view clears my mind.' The day was fine indeed; 'twas late March and the sun warmed my cheek like a lover's hand. At least, I yearned for the hand of a particular friend upon my cheek, as I looked upon the rolling hills beyond Middleham castle.

She laughed. 'Pray, what fills your foolish mind so much it needs to be cleared?'

'Thoughts.' I cared little for her tone.

'Of what?'

I had no desire to continue this conversation. My sister and I had little enough in common, I did not care to pretend to a friendship. 'What is it you want, Isobel?'

She looked into across the rolling country surrounding Middleham, fixing her gaze upon two circling hawks some way distant. 'I want nothing from you, Anne, save a little respect. However, our lady mother desires you attend her directly.'

'Why?' I cared not my manners were lacking.

'How should I know that? She does not disclose all her mind to me.'

'She discloses a great deal more to you.'

Isobel sniffed. 'But I am the elder, and almost a woman. It is only to be expected she should disclose more to a woman than to a child.'

This conversation was not what I had expected it to be. 'Pray what do you mean, 'a woman'? You are fourteen, Isobel. That is not yet a woman – because you are not wed.'

She laughed again. 'I have been a full woman these last six months and so am ready to be wed. Did Mama not tell you?'

I turned and looked deep into the hills beyond. 'Why should she tell me of such matters? I am but a child of ten.'

Laughing once more, Isobel stood before me, blocking my line of vision. 'Mama will have spoken of the journey awaiting your body. She must have readied you for the gift you will receive in time, and the fruit you may one day bear because of it.'

I had indeed been made ready for the next step in life. And it terrified me.

Mama informed me we were to leave Middleham forthwith, so I should pack whatever personal effects I wished to take. It seemed she had grown bored of the moors and yearned for different comfort. With Papa away so frequently, it was decided Warwick Castle would better suit our needs. I did not understand this decision, especially as many of Papa's wards had left in recent weeks, returned to their families, sent on to further their education, or like Francis, to reside with the family of his new bride. As we would be a small family party, moving to the great castle at Warwick seemed wholly unnecessary to me, but my position was not to question and so I did as told.

I missed Francis. Not so much for his company, though he was unfailingly kind to me and we always found some diverse entertainment to pass the hours, but because of his connection to Dickon. While my dearest friend did not write directly to me, there was always a kind word, an enquiry, or even a small token enclosed for me inside the correspondence Francis received. Now, I should have no further word of Dickon, though I held to the hope Francis might write from time to time. But with a wife demanding his attention, I doubted he would think of me.

There was some small comfort to be found in that Papa had secured my cousin as bride for Francis. The young viscount was now husband to Anne Fitzhugh, a daughter of Papa's younger sister, Alice. The Lady Alice was an aunt I held dear; for she took trouble to speak with me whenever we met and I enjoyed her lively and diverting company. Moreover, at least I might still see Francis occasionally, for Aunt Alice and Papa were close and many a saint-day feast or family gathering had been brightened by the presence of the Fitzhugh family.

Now though, I must pack my paltry treasures before the journey south with Mama and Isobel. This pleased me not, for I had no love for Warwick. Though the place of my birth, it was vast and cold – in atmosphere, not in temperature, for it was luxuriously furnished. Yet the castle put me so much in mind of Mama's moods, I came to wonder if its air was the reason she behaved in the cool and aloof manner she did. But go I must, for I could not stay upon the moors alone, as much as I might wish to. Inside my head a small voice suggested Papa wanted us at Warwick, not because it was in the centre of the country and easier to communicate with, but because its grandeur far better suited his mind-set. As I thought on this, Francis' words about demonstrations of power echoed loudly.

And so in the cool comfort of Warwick we stayed for many months. Mama and Isobel settled quickly into its splendour, as though this was where they had desired to be all along. I could find no solace inside its deep stone walls, for though nearer to my dearest friend at the court, the grand rooms and halls held no memory of him.

Papa had been long gone, across to the Continent conducting negotiations with the French and Burgundians. Mama spoke many times of how she was so proud of Papa, trusted enough to oversee negotiations centred round a marriage for King Edward's sister, Margaret. So loudly and frequently did Mama speak of the matter, it began to seem as though she hoped to convince all of Papa's continuing loyalty.

'Why do you not ask of your father?' Mama demanded as I joined her for supper one evening.

Unprepared for such a question, I balked, mindlessly staring at the brightly-coloured tapestries as though I wished I was elsewhere. I could not disclose the truth for she would be hurt and insulted. I missed Papa, I missed his fond attentions. I missed how he looked at me; a direct, intense gaze only he possessed, that left me feeling I was the one person in the room who mattered. And whether he meant it or not, I missed being told how much he had missed me.

Mama's eyes narrowed as she waited for a response. 'Speak up, child. Anyone would think you care nothing for his achievements and status!'

'It . . . it pleases me to hear he sits so high in the king's favour.'

'Does it truly please you?' she peered at me, the pale blue eyes still cold. 'You show little enough interest.'

'Of course, Mama, why should I not care about Papa?'

She leaned back, nestling into a mountain of silken cushions alongside her on the settle. 'Yet you no longer ask of him. Once upon a time, every time your mouth opened it was to demand news of when Papa returned. Nowadays, you make no effort to ask. Why should that be, I wonder?'

Once upon a time I would have crumpled under the withering gaze but, on this day, I stood tall, though where I found the strength I knew not. 'You read from his letters so often, Mama, speak of his business so often, I have no need to enquire.'

She did not appear convinced, asking in a low voice, 'I presume you understand the concept of loyalty, Anne?'

How could I not? Loyalty was the very thing that kept a smile upon my face when my heart was heavy and all seemed lost. Loyalty drove me on through the long hours of my life, hoping each new dawn brought me nearer to a day when I might share confidences with my dear friend once more. Loyalty tied me to him, kept memories of him alive in my mind and, above all, gave me hope. Loyalty was something I understood more deeply than Mama knew.

'Good,' she scowled. 'For you might soon need to draw on that loyalty.'

'Why, what has happened?' I dreaded what news she might impart next.

'It seems your father has been made a fool of once again.' Mama's voice was as cold as a December day. 'His Grace, King Edward, continues to make decisions without proper counsel.'

She gave a high-pitched laugh. 'I should correct that, perhaps. King Edward no longer seeks your father's counsel, having so many offering advice while your father is absent from court. He is utterly unable to counteract their schemes and 'tis no wonder my husband believes the king behaves in this way deliberately.'

'I do not understand, Mama.' The feeling of cold water running down my body returned and I shivered though the sun shone through the window with all the warmth of an early autumn day.

'Though your father favours a marriage between the king's sister and French nobility close to the throne, others have differing views.' She pursed her lips as though the next words would sour her mouth. 'It seems the king listens to those who have been at court for mere months. He takes note of those whose birth is nothing. The great and noble families of England are rapidly being polluted and diluted by a filth that also affects the king's mind!'

I said nothing, watching the banshee before me, her eyes wild with fury. 'Mama, what is this?'

'My clever husband has worked tirelessly to befriend the cunning King Louis, and so, of course, benefit England. He nursed hopes the Lady Margaret's marriage would also benefit this realm, keeping diplomatic relations with France cordial, but now . . . ' she spat the final words, unable to continue her tirade.

There was nothing I could say to calm her, nor would I have dared. I had witnessed Mama in this state before and she was best left, allowing her fury to burn away. I cast my eyes downward, waiting until she deigned to inform me what grievous slight had inflamed her ire.

'Edward . . .' she continued, without any proper address of our king. '*Edward* has already reached an agreement with the Burgundians. Unknowing of this, your father has brought King Louis' ambassadors back from France. Edward has wilfully shown such lack of interest, he risks insulting the French. In the midst of all of this, your father is forced to continue negotiations, knowing them to be as hollow as a rotten log.'

Rising from the table, Mama paced the solar with such determination I hoped she had forgotten I was even there.

'Not only that,' her voice rose higher still. 'Edward has taken the Great Seal from your uncle.'

She made it sound as though the king had no right to do such a thing.

'Why would that be?' My voice was barely a whisper.

Mama did not answer directly, staring across the room, her thoughts far away. 'Edward even went in person to take it from your uncle, citing your father's obstruction of royal plans as the reason. The situation is absurd and insulting, yet all the while, he cannot see what distraction sits before him, cannot see he is being manipulated.'

In this state of feverish agitation, Mama could be volatile. I stayed silent and kept well back from her hands.

'The Great Seal was given to your uncle after the battle of Northampton, presented to him for safe keeping. How dare Edward then take it back in so rude a fashion!'

I was motionless, praying she calmed down, praying Isobel would come into the solar, anything to take her mind off this matter. The Great Seal of the Realm was an important artefact, used quite literally to symbolize the king's approval of important state documents. Bigger than a man's hand, it was a mould into which wax was poured and set, attaching the king's seal to the document by a cord or ribbon, thus approving said document. I had held it once. Papa had it in his possession, I know not why, but he showed to it Isobel and me, a broad smile upon his face as he did so. As I recalled the brightness of his eyes that day, I was filled with sadness, for Mama's words did not sing of trust and comradeship betwixt my family and the king.

'As if all this did not insult our family enough, there is worse to come.' Eyes wide and bright, my mother shrieked the words.

Silent I stayed, head bowed as if in playing a childish game of if I could not see Mama then she could not see me. But she did, venting her fury as though these matters were all of my doing.

'Edward has also refused to wed his brother, George, to Isobel.'

That I did not know. Raising my head a little, I saw the visage my mother wore was dark indeed, one to instil fear in the most steadfast. I dropped my gaze, wishing to be anywhere but here.

'How dare he refuse the only match in the land worthy of my daughter. She is the offspring of noble houses, of bloodlines ancient and renowned, yet we are ignored and insulted at every turn.' Mama paced the floor while I remained motionless and, I prayed, invisible. 'This is all her doing. That wretched enchantress influences Edward's every move and thought these days. We had such high hopes for him, such great aspirations . . . but more and more our efforts come to naught.'

At last I understood some of what had occurred. There was a name Mama spoke only when she had no choice. A name Papa had also come to despise, a name that was close to the king and smothering him - Wydville.

After admitting to a secret marriage, King Edward had soon married off the heirs of the noblest families to his wife's many sisters, the heiresses of the land to Wydville sons. Many nobles complained how the finest bloodlines of England had not escaped the Wydville offsprings. I had heard my parents discussing this matter on several occasions, made furious as much by the fecundity of this family as by their lowly blood mixing with the ancient lines of England. Also of concern was the rapid rise of Elizabeth's father, Wydville himself, favoured and soon elevated to positions beside the throne. Though I had taken little notice until more recent times, it appeared Richard Wydville, now Earl Rivers and Edward's chancellor, had counselled favour for the Burgundians. And unbeknown to my father, Edward had signed a treaty. Coming a paltry second to the Burgundians, Papa was forced to mask his thoughts and entertain the French as though naught was amiss.

'We must do what we can to stop the surge.' Mama had become a madwoman, striding about the solar as though she set off for the hunt. 'All too soon there will be no-one left worthy of my daughters and the inheritance they shall one day receive!'

My hopes of seeing Dickon again withered away like a flower in the frost.

Over the coming days, I mulled over Mama's words. Something in there had struck a chord but I could not discern exactly what until the day I came across Isobel lounging on the settle, scoffing comfits with a look of satisfaction across her plump face.

'Sister, how good to see you.'

Isobel rarely acknowledged my presence, so I was somewhat surprised by her words. I nodded but did not return the greeting.

'Did you want something?' she asked sweetly.

I held up the book I had come to collect but still did not furnish her with a reply. I was almost at the door when she let slip her little jewel of a comment.

'If I should wed, you will need to curtsey to me, sister. How should you feel about that?'

I turned and stared at her. That she would wed was never in any doubt. Where she would wed was another matter entirely, given most suitable young men of the land had been taken and His Grace had forbidden the one match my family desired.

'I am the daughter of an earl, as are you. Should you wed an earl, I do not need to curtsey for we should be of equal rank.' I refused to play along with her game, for I had a suspicion where this was heading.

Isobel gave a thin smile. 'And if I did not wed an earl?'

'Then you would most likely need to curtsey to me, for I should have higher rank.'

'La, Anne!' she cried. 'You are no fun. Let us hope I secure a duke, for then you will have to curtsey and I shall enjoy it greatly.'

I still refused to play her foolish game. 'From what I have been told, such a marriage is not to His Grace's liking. Perhaps the queen has other plans for her dear brother-in-law's hand and will persuade the king to it, sister.'

Despite my rare moment of provocation, Isobel laughed. 'I think Papa has had quite enough of that widow's influence upon the king and will see it done no more.'

'His Grace will be wroth if Papa takes it upon himself to arrange a match with any man, especially if he knows naught of it.'

'And what of the king ignoring our father's advice?' My sister's sudden words echoed those of Mama so closely, I suspected she had been well-schooled in the matter. 'His Grace sought no consultation when he wed that widow, and the kingdom suffers as a result. Moreover, as we are oft reminded; those whom God has joined together let no man put asunder. Remember sister, the law of God applies to kings as much as to the rest of us.'

So my sister would wed a duke whether His Grace agreed or not. All the dukes in the kingdom already had wives save two, both brothers to the king. In that moment, I knew my Uncle George, the Archbishop of York, would obtain the necessary dispensation from His Holiness, the Pope, for Isobel and the favoured duke were well within the degrees of consanguinity. The problem was obtaining such a dispensation without the king's knowledge, but George Neville was a man of power and influence, and no doubt knew men at the Papal court willing to assist for a price. And Papa had means enough to make it worth their while, without depleting his coffers noticeably. At that moment I knew all this would be done without His Grace's knowledge, let alone his permission. My heart sank. If Papa offended King Edward by marrying Isobel to George, then Dickon would be as far away from me as he ever could be. Edward would make sure of that to thwart Papa once and for all. A tiny voice inside my mind suggested the king may actually approve the match, but in my heart I knew different. Queen Elizabeth had already given the king two daughters. It was said the royal couple had delighted in the arrival of the young Elizabeth and more recently, of another daughter, Mary. Celebrations had been ordered after both births and there seemed no great concern over the lack of a male child. The queen already had two sons from her first marriage, enough to establish her fertility and the likelihood she could still bear sons aplenty. It was only a matter of time before she birthed the all-important heir.

In the absence of a son, George, Duke of Clarence, was heir to the throne of England, and had been since Edward claimed the throne. Though the queen had since birthed two children, it appeared this lack of a male heir was of greater interest to my father than it had been previously. Perhaps the king had suspicions about my uncle's business as archbishop. Perhaps the king trusted my father no longer, persuaded by Wydville influence that Papa was better employed elsewhere. Perhaps the king could no longer discern where his trust ought to be placed. Whatever the reason, a flat refusal over the marriage had been the outcome, along with more questions than answers and a growing uncertainty about the future. From Isobel's comments, I was forced to presume my father had finally decided upon his next move in this real-life game of chess, and would exploit the lack of a direct heir to establish a firmer connection between our family and the throne. It mattered not what the king or queen thought, if indeed, they even knew of it till afterwards. Papa was about to play his hand – and in secret. That Isobel and I, and probably Mama also, were merely pawns in his game seemed to concern none but myself.

The discontent continued. In the privacy of our home, Papa often vented his frustration with the court and a family he despised. Though he was careful never to besmirch the name of the king, he was far less discreet about the queen's family. He also kept up his correspondence with the French. Indeed, he seemed rather proud of his connection at the court of King Louis, often dropping into conversation names guaranteed to impress. Mama would nod and smile, her pride clear, but I could find no solace in it, for my father's allegiances appeared to be shifting in a direction I could no longer understand.

I was not the only one concerned with my father's French connections. Rumours abounded that he harboured Lancastrian sympathies, inflamed by the capture by Lord Herbert of a messenger from the deposed Queen, Margaret D'Anjou, who alluded to reports heard overseas of Papa's support of the lady. The messenger was captured as Lord Herbert besieged Harlech Castle in Wales, a final stronghold for the Lancastrian cause. I did not believe such vile aspersions for one moment; Papa despised the deposed Queen Margaret with a venom he reserved for very few, but even I could see how his communications with the French court, where Margaret had sought support, might be misconstrued.

King Edward was concerned by these rumours, summoning my father to attend court to clear himself of the accusation. For days after the messenger arrived, my father walked around in a black haze, uncommunicative, surly and miserable. I knew he had not yet chosen a move. Cornered, he sent an angry response to the king, refusing to attend. Mama was on edge, moody and fearful until we received word the king had accepted Papa's written account of events, even sending the accuser to meet with Papa at Sheriff Hutton castle.

This was a difficult time for us all. The mood within our family was heavy and dark, so I often sought a place of quiet, well away from my elders and betters. I could find no words of solace or support to offer my father, for my heart was heavy. In staying away from his company, I wilfully deprived us both of the affection we had always relished, but I could not be false. I could not assure Papa I loved him no matter what, for the fear seeping into every corner of my life, tainted all it touched – and that included my love for him.

# Chapter Five - Indiscretions

## 1467

As the weeks passed, Mama became less discreet with her letters than she ought to have been. While Papa's fury was cold and detached, simmering beneath the surface till he had decided upon a response, Mama bemoaned and decried everyone who had offended her to anyone who would listen. Though Isobel and I bore the brunt of her dissatisfaction, I feared she would speak too much in the hearing of one who would happily sell knowledge to those who buy such things.

Fortunately we moved betwixt the castles of Middleham, Warwick and Sherriff Hutton so frequently her outspokenness did no lasting damage, for we were not in one place long enough for her indiscretions to be passed on. At least, I prayed that was the case.

Our Uncle George, the Archbishop of York, was also mired in the dissatisfaction affecting our family. The wounds caused by King Edward's retrieval of the Great Seal had barely healed, when the king, accidently or otherwise, send papal papers to our uncle revealing the election of Thomas Bouchier, Archbishop of Canterbury, into The College of Cardinals. This eminent position was one our uncle had much desired and, if Papa's inferences were anything to go by, had been scheming to achieve. Though our uncle was gracious and restrained in his defeat and the king's unkind reveal, Papa was far less generous, citing the poisonous influence of the Wydvilles as sole reason a clever man was precluded from a deserved role. He spoke of this matter with such venom and fury, I was relieved it was only when our family was alone.

Mama however, showed no such discretion. As Isobel and I sewed beside the fire, she waved a recent letter from Papa in the air, scarcely aware of the servants in our midst.

'Your uncle works tirelessly in his position as archbishop,' she announced, to no-one in particular.

I concentrated on my stitches, suspecting this conversation would not benefit me in any way. Isobel however, took great interest.

'Indeed, Mama, in what way does he work?'

'In the ways that matter most; the good of the family.' Mama leaned forward, staring directly at her eldest daughter. 'Indeed, he writes most encouragingly to your father of a man named James Caldwell, the king's own representative at the papal court. My heart is gladdened to hear such tidings.'

Isobel's embroidery slipped from her lap. She reached over to clasp Mama's hands. 'It gladdens mine too, Mama.'

Mama smiled. 'I am contented you should think so, my dear.'

Head bending lower over my stitches, I concluded the wily archbishop had made progress at last. Efforts to procure a papal dispensation for Isobel and George of Clarence to wed had been languorous at best, especially as one of his emissaries to The Curia, governing body of the church in Rome, had been rebuffed in no uncertain terms. This time, the future seemed a little brighter — at least for Papa and Isobel. But as each step was taken towards my sister's clandestine marriage, our risk of offending the king became ever greater, pushing Dickon farther away from my reach.

Little else was heard on the matter for months, but that was not unexpected. Such matters often moved slowly for the church worked as a law unto itself, but if discretion and coercion was needed to attain a dispensation, then patience was needed in greater quantities than the gold to pay for such procurements.

The year passed with little else to distract my sister and me. We learned our lessons, practised our manners, prayed to our Lord and obeyed our mother. Papa came and went, sometimes returning in a particularly foul mood, sometimes merely unhappy. I learned to avoid his first evening at home, for it did nothing to lift my spirits. Often, he had mellowed by the next morning, and a quiet encounter as he sat attending to his papers might draw forth a smile but for the most part, I behaved as a good daughter ought; doing exactly as bidden and saying nothing till asked.

My eleventh birthday, falling in June of that year, came and went unmarked. Papa was away once more, Mama engrossed in the matters he relentlessly wrote of, and Isobel seemed not to recall I had a birthday at all.

Little news came my way over the second part of the year, for my mother kept much of Papa's business to herself. Other than showing surprise that John, Lord Wenlock, was implicated in a Lancastrian plot, she became increasingly frugal with news within my hearing. Wenlock was Papa's deputy at Calais and had accompanied Papa on many of his diplomatic missions besides negotiating a truce-at-sea with the French some years before. As Mama listed the qualities of the man, it became clearer to me how dissatisfaction was spreading across the kingdom like a disease.

In December, King Edward moved north to Coventry to keep Christmas. There, he was joined by the Duke of Clarence, his Wydville relatives and his council. Though nothing was said of the king's youngest brother, I dared to hope Dickon had come north too. Still half a realm away from where we celebrated the birth of the Christ Child at Middleham, it cheered me to think my dearest friend was not so far away.

Though we marked the season with the lavishness I had come to expect, the feasts, music and entertainments seemed hollow and false despite numbers of Papa's retainers and invited guests from both City of York and families of importance from across the county. Yet my father was on edge; surly and agitated, and marking time as if he knew something was about to occur, though he kept it well-hidden most of the time. Mama, tuned into his moods as any good wife should be, was stern-faced and hard to please. Isobel, I took no notice of, and avoided at every opportunity. It was only as Twelfth Night approached, when my beloved Aunt Alice, her Fitzhugh husband and family joined us, did my heart finally hope for some joy this season.

'Anne.' Francis held out his hand to me.

I smiled, allowing him to kiss my hand in greeting. His young wife watched our every move, her eyes flicking nervously between myself and Francis.

'You look well,' I said, ignoring the plain, sullen girl beside him. My cousin Ann was even more reluctant than I to make conversation, and though we had grown up together, we had little in common and I much preferred her mother's company. Not that I held back on the courtesies, for my own dear Mama watched over proceedings like a hawk.

Francis grinned. 'I am well, and would ask for your hand in the dancing later, if I may?'

'If your lovely wife does not mind, for as a new husband you must dance with her as often as she wishes it.'

72

If I had hoped for some response or protest from Francis' young wife, I was to be disappointed. She simply stood beside her husband, eyes never leaving my face. Though of similar ages, Cousin Ann was shorter than I, and rather heavily built. Her thin brown hair was scraped back so tightly beneath the headdress it strained the skin at her temples. Over the dark mossy-green of her gown, the plump pale face reminded me of a full moon rising over a lake. I almost pitied the girl greeting my beautiful sister but instead, straightened my back and prayed for a little humility. My cousin was a viscountess and a married woman, whereas I, though an earl's daughter, was still an unwed maid. I smiled, trying to remember my manners.

'It is hardly our first Christmas as husband and wife.' Francis laughed. 'I am certain Ann will not begrudge you one dance.'

As her pale green eyes swept up and down my form, Ann Lovell gave a thin smile suggesting she begrudged every moment her handsome husband was not attending to her. I cared not, desperate only for news of Dickon. As she finally turned away to join her mother, I looked to Francis, studying his face for clues.

'I wish to hear your news, Francis, far more than I wish to dance. It is some time since we met and there must be a great to tell of your new life.' And old life, and old acquaintances, one in particular, but I clamped my lips together for I dared not reveal myself before my family.

He nodded. 'I will find a moment when Ann is not watching. She is rather in awe of you.'

I could not imagine anyone, child, adult or even the dull Ann Lovell, being in awe of me. I was one of God's least interesting creatures, without height, looks or wit to draw notice in a room filled with people. I forced a laugh.

'Very well, my friend, whenever you think appropriate. Do not forget though, for I shall be saddened not to hear of your news.'

'And those whom I have seen lately perhaps?' he murmured, bending low over my hand.

I snatched it away, fearful I should reveal my innermost thoughts. But Francis already knew and had known of my deepest secret for years. Stepping back, he bowed low.

'Till later, Lady Anne. Be assured I shall not forget, for yours is not the only wrath I must face if I do.'

I gasped, turning my face to the wall so none would see. Though he had disclosed nothing, it was clear Francis had either seen or received word from Dickon over Yuletide. His inferences led to no other conclusion. I could scarcely breathe, heart pounding beneath the wine-coloured gown that was my Christmas gift. Beads of perspiration trickled down my temples, spotting onto what little décolletage I owned, running past the pearl-drop held around my throat by a silk ribbon I had also received. Papa had demanded my wardrobe be furnished with new gowns, after commenting how too often I dressed like a serving-girl, not the daughter of an earl. He did not ask what I might prefer to wear before this instruction, but neither did Mama inform him there were already fine gowns in my possession, but I wilfully chose to wear more comfortable attire instead of that befitting my rank and status. Though it pleased me not at all, I had the sense to stay quiet about the matter.

'Anne, are you quite well?' Mama's chill tone rang out and I clutched at the pearl.

'Indeed, Mama, though 'tis too warm in here for a brocade gown this heavy.' I bowed my head so the dark silk veil of my headdress fell forwards to hide my face.

'Step outside for a moment and take some air lest you take ill and shame yourself before our guests.' A hand grazed my forehead as Mama gave a deep sigh. 'There is always something wrong with you child, always when you ought to be at your best, representing our family. For certes I do not know what to do with you.'

Though my aunt laughed at my mother's comments, I knew those undertones so well. She was displeased and disappointed I was not growing into a fine lady like Isobel. My sister was almost as tall as Mama, slender and willowy with cornflower-blue eyes and a clear complexion. Her hair was a light brown, a shade somewhere between copper and honey. When brushed, it hung in shining tresses to her waist. I, on the other hand, was short and small boned with unruly mouse-brown hair and dull hazel eyes. In one of her less kind moments, Mama had proclaimed how, if my hair was a little shorter and I wore a tunic and hose, I could easily pass for the sergeant's young son. Though I yearned for a day when my appearance pleased her the same way my sister did, especially as I had been making an effort of late, I was thankful for more height and bearing than my poor cousin possessed.

It was almost the end of the evening before Francis approached me again. Though we had danced many carols, Ann Lovell had joined in each one leaving no opportunity for private conversation. I resigned myself to a long wait for Francis' news.

Towards the end of the evening, with still no opportune moment presenting itself, I began to despair of ever hearing of Dickon. My aunt and mother were in such deep conversation I suspected they plotted some entertainment I was guaranteed not to enjoy. Soon after, they called over my father and uncle-by-marriage, Henry, Baron Fitzhugh. As the adults stood laughing and chatting together, I did not see Francis approach.

'If the ladies have their way, we shall be imposing upon your hospitality well beyond Twelfth Night,' he smiled. 'I do hope so, for that will give us time to become re-acquainted.'

As I murmured my delight at such a scheme, out of the corner of my eye, I saw Cousin Ann approach.

Francis had seen her also. He greeted his wife before bowing low before me. 'It grows late and I bid you a goodnight, Lady Anne. Perhaps you might find an hour for chess sometime tomorrow?'

Nothing delighted me more. As I politely and demurely gave assurances to meet for a game, I watched the young woman's expression change. Upon close inspection, her wide features revealed this was not shyness, this was envy, and a great deal of uncertainty.

'Cousin Ann.' I gave what I hoped was a gracious smile. 'Your husband has challenged me to a game of chess for old times' sake. I am sure he has mentioned how we played often when he was my father's ward here. Since his departure I have little chance to hone my skills and fear defeat too soon. Pray come and advise me.'

Ann screwed up her face. 'I do not play and cannot understand why others find pleasure in such a difficult and uninteresting pastime.'

I took a deep breath. 'Then perhaps you would come to support me?'

'I think not,' she declared. 'We have all been invited to join your mother and sister in chapel and then ride up onto the moors to meet our men. As their hunt commences the festivities for Twelfth Night, I confess surprise you failed to recall this, Cousin.'

With nothing left to say to either my cousin or her husband, I made excuses and hastened to my bed, warm with dreams of Dickon and the hope Francis' news was good.

The men set off to hunt at dawn, while we ladies enjoyed chapel and a morning of idleness before riding out to wait for the hunt's return. Though the morn dawned clear and white-over with frost, its chill did not leave me, no matter how close I sat to the fire.

Yet I was not unhappy. Francis was still a guest within our walls and, though he had spent most of his time here dancing with his wife or drinking and talking with the menfolk, he would, I was certain, find a moment to speak with me. I also discovered the women had much to reveal.

Sitting at a table with the reticent Ann Lovell, my ears unexpectedly tuned into a conversation between Aunt Alice and Mama.

'Is that so?' Mama declared, far louder than I am sure she realised. Fortunately, we were only a family party sat in the warmth of the solar; Mama, Isobel and I, Aunt Alice, Cousin Ann and her youngest siblings still in the care of their nurses.

'Indeed.' Aunt Alice sat back in the chair and sipped her wine. She put so much feeling into that one word, I stopped, hand poised as if consicering my next move over a game-board.

'Pray when shall I see these famed cards?' Cousin Ann sniffed, staring at the pack still clutched inside my hand.

Jolted back to the moment, I somehow found a smile for my sullen cousin and spread out the playing cards before her. After one of his more recent trips across to the Continent, Papa had returned with a particularly fine pack of cards that he was much taken with. Though he steadfastly refused to teach us any games, deeming wagering especially sinful for women, he allowed us to admire the delicately painted pictures. While the numbered cards were decorated with hunting symbols like horns, hound tethers, collars and game nooses, the picture cards showed nobles resplendent in their finery. These costumes depicted lords, ladies and knaves, all brightly coloured and finished with gold or silver paint. Isobel would often sigh over the ladies' gowns, quite different from those Mama owned. I, on the other hand would look at the faces of the lords, wondering if they wore the faces of this land, or another. Neither of us took much notice of the knaves. As I turned over the pack searching for those showing the elegant ladies Isobel admired so much, my ears strained to hear Mama's conversation.

'But are you certain of this?' Mama still failed to keep her voice low.

'Henry assures me it is true,' Aunt Alice smiled. 'He has relayed all to your husband but it seems we are not the only nobles of the land unhappy about the influences of that family over His Grace.'

Mama sipped from her wine cup. 'Alice, you cannot imagine how it pleases me to hear this, and I have no doubt my husband feels the same way. What more do you know?'

Aunt Alice proceeded to enlighten Mama, which I was apparently privileged to receive direct from her mouth later as we dressed for the feast.

It seemed an increasing number of noble families grew disenchanted with the meteoric rise of the Wydvilles. King Edward's casual and often flippant dealings with both the French and the Burgundians had impacted upon England in ways he had not foreseen. As Charles of Burgundy evaded coming to terms over English cloth, Edward was forced to revoke edicts of Parliament prohibiting imports of Burgundian goods, and so impacting upon those made in this country. The Merchants of London and further afield complained loudly, and threats were heard against those who had counselled the king in this matter. The mutterings grew, inflamed by Duke Charles' delay in signing a marriage agreement for the king's sister's hand, besides signing a six month truce with the French, compounding an already complex situation between the Dukes of Burgundy and Brittany, and the Kings of France and England. It was being said across all classes of England how the Wydvilles had estranged the king from his true lords and the realm was being betrayed.

I said nothing as Mama relayed her news. Her face was a picture of triumph and justification, leaving me in no doubt she and Papa had been waiting to hear such tidings. It seemed odd to me, though perhaps my youth could excuse such wide-eyed innocence, how Papa seemed unwilling to counsel restraint and loyalty amongst his friends, retainers and family and, that he too, relished the discord his protégé was inciting.

Mama had more to reveal, though much of this was old news, taking a while to reach our northern ears. More recently, the Duke of Clarence, and my sister's intended, had blazed his own trail against Wydville supremacy. Now in his late teens, George had begun behaving as though he had already come of age, offering his hospitality to the magnates of Gloucestershire and Somerset, clearly trying to enlarge his own following. He had also meddled where he should not, delighting in inflaming one ancient house against another, especially if that house showed any support for the king.

While Mama and Isobel appeared pleased George had become so active in affairs of the realm, I could not help but wonder what he sought from it all. Bless my innocence. Having experienced the directness and openness of the likes of Dickon and Francis, I could not comprehend why men must stir a hornet's nest in the vain hope their adversaries are stung. In my limited experience it seemed such things were simply best left alone, and I could have sworn Dickon's voice rang out its concurrence in my mind.

The festivities of Twelfth Night did little to placate my misgivings. Though lavish and entertaining, my mind was preoccupied with what I had learned that afternoon. As once before, it was as though cold water ran down my spine, chilling me to the core. There was nothing I could do or say to my family, for I was the least of them and worthy of no notice, but I began to fear for us.

'Would you care to dance?' a familiar voice asked. Francis' smile drew me from my melancholy but I declined his kind offer.

'Why?' he frowned. 'Ann has retired for the night, a headache brought on by the music so I thought it opportunity to seek you out.'

I smiled again. 'Dancing I can do without, but cooler air I need most urgently. It passes all understanding how fine ladies survive in these garments.'

'And I was about to compliment your attire,' Francis laughed. 'But I see now that would be quite wrong. You are the only lady I know who cares little enough for possessions and is not given to the sin of vanity!'

'You know me so well,' I accepted his hand and we left the great hall, much to the consternation of Mama.

The night was fine, clear and bitterly cold. Up on the battlements, muffled in thick cloaks, we stole a few moments of privacy.

Francis talked little of his new life, save how he was growing fond of my aunt and her husband. He said even less about his bride and I was left to conclude they either had little in common or he cared for her not at all. That was hardly surprising. The women of noble houses did not marry for love and expected none. They married to secure their houses and fortunes; love was not a consideration. If we should ever be fortunate enough to experience love, it would be for our children. Respect, obedience and a fine dowry; that was all our husbands demanded - and of course, an heir.

'You are not listening to me, are you, Anne?'

My head shot up, searching for Francis' face in the darkness.

'And have no interest in my hounds or fine new horse,' he laughed.

I spluttered an apology but he laughed once more. 'There is no need for apologies, I know what you wish to hear, sweet girl, and you have been made to wait long enough.'

My response was barely intelligible.

'He is well enough,' Francis began. 'Striving to understand all he can of statecraft and, when His Grace has time to spare, Edward makes a good teacher to those willing to learn.'

Barbed words, and no doubt directed at the king's other brother, George. But I had no concern for that particular brother. 'What do you mean, "well enough"? What ails my friend?'

Francis sat in silence and though I could not see his face, I knew his expression was dour. For several minutes we stared up at the moonless sky, the stars bright in the freezing air.

'I ought not to keep you out here.' Francis reached for my hand but I refused to take it.

'Not until I know what ails Dickon.'

'You will catch cold and your lady mother will be wroth indeed . . . '

'I do not care and nor will she. I only care whether my dear friend is well.'

Francis sighed. 'I see you will not give in, Anne. You have always been a stubborn creature, indeed, Dickon has remarked upon it more than once.'

My heart leapt, for I was remembered! If Francis was to offer nothing else those few words would have satisfied me. But he had hinted at more and I needed to learn all I could about the health of my friend.

'As I said, he is well enough. He strives hard to be the best at whatever he does, though as the king's youngest brother he is still seen – and often treated – as a child. That frustrates him, though I suspect Edward has observed something in his nature that he likes, for he often includes Dickon in private discussions, much to the irritation of others at court.'

'And?' I was not yet placated.

'He works like no other of his age. When not attending the king, he is diligence itself at his lessons, for he esteems learning and wishes to improve his knowledge of languages, scripture and literature. He also practises harder than most in the yards.'

'How does he find time enough?' I cried, imagining Dickon exhausted from his labours.

'How indeed,' Francis murmured. 'And therein lies a greater issue.'

Exasperated he had once again ceased speaking, I recall clasping poor Francis' cloak and threatening to reveal our meeting to his wife should he not furnish me with the detail I needed.

'Dickon suffers,' Francis began. He tugged at my hand but I still clutched his cloak, dreading what might come. 'But as he is wont to do, says naught of it.'

'How, what causes him such distress?'

'Oh, Anne, I do not know where to begin.' Francis drew breath, relieved I had finally released hold of him. 'Dickon enjoys the ritual and order of court, of law-making and ruling, but he does not enjoy the stratagems and, as he puts it, unnecessary talk about everything under God's sun but what truly matters. He wishes men would speak plainly and fairly and without rancour for then they could accomplish far more, though he knows it will never be so.'

In the darkness, I nodded. Francis had described the Dickon I knew so well.

'He is often frustrated by Edward's distractions, not understanding why His Grace spends so much time indulging himself instead of dealing with what matters. And then there is George . . . '

I had no desire to hear about George but, if it gave me the smallest window into the mind of my dearest companion, then Francis might speak of George all night.

'What is the matter with George?'

Francis laughed out loud. 'What is not the matter with him? He is an arrogant, ungrateful whelp, and will not be satisfied however much he receives.'

Once again, the words coming from Francis' mouth were most assuredly not the words of a fifteen-year-old youth. I shuddered to think the shallow and grasping character they described was the proposed husband of my sister and prayed there might be more to recommend George. But I knew the truth already; his dukedom and proximity to the throne were recommendation enough for my father.

'Is that all?' I asked, still suspicious Francis might think it better to shield me from the truth about Dickon.

Knowing he had been exposed, Francis cleared his throat before speaking, as though he preferred not to reveal what was on his mind. 'He is experiencing some difficulties with his back.'

'Pray what exactly are these difficulties? Is he hurt or crippled?' I could hardly speak, fearing Dickon had suffered some terrible injury none thought it prudent to speak of.

Francis drew another deep breath. 'For some years now, since we were here in your father's service, he has suffered pain around his spine. It does not trouble him all of the time, but it is getting worse. I have learned he has consulted physicians since his arrival at court, sourced I believe, by his lady mother.'

'But what has caused this? Did he fall from his horse, or sustain injury in the tilt-yard?' I could barely get the words out, so deep was my worry.

'He has endured no injury, nor is it due to his continued exertions. Indeed, when we were wards here there seemed no obvious reason for it, save his spine appeared to be a slightly different shape from the other boys'. When last we met, he seemed in excellent health, and has not spoken openly of it for some time. Understand, Anne, I would not dare insult him by asking.'

'Then how do you know it still troubles him, Francis?'

'Though riding is no problem and he can suffer a hard day in the saddle as well as any I know, when he has endured an arduous day's practise with the sword or other weapons on foot, he is fatigued and sometimes suffers pain. He makes only the merest mention of it, occasionally followed by a request for strong wine, but knowing him as I do and, watching his face when he thinks no-one can see, it causes far more discomfort than he will allow – even to me.'

I could not respond. My dearest friend endured something I knew naught of, something he could not explain, nor expunge, and there was naught I could do to console him. I wanted to weep.

Through the darkness, Francis sought my hand. 'He would be most unhappy to learn I have spoken of it, Anne, so mention nothing of this matter especially to your family. Clothed, Dickon appears much as another of his years and so almost no-one knows of this. I heard of the physicians' attendance while in company with the Duchess of York but I do not think she intended me to learn of it. 'Tis a private family matter but, whatever its cause, know that it does not hold Dickon back. Indeed, I am inclined to believe it urges him on to succeed, to be better because of it, not in spite of it.'

Fine words from Francis, but little comfort when there was nothing I could do to help my friend.

'There is something I must say to you, dearest Anne.' Francis' tone had changed – and not for the better. I turned towards the sound of his voice for I could barely see him through the night.

'While many of those beside the king dislike the spread of Wydville influence and blood,' he began. 'They try to counteract what they can by just and sensible counsel. However, your father. . .'

'Is becoming more discontented with each passing month,' I spat, before realising I ought to keep my lips closed. But this was Francis, a ward of my father, now his nephew-by-marriage, and one close enough to see it too. 'In private, Papa is recklessly open in his disdain towards the queen's family.'

'And he is showing that disdain farther abroad than the solar,' came Francis' reply through the night. I braced but he reached for my hand, offering silent reassurance. 'Ah Anne, I know that is not what you wanted to hear but it is the truth, and you should be aware of it. I must also say, should discontent spread to a point where men must choose, know that I shall choose the House of York, despite marriage to your Neville kin. Edward is our anointed king and, as such, has my full allegiance, whatever faults he is said to have. In this, Dickon and I are in full agreement.'

So, they had discussed the fickleness of my family. My exhale was so loud I feared we should be discovered. 'Is it that bad, Francis?'

'Not yet,' he said, and I suspected he smiled. 'But a disaffected noble, especially one of the most powerful, can easily inflame others. Once a fire is fuelled, it will burn for a long time.'

So, the viscount was not to be turned and that gave me much comfort. No doubt my Cousin Ann would have a great deal to say on the matter when she learned of her husband's fealty, but I cared not for her. I cared only that Dickon's friend valued loyalty as much as Dickon.

Francis leaned in towards me. 'Dickon fervently wishes you to understand this, for he would not see you hurt. But if your father insists on walking this path, not only will we all be hurt but it is likely we shall find ourselves on different sides.'

# Chapter Six – White Roses

## 1468

My father received a message on the day before Twelfth Night. Whilst this was not unusual, his reaction was. Henry Fitzhugh and his son-in-law, Francis, were summoned to Papa's chamber and the men shut themselves inside, ordering food and drink to be delivered there. Sometime later, Mama and my aunt joined their menfolk, leaving Isobel, Cousin Anne and me, to entertain the remaining guests. Though I could not say why, I knew trouble was brewing.

Papa and Henry said nothing as they returned to their guests. Indeed, my father conducted himself with such delightful manners, only one who truly knew him well understood the brittleness of his façade. As usual, Mama found it difficult to keep her emotions under wraps but several sharp glances from my father and aunt seemed to keep her in check.

Much news had come their way, though not all of it good. Keeping a quiet Christmas in the bosom of his family, my father had deliberately set out to give the impression trouble was the last thing on his mind. Yet there were many throughout the land who acknowledged no higher authority than Papa, and he had received word that men were available whenever he should have need of them. Moreover, it transpired upon New Year's Day, those supporting my father in the County of Kent had taken it upon themselves to attack a manor belonging to Earl Rivers, killing his deer and ravaging the land thereabouts. Only the quick-thinking of the servants prevented the earl from losing much of his possessions, carrying away his valuables as they fled.

Shifting my seat a little closer to where aunt and mother settled themselves, I listened to their talk. I ought not to have done such an ill-mannered thing but I was overcome with a need to learn what had occurred to require a sudden and clandestine meeting in the midst of festivities.

Though relishing this small but pertinent attack on Wydville power, my father had far more to worry about. As Francis sat down beside me, I knew instantly things were amiss.

'Your father is not happy.'

'That much is clear,' I smiled, trying not to react to his dour expression.

'It seems Robert Neville, your father's secretary, has returned from France with a certain William Menypeny; a Scotsman high in King Louis' service . . . '

I already knew Papa's secretary was on his way back to England, for I had overheard another of Mama's indiscretions. I did not know this man, where he had been nor that he brought company, but the hairs rose on the back of my neck. Twisting my fingers together, I waited for Francis to reveal more. No doubt this man's return was the true reason behind my parents' withdrawal.

'Though Menypeny may have hoped his visit remained quiet, friends in the south advised him to make his presence known to the king. He is at Coventry as we speak.'

I tried to stifle a gasp. I had little knowledge of my father's business, and especially that which he conducted with the King of France, but even if it was genuine, and innocent in nature, it could do no good for it to be brought to the attention of His Grace. Francis' face reflected my darkening thoughts.

'The secretary sent word ahead. Though Menypeny was treated with all the respect an emissary should expect, Edward asked directly if he carried letters for your father. Menypeny freely admitted he had some letters upon his person though for reasons we cannot fathom Edward did not ask him to hand them over nor to open them. Your father can only conclude His Grace was satisfied with Menypeny's explanation of why the King of France should be communicating directly with an earl in his service.'

'Whatever did he say to secure such belief?' I could barely get my words out, so appalled was I to hear of this. If relations between my father and the king were becoming so strained and suspicious, I was right to be fearful.

Francis stared at his hands, clasping them together as he spoke. 'Menypeny is wily and quick-witted, but that is hardly surprising considering he serves one of the most cunning kings under God's sun. He admitted he knew nothing of the contents himself but supposed they contained little more than Louis' astonishment that England, meaning of course, King Edward, had not responded to proposals put forwards by his ambassadors last year.'

After the king's poor treatment of the French Ambassadors my father had brought over, Francis' news was hardly surprising. Edward had infuriated my father with his behaviour towards the diplomatic party and, indirectly, infuriated the King of France.

This political tempest was beyond my understanding despite being assured I had wits aplenty for a girl of my years. To me, the stratagems, designs and policies of kings always appeared unnecessarily complex, as Dickon had once remarked. Though I knew board games such as tables and chess were encouraged to broaden the minds of the children of those who rule, I could not help but wonder if war would be a less frequent thing if this desire to out-manoeuvre one another was curbed. But perhaps that was purely a woman's view, for it was common knowledge men loved nothing more than to sport with their peers, at hunting, politics and power. My desires for a peaceful life would solve nothing here; the delight with which my father had received news of the attack on Earl River's property had been fleeting. As I looked upon his face, it was clear every thought was concentrated upon his next move. His mind whirred away, deliberating how he could deal with the king's wilful interference without losing face or offending His Grace beyond forgiveness. Once again, fear clamped a heavy hand onto my young shoulders.

If Francis had any more news of Dickon, he said naught of it. As I retired for the night, the feeling he had no more to say would not leave me. Perhaps Francis was simply being kind, relaying snippets about the health and welfare of my friend for old times' sake, and because he knew it pleased me. But as I recalled the confidence he had broken disclosing Dickon's ailment, I doubted myself all over again and prayed to the Lord above Francis had more to tell.

The day after Twelfth Night dawned bitterly cold, with a north wind that promised to bring the worst of winter. The temptation to remain at the fireside was great indeed but our home was still filled with guests and they must be entertained.

After attending chapel with Isobel, Mama insisted we both spend time in the great hall conversing with the remaining guests. It seemed she, Papa and my aunt and uncle had further business to discuss before departures began in earnest.

The morning flew I know not how and, to my relief, soon it was midday and the dinner was served. Thankful for a simpler fare than we had received for days, I ate more than usual. Isobel made barbed comments as she saw this but I said nothing, caring little for any speech with her. She devoted herself to our cousin Ann instead, for which I felt some small gratitude. After eating my fill and passing the time speaking with those sat to my left, it occurred to me Francis had not appeared that morning.

As Isobel left her chair to speak with my aunt, seated the other side of her daughter, I leaned across to speak to Cousin Ann.

'Is your husband quite well this day?'

Ann's face soured at the sound of my voice. 'He is well enough, thank you.'

'Does he not eat?' I could not help myself, concerned something had taken Francis from me too soon. 'Dinner is finished and he will have taken nothing before departing . . . '

'That is hardly your concern, Cousin,' Ann snapped. 'But as you seem so keen to take on the worries of a wife, know he attends your father. If the earl will release him, perhaps you should ask he join us, for my husband takes more notice of you than he does his own wife.'

Flying back into my seat, I was stunned into silence by my cousin's venom. That she resented me was clear as day. I sat in silence, wondering what I had done to offend her so deeply. After a few moments I felt a light touch upon my arm.

'Cousin, forgive my poor manners,' Ann croaked. The effects of her mother's chastisement were still clear upon her unhappy face. 'Upon reflection I see you were only acting with kindness as a hostess ought. I believe a messenger from the king arrived here a short while ago and your father summoned the men of my family to attend him. Food was delivered to them some while past.'

King Edward had sent an urgent summons to Papa, ordering him to Coventry directly. There were no courtesies, no polite invitation, just an abrupt and direct summons to attend His Grace forthwith. Papa's reaction was equally abrupt and, despite the numerous guests, our home now felt as though it sat in the centre of a military campaign.

The Fitzhugh family departed later that day, taking Francis away too. As Mama, Isobel and I stood in the ward watching them leave, my heart was heavy. Not another word had been said to me of Dickon, and nor was it likely to be. The wind still tore through us as though we wore nothing, flakes of snow fluttered violently across the yard without even touching the ground. I could not stop shivering, desperate for the ladies to cease their fussing and get into the carriage, though it also mean Francis' departure was imminent. Once the ladies were settled and wrapped up well for their journey, my uncle made his farewells. Appropriately brief, he thanked Isobel and me, lingering barely a moment longer with Mama. Francis followed behind, though his farewells were slightly more gracious. I braced, vowing not to give in and reveal just how hungry I was for news of my friend but, as Francis approached, the tears welled up in my eyes and I could no longer keep them at bay.

'Hush, Anne,' he whispered, bowing low over my hand. 'I am aware of your disappointment, and you care for not amongst us.'

He planted a kiss upon the back of my hand, limp as a wilting flower. As he rose, he murmured so softly I had to strain to hear his words.

'It pleases me you are in such good health, and to see you grow into a fine and accomplished lady.' There was a twinkle in his eyes as he spoke. 'Be assured, should any ask after you, I shall make it my business to relay every detail.'

Was I supposed to take comfort in such vagaries? Was I supposed to be satisfied with an inference that should an enquiry be made after me, Francis would respond well? It was scarcely enough to feed this rapidly emptying soul but I must make do, the for there was no alternative.

Francis stepped back, reaching for his horse's reins. About to mount, he turned back, much to my surprise.

'I ride south.' He stared at me, eyes so dark and deep I was forced to conclude he needed me to understand far more than his words said. 'My estates are in dire need of attention so I do not expect to be in the north for some time to come. No doubt my wife's family will miss me but that cannot be helped. As God is my witness, I must attend to what I hold dear without delay.'

I doubted The Lord above would worry over Francis' estates. Indeed, I did not believe Our Father would be overly concerned with Francis' absence from the north of this great land. What struck me most was the severity of his tone and look in his eye. My friend was trying to tell me he made for the court and our king, I was certain. He had sworn allegiance before God to the House of York and Francis would not break that oath, no matter which family he had been married into.

He was also trying to tell me my father did not have his support, whatever came to pass.

Papa did not take kindly to being summoned to court like a dog to his master, especially when that master had surrounded himself with many who resented my father's power and influence. I learned later that day, Papa had responded to His Grace with a brief but curt reply, saying he would not enter the court until the enemies of him and his policies had been dismissed.

As before, our days were spent walking upon egg-shells as Papa waited for a response. He despatched riders carrying messages near and far, pacing the battlement watching for their return. In the darkest of moods, my father became unbearable company and so I retreated to my chamber more often than not. On the brief occasions I ventured into the hall or solar, I stayed only as long as I could bear it, though Mama demanded my presence more often than I would have liked. Whispers abounded that my father communicated with James III of Scotland in the hope of procuring more men to support him. Whether there was truth in that or no I could not say, for I was told nothing, but it was clear even to a child of my years that troops were being assembled for something particular.

Fearful this could escalate beyond his control, my Uncle George, the Archbishop, used his guile and position to broker a truce as it transpired Papa's response had unsettled His Grace as much as the summons had unsettled Papa. Archbishop Neville had read the signs correctly, putting himself out to arrange a secret meeting at Nottingham with Earl Rivers, compromise being the order of the day. Uncle's returning message was direct; Papa would be welcomed at court if he would arrive in good mood enough to graciously accept the welcome they offered. Though Mama was scant on detail as she relayed this, the relief in her eyes was evident. Papa could retain his dignity without capitulation or a clash of forces with the king that would change everything irrevocably. Time had been bought for us all by the archbishop's careful thinking, though as I saw my father's face as we made our farewells, I knew he had not decided upon his next move despite the archbishop's intervention.

And so it was, Papa rode away from Middleham, accompanied by a great many more men than was appropriate for such a visit. I later learned that before he left, Papa had still found time to write to his friend the King of France.

'Anne, come here. I have news to share.'

I left my sewing in the window seat and joined Mama on the settle. In her hand was a letter and I knew she was pleased with its contents simply by her tone of voice. It would be foolish of me to waste a rare moment of conviviality.

'Is the letter from Papa?'

'Who else?' Her thoughts were far away, her unseeing eyes fixed upon a tapestry hanging on the far wall.

'Pray, what does he say?'

It was a moment or two before she registered I had even spoken.

'Should you care to visit London, child?'

Even though the surrounding meadows were awash with springtime colour, I was trapped inside the suffocating comfort of Warwick Castle, wanting to be anywhere but here.

I smiled at her, with genuine delight for once. 'Of course, Mama.'

She returned the smile. 'Though we may not join Papa as he escorts the Lady Margaret on her bridal journey, we are to accompany him south and await his return in the city.'

This was good news indeed. Papa and King Edward had continued in the spirit of reconciliation brokered by my uncle at the start of the year. Though I was in no doubt Papa's dissatisfaction with the Wydvilles would rear its ugly head again, these last months had been far more settled than the preceding year. In all matters pertaining to the court, the king, as well as the queen and her family, Papa had conducted himself with all the congeniality and good manners his position and breeding demanded. After the marriage agreement between Charles, Duke of Burgundy, and Margaret, sister to King Edward IV, had finally been agreed and signed, preparations for the wedding began, and my father was granted the honour of escorting Margaret's bridal journey to the end of English lands.

We were not invited to the festivities, though Papa would join the Lady Margaret, His Grace, King Edward, the Dukes of Clarence and Gloucester and other hand-picked lords and ladies of the bride's retinue. To my surprise, Mama was not put out nor offended by this and I could only conclude there was some protocol or tradition that precluded us, for the queen did not attend either. I am certain Mama drew much comfort from the fact Queen Elizabeth was also to remain behind with her young daughters, forced to hear of the lavish celebration from others' mouths.

In late May, we left the luxury of Warwick, travelling at a leisurely pace down ancient roads to the city of London. Though happy to be away from the soulless fortress I had inhabited for most of the spring, I found no solace in the city as hoped. To be so close to my friend and not able to so much as look upon him even from a distance, seemed almost cruel. My childish nature resented this bitterly and I would far rather have remained in Yorkshire, where by will of God and the many miles between London and Middleham, I could do naught to change the world. In London, Dickon was but a short boat ride from the end of the garden where I frequently sat, and thoughts of him were larger in my mind than ever before.

Just before Midsummer's Eve, the Lady Margaret began her journey from London to Burgundy. My father had left us some days before to ensure he was fully prepared. The procession began right in the centre of the city, whereupon Lady Margaret crossed to St Paul's Cathedral, to make offerings. From there, she travelled the length of Cheapside, where not only the Mayor and Aldermen were waiting, but scores of Londoners, Mama, Isobel and me. We might not be playing a part in all this magnificence, but Papa had arranged for us to watch the procession, paying a merchant handsomely for the use of his house. Mama, Isobel and I were able to view the procession from the rooms of this house, comfortably settled at upper windows, where we were shaded from the worst of the sun, and served cool refreshments whenever we wished. Though Mama and my sister turned up their noses at the smallness of the rooms and tastelessness of the furnishings, I found the merchant's house comfortable and unpretentious. It reminded me of the less opulent rooms at Middleham, a place I missed dearly.

Papa rode at the head of the procession, the Lady of York positioned behind him on the same horse.

They were followed by a train of lords and I would have given all I owned to be with that fine procession. The colours and splendour of the train were a feast for the eyes, Lady Margaret attired with the livery of her house, the horse dressed to match. The sun shone bright that day, highlighting the lords in their finery, the gilding of the horses' trappings glinting as they passed. The crowds cheered loudly as the last unwed daughter of York passed by, for London dearly loved a display and a beautiful lady but, as Mama proudly observed, they were also inordinately fond of the Earl of Warwick. Under a cloudless sky, hope soared as high as the larks above.

Once the procession had passed and the crowds dispersed, we left the merchant's house and returned to our own. In the heat of late afternoon, I retreated to the gardens, finding an isolated but shady spot beneath the trees. There I idled, dwelling upon the fact my dear friend was but a mile or two from me as I sat daydreaming. Papa had relayed the details of the procession to us, so I knew the Lady Margaret was to be entertained at the Abbey of Stratford before setting out on her journey in earnest. After crossing the River Thames, she was to travel down the ancient Roman Road, resting overnight at Dartford, Rochester and Sittingbourne before reaching Canterbury, and the Shrine of St Thomas. There, too, would she make offerings before continuing through Kent to the coast whereupon she would take a boat across the sea to her new life as a wife and a duchess.

Both Isobel and I much desired to visit the famous shrine of St Thomas, for we had learned of this martyr in our lessons. Drawing pilgrims from across the country and even from the Continent, all knew the story of how this son of the lower classes had risen to serve a great king as Chancellor. As time passed, conflict arose between King Henry and Becket, appointed Archbishop of Canterbury some years before. Accusations and threats were issued by both parties, resulting in Becket fleeing across the Channel. After the intervention of the Pope, King Henry offered a compromise allowing Becket to return from exile. But when Becket took the drastic step of excommunicating the Archbishop of York and Bishops of Salisbury and London for crowning young Henry, the heir-apparent in his stead, the king supposedly uttered words out loud that led some of his men to believe he wished the Archbishop dead. Becket was slaughtered within his cathedral. England was rocked by a crime of this magnitude, committed against a man of the cloth and within sight of God. Becket was proclaimed a martyr and within two years of his death was canonised by Pope Alexander. Soon it was said, miracles were being performed at the shrine; cripples healed, wounds vanished and eyesight restored. Even now, centuries later, Becket's shrine drew pilgrims from far and near. The thought that Papa would return to us direct from the shrine seemed almost a small miracle in itself, and my musings about Dickon faded a little, knowing Papa would have much news to relay.

The endless days of Papa's absence were bittersweet. I was content he should be serving King Edward so closely once more, but knowing he spent so much time in Dickon's company while I could not, was difficult indeed. I prayed for patience and humility, hoping the days would pass swiftly till Papa's return.

As I returned from my prayers one morning, Isobel's cry shattered my thoughts. 'Anne! Come this instant, Mama has summoned us.'

Out in the gardens, Mama was comfortably settled beneath an arbour weighed down with newly-opened roses.  The blooms were purest white: the emblem of the House of York.  Whether by deliberate choice or accident I knew not and, as I breathed in the heady scent, it was as if The Lord himself had sent us a sign.  Intoxicated by this heavenly perfume, I curtsied to Mama and waited to see what she would reveal.

'Your father has sent word,' she murmured. 'He relays how all went well and the king was so delighted with the festivities, at the last moment he decided to accompany the procession to Canterbury.'

The unexpected presence of the king would cause mayhem to those organising accommodation and feasting, but I gave little thought to His Grace, my mind drifting onto what Dickon might have thought of events.

'He also wrote that the Lady Margaret continued safely on her journey, boarding her ship to The Low Countries.  He writes how sixteen ships there were in total, containing not only the bride and her entourage, but horses and men enough to guard them all from French pirates . . . '  Mama stopped speaking to cross herself.  Thankful we had not needed to visit Calais for some time, I was reminded what a dangerous business travelling was.

She mouthed a silent prayer before continuing. 'It is as your father suspected.  Anthony, Lord Scales, is her presenter and Sir Edward Wydville goes with him too.  No doubt the queen will be well pleased her brothers have been entrusted with such responsibility.'

I said nothing at Mama's acidic comment.  The queen may well be represented but Papa had been granted a high honour indeed by leading the procession despite his refusal to assist with lady's great dowry because of the continuing frustrations as King Edward carved his own path through the political maze of England, France and Burgundy.  I knew we should take solace that our family had not been ignored or excluded, so the spite in Mama's tone was quite beyond my comprehension.

And so we awaited Papa's return, filling our days as best we could despite the never-ending heat of summer. Though excused most of our lessons for a few weeks, we still read, sewed and practised our manners and our dancing, and conducted polite conversation with the few visitors we did have. Each afternoon seemed hotter than the one before and even to walk out in the gardens was exhausting. Dressed each day in my finery, I suffered in the heat despite the lightweight cloth of my newest gown. Sitting beside Isobel on the bench, I fanned my face with the book I had brought to read, thankful to be out of the sun but despising the elaborate headdress and veil my advancing years demanded.

'How I wish we could have accompanied Papa.' Isobel uttered the words I had not dared to think. 'I should have liked to have seen the bride sail away on her journey.'

As her thoughts drifted away, I opened my book and pretended to read. Isobel cared nothing for the king's sister, wishing only to become a bride herself, with a beautiful gown, a handsome husband and the eyes of all upon her.

'It is unbecoming for a lady to be so obvious,' Mama murmured, and I knew she had drawn the same conclusion as I had. She patted Isobel's hand. 'You may not be a blushing bride yet, daughter, but perhaps Papa might return with company to please you.'

My sister had never appeared so lovely. Sitting bolt upright, a smile curved the corner of her mouth and her eyes brightened as they flicked across Mama's face. 'George comes *here*?'

Mama inclined her head, clearly approving Isobel's excitement. 'Though your father is not due back for several days, occupied with matters of business in Kent, he writes how has extended an invitation and is confident it will be accepted.'

Isobel's smile fell away. 'But what of the king, might he not gainsay such a visit?'

Clutching my sister's hands to her bosom, Mama smiled for the second time. 'Sweet girl, all know the Duke of Clarence is his own man. If he wishes to pay his respects to the family of an old friend he may do so without seeking anyone's permission, if indeed, such paltry matters become known beyond the duke's household.'

So busy was I wondering whether the duke would attend alone, I barely heard the acid edge to Mama's voice.

Isobel was almost unbearable that evening. Forced to view almost every garment in her coffer, I was relieved to hear Mama's voice calling us for prayers. As we knelt before the prie-dieu, the monotone voice of our priest reminding me of insects swooping through the evening air, I prayed with all my might Dickon might accompany his brother.

Forced to endure further duties as lady-in-waiting to Isobel, I suffered some regret in not asking The Lord for more than Dickon's company, desiring peace and solitude as well. It was not to be. I attended many more consultations till I grew heartily sick of it all and found it increasingly difficult to maintain civility when asked yet again about the colour of a particular veil or headdress.

Next day while my sister still slept, I crept outside to the rose arbour direct from prayers. Though I had not yet broken my fast, the temptation of a moment's quiet while the day was still cool proved too much for me to ignore. With my psalter, a precious book of psalms clutched in my hand, I sat watching a thrush searching through leaf-litter for snails, my mind as still as the morning.

All too soon the peace was shattered. Loud voices carried on the air and I knew something was amiss. Though duty-bound to go to my mother, the stubbornness she tried so hard to expunge came to the fore and I remained beneath the roses, their delicate white petals dotted around my feet like summer snowflakes.

All was quiet once more, save for the tap-tap-tapping of the thrush breaking his hard-earned gains upon a stone.

'So this is where you hide.' Deep tones shattered the stillness.

Time seemed to halt, as did my breathing. Before me stood the one man in Christendom I most desired to see. Dickon. Certain this was a trick of the light, or of my mind, I almost fled from the seat.

Yet there he stood, a grin spreading across his handsome face. Though I opened my mouth, no words came out. Face flushing with heat, my head dropped so he would not see my shame.

'Ah, Anne, I had hoped you would be pleased to see me. Should I leave you be?'

Fear he had misinterpreted my actions choked me. *'No!'*

'Should I escort you back to the house instead?'

'No.' My foolish mouth said once more.

Dickon's brow creased, shadowing his eyes. 'Francis led me to believe I might receive a warmer welcome . . . '

If I did not take myself in hand, he would be gone, thinking me unhappy about this visit. I lurched forwards, the psalter slipping from my lap.

'Have a care, Anne, or you will fall from the bench.' He placed a hand on my shoulder and I trembled beneath it. 'If I have disturbed your peace please say so and I shall leave this instant.'

'No!' I cried once more. Dickon must think me a simpleton but in truth, my tongue would not work. So many times had I imagined this moment, so many times had I yearned to see my dear friend, but now he had come I was rendered dumb.

To my eternal joy, Dickon lowered himself onto the bench. His eyes had not left my face and though I felt their heat, I dared not look at him, dared not look upon the face I saw in my dreams.

'We should return,' he said soft and low. 'Your lady mother was most unhappy you were nowhere to be found. She has servants looking high and low, though I doubt any will have searched the hayloft as I did.'

My head turned slowly. At last my eyes looked into his. Still dark, even with the brightness of this summer's morn, they glinted with amusement.

'Though you have indeed grown into a fine lady, I suspect beneath these silks still lurks the urchin I knew, determined to wilfulness and disobedience.'

The words could have been my mother's but the tone was most assuredly not. Moreover, I was certain a hint of admiration lurked in Dickon's tone.

I took a deep breath, and then graced him with a smile. 'I . . . I meant no offence by my silence but your appearance surprised me beyond words, appearing like an apparition in the night. Indeed, I can still scarcely believe you are here.'

The light tone still ringing with good humour, he murmured, 'For certes I am no apparition.'

Laughter burst from my mouth. 'I can see that now and shall thank The Lord most heartily for it.'

Dickon reached down to retrieve my psalter, turning it over and over in his hands. 'This is a most comfortable spot to read and take the air. I wish for nothing more than time enough to enjoy your company.'

My heart pounded so fiercely, Dickon must have heard its beat. Swallowing again and again as perspiration formed upon my brow and beneath my gown, I fought for some composure. After what seemed like an age, I was finally able to speak to the person beside me, who I had yearned to see for so many months. Yet I dared not say what was truly in my heart for propriety would not allow such disclosures. Nor could I pour out my woes and grief, for duty would not allow such betrayal. Instead, I sought solace in courtesy, praying my dearest friend could read through the veil.

'Then stay awhile and dine with us . . .' my voice was barely more than a whisper. I knew not from where the courage came to issue such an invite, yet I had to speak those words, had to keep my dear friend here a moment longer if I could.

His handsome features dropped. 'Ah, Anne, this visit is only brief. I have a king to attend and you have a mother, one who was less than happy to find you absent.'

Dickon spoke the truth of Mama's dissatisfaction with me, I was in no doubt. Though bitterly disappointed our reunion was to be so brief, I sought to redeem my lack of conversation. 'She can be quite disagreeable these days, pray how did you secure her agreement to join me out here?'

'I offered to search for you, hoping to find you first and have a moment's quiet conversation.' Dickon smiled and my heart skipped a beat or two.

Nothing would be more delightful than to detain my dear friend awhile, but I was aware any delay would cause only trouble for both of us. Forcing myself up off the seat, I stood barring the way and drinking in all I could before he was gone from me. Dickon stood too, his eyes still flicking over my face. Reaching out, he plucked a newly-opened rose from the bower above us. Stripping the thorns from its stem, he placed the white flower in my hand.

'This month has seen your birthday,' he grinned. 'And if I recall correctly, you have now attained the great age of twelve.'

Trust my friend to remember such a trivial thing while the family had missed it yet again. Only Mother Nature had marked my birth-month, presenting me with the gift of womanhood for which I was inherently ungrateful. Exhausted by a particularly arduous day of travel on our way to London, the day had been miserable enough already without her unwelcome gift.

Heart still pounding, I took some comfort that Dickon had remembered me at all, but also another moment to look at him properly. Since our last and rather brief meeting, he had grown taller again though he was still not even as tall as Papa. Broader across the shoulders than before and dressed in fine calf-skin riding boots, grey hose and a wine-coloured tunic made from the finest lightweight wool-cloth England could produce, he appeared every inch the royal duke. Yet beneath the auburn-streaked hair curling to his collar, the dark blue eyes still sang of the boy I once knew. He was, for I thought of it each day, more than sixteen years of age and almost a man. A man I knew nothing about and, for a heartbeat, I mourned for those lost conversations, chess games and shared tales of chivalry, for we could never regain those lost years.

'Anne?'

As my eyes took in more of this apparition, I saw Francis was right; whatever affliction had caused physicians to be consulted and clothing altered, there was no sign of it as he stood before me on this beautiful summer morn.

'The day is already far too hot for my liking,' Flustered by his presence and unnerved by the depth of my regret, I fanned my face in a feeble attempt to hide the discomfort. 'I should have sought a cooler spot.'

Dickon looked up at the roof of white flowers above us, as if to say there was nowhere more shaded to be found. He smiled once more. 'In my mind, I have pictured you as the little girl I last saw at Cawood. Though Francis has supplied more than sufficient detail on how you have grown, I confess to some surprise.'

'In what way?' Pray to God he was not disappointed.

He paused for a moment, clearly choosing his words with care. 'I did not expect to see you so refined, nor so poised and elegant. The little girl has quite vanished.'

Perhaps Dickon meant his words to compliment, perhaps he meant to be kindly but I sensed he felt cheated somehow, as if he wanted to see a child and not a girl on the cusp of womanhood. Yet why he should wish this, I did not know.

Dickon gestured towards the house and side-by-side we moved as slowly as snails might. It was as though neither of us wished to reach the cool of the building nor the stares of the others, knowing our time alone was at an end.

'We received word your brother George might pay us a visit,' I blustered as we walked. 'But we did not expect the honour of receiving you also.'

He halted right in the middle of the path. 'Your father may have felt it better I left Middleham but that does not change the fact your family, and most of all you, Anne, were always kind to me. I have long desired to pay my respects to your lady mother and our return from Canterbury offered such an opportunity. The fact your father is absent made it an easy decision.'

'My Lord, you are always welcome in our home.' Unsure why he was here, I sought refuge in a more formal courtesy. If Dickon had come merely to pay his respects because of past kindness, then hope was lost.

He did not move. 'Have I offended you in some way?'

'Nothing could have pleased me more than this unexpected visit, but . . . '

Dickon nodded, his expression pained. 'So much has happened since last we spoke, perhaps like myself, you do not know where to begin.'

I let out such a sigh he reached across and clasped my arm. 'I understand, dear friend, and it pains me too that we are little more than strangers. You and I are further casualties of that wretched secret wedding.'

And of my father's growing dissatisfaction - but I dared not speak those words out loud.

As I stifled a sob at his honesty, he released my arm as if suddenly aware of the impropriety. 'Our families would have kept us apart even if I was still your father's ward, for by now they would have decided where we were both to be wed.'

No doubt they would, though I suspected my father harboured the same hopes as I did, but whether the king saw me as a suitable bride for his youngest brother, only the Lord above knew. Dickon gave nothing away on the matter and for that I was grateful. If my father continued with his dissention, no marriage could happen while King Edward sat on the throne.

'Come,' he ordered, snapping me from darkening thoughts. 'We must not tarry or your mother will ensure we are kept apart whether I discovered your whereabouts or not.'

'I still have it!' I blurted out.

His brow creased once more. 'What do you still have, Anne?'

'The pin.'

Dickon's expression was blank for more than a heartbeat before his eyes lit up. 'Ah, the silvered boar, I presume?'

I nodded, wondering if I had made a fool of myself.

'And do you wear it?' he asked in such a low voice I could barely hear the words.

Under the intensity of his gaze, I blushed and dropped my head. 'Since the day it was put into my hand.'

'I confess surprise you have not lost or discarded such a trivial thing.' His hand reached out to my chin, lifting my face up. Still looking at me with intent, he murmured, 'But it pleases me to know you keep it close.'

Glancing down, I hid my awkwardness once more. As if he knew of my discomfort, Dickon's hand fell away, reaching for the leather pouch suspended from his belt. From within he drew something small.

'Hold out your hand,' he ordered.

Into my outstretched palm he dropped something small and made of metal. Memories of that night in the darkened solar with Francis flooded back into my mind for in my hand sat another pin. I frowned, holding it between my fingers to see the detail.

'From the shrine of St Thomas,' he smiled. 'I bought more than one, though at the time I did not know why. Now it is clear why I did such a strange thing.'

So delighted was I with this precious and unexpected gift, once again words failed me. Though produced in great numbers and not especially finely made, these pins were sold to those who visited the shrine, often travelling miles to pay pilgrimage. The badge was in the shape of a pair of gloves, representing the saint's vestments I presumed, and was now as precious to me as that tiny silvered boar.

'Think of it as a late birthday gift,' he smiled again. 'For it may last a little longer than a flower in this heat.'

Turning, he stepped into the house while I remained on the step a moment longer. As I looked down, the rose he had plucked earlier was still clutched in my hand. I dared not walk inside with it for Mama and Isobel would make much of such a simple gift, so I enclosed it carefully inside my psalter, beside the word of The Lord. The pin I secured inside my gown and would attach it to my chemise at the earliest opportunity, as close to my heart as it could be.

After a cup of ale and a plate of food, my dear friend made his farewells while George lazed on the settle, announcing how he needed a bed for the night. Dickon was merely passing through on his way back to the king, meeting him at The Tower where they would take a boat upriver to Shene to join the queen. George was here at my father's invitation and was not about to make the effort to come back another day.

Mama bade me see Dickon away, declaring it far too hot to venture out of doors. I suspected she wanted to chaperone Isobel, for though there might be secret plans to wed the young couple, propriety must still be observed. It did not occur to her the youngest daughter might be more in need of a watchful eye, and I said a silent prayer of thanks for my mother's failings this day.

Out in the stable yard with Dickon, I still struggled to believe he stood before me but, moreover, I was fearful it might be another three years before I set eyes upon him once more. Taking in his countenance in the moments before he departed, I realised he had grown taller than George. 'Twas only a little, so little it would not be noticed by most, but I had noticed, and so had George if his barbed comments were anything to go by.

'Farewell, my Lord.' I said, seeking refuge once more in politeness. 'Travel safe and may Our Lady of Heaven watch over you.'

He stared at me. 'Just because you dress like a fine lady does not mean you need to speak like one with me. It is I, your childhood friend, the one you revealed your secrets to.'

All save one secret – the greatest of them all. I stared at the ground, not brave enough to look into those dark, all-knowing eyes.

'I have missed you,' I admitted. 'The Lord knows how lonely these last years have been.'

He gave my arm a gentle squeeze. 'And I you, little Annie. Hardly a day passes when I do not think back to those days. They were precious times.'

Precious times indeed.

'I recall our lessons with clarity . . .' he continued without giving me a chance to respond. 'Though our lessons were separate I am certain yours reflected ours in one aspect especially.'

'What aspect is that?' My voice was barely audible so great was my fear of what he was about to say.

'How we must always do as bid by our elders and betters.'

'We must do as bid,' I repeated like a child.

Clasping my hand, Dickon murmured, 'Remember those words, for I most certainly shall.'

My head jerked up and I looked deep into those eyes. Here was another trying to tell me something without words. In the confusion, I felt my brow crease.

As he saw this, Dickon gave a quiet laugh. 'I see you despise subterfuge almost as much as I do. Rest assured, Anne, no harm is intended by my words, saying simply I consider the sin not yours to carry.'

With that he mounted his horse and turned from me. Stunned, I stood in the same spot, the sun beating down upon my head and so much sweat dripping into my eyes it seemed tears streamed down my face as he rode out through the gate.

Only as I lay in my bed later that night did I understand what Dickon had really said. He needed me to understand whatever path my father chose from here on, he did not hold me culpable. The sins of the father would not rest upon this child; at least in the eyes of the Duke of Gloucester. My heart rose and sank at the same time. Dickon knew I had no choice and must do as my father bid but he also knew, or at least suspected, my father was marking time and that I could do naught to halt the coming storm.

# Chapter Seven – Old Father Thames

### *1469*

I began to believe it might well be years before I set eyes upon my dear friend again. Months had passed, as had the feasts of Michaelmas and Christmas. Back up in our northern fortress of Middleham, winter held us tight in its icy grip and it was as though those precious few moments in a summer garden had never happened.

Though my father had maintained an air of congeniality for the first part of the previous year, after his triumphant escort of the king's sister, the bitterness lurking beneath had risen to the fore and he had taken every opportunity to undermine Edward's advantages from the Burgundian match. Rumour was rife, some saying how Edward planned a strike while others suggested the wily King Louis of France would take up arms on behalf of the Lancastrians. None knew what to believe, especially when further tales told of the deposed Queen Margaret being poised to sail from Harfleur. Lord Scales, another Wydville sibling, was forced to put the fleet to sea, monitoring the water between England and Normandy for several weeks, at enormous expense to King Edward. Taking her cue from Papa's letters, no doubt, Mama relished relaying events such as these, though I tried not to react to the delight in her tone as she did so. However, she was far less gleeful when telling us of the recent arrest of John de Vere, Earl of Oxford, husband of Papa's younger sister, Margaret.

It also transpired the Wydvilles succeeded where my father had not; by tainting their own reputation. Informed by my father's letters, Mama relayed how, sometime past, the queen's mother had coveted a particularly fine tapestry belonging to a certain Thomas Cook, previous Lord Mayor of London and purveyor of tapestries and cloth. Cook refused to sell at the price demanded and when he was later arrested upon suspicion of plotting with Lancastrians, the queen's father, Earl Rivers, seized the opportunity to plunder Cook's houses, taking many valuable goods, the tapestry included. Though Cook was later pardoned, he was kept in prison until Rivers had extracted a small fortune in fines from the man. At the same time, a tale circulated that tarnished the queen's reputation directly, telling how she had exacted revenge upon the Irish Earl of Desmond, whose reckless comment about how Edward might have done better to marry a king's daughter had resulted in his execution. Though Desmond had also been accused of treason and other crimes by his enemies, it suited a great many at this time to believe his death lay firmly at the feet of the queen. While no doubt embellished and exaggerated, tales of this nature did nothing to endear the Wydvilles to the populous, and the relish with which Mama relayed them to us discomforted me deeply.

I, of course, only learned about events much later than they had occurred, and even then had to piece together Mama's snippets with gossip overheard from the servants, but it still was as if a dagger was forced into my flesh. Each thrust Papa made at the House of York, and of course, the Wydvilles, was another at Dickon. There were many, many nights when I cried myself to sleep.

Revelling in King Edward's discomfiture and misfortune, my family became ever more tightly bound and far less open in discussion when I was in their company.    Mama, however, still let enough slip to pepper my dreams with nightmares.

'Isobel!' she hissed across the solar one grey afternoon as we sat by the fire, clearly believing I was absorbed in my reading. 'I have heard from your father. Come here so I may relay his news.'

Eyes cast down I kept reading, knowing Mama was deliberately ignoring me.  A few weeks before at the beginning of Lent, Papa had sailed for Calais where he had been commissioned to survey the boundaries of English territories.  Whilst there, he had taken time to travel to pay his respects to the Duke of Burgundy and his letters to Mama had been many, for he had much to relay of this business.  Most from his letters she willingly shared; the weather, the duties he had to perform, the route he travelled to St Omer to meet with Duke Charles and his honoured guest, Sigismund, the Archduke of Austria.  It was with great pride Mama declared how Papa then accompanied the duke a short distance south to Aire, to meet with Duchess Margaret, sister to King Edward and who was the lady he had so recently escorted in her bridal procession.

Up until this moment of secrecy, Mama had always included me in the sharing of news.  Indeed, she had actively encouraged me to hear, insisting it was a part of my education.  Today it was as though I was not in the same room.

'Pray what does Papa say?' Isobel was eager for news.  I sensed Mama's eyes upon me and kept my eyes upon the book, though I read not a word.

'He has received word from his brother, the archbishop,' she murmured.

Isobel drew breath. 'And does Uncle George send good tidings?'

'The best we could wish for.'

116

If the required papal dispensation had been procured as Mama had alluded, then it was only a matter of time before my father held the document in his hands. Eyes still cast down upon my book, I gave what I hoped was a good impression of someone utterly oblivious to events around them. But inside I quaked with fear. We were about to set out upon a journey that might not have a way back.

'Anne.' Mama's cold tones came across the solar. 'While the roads are dry we shall make for Warwick Castle. Ensure you are prepared to leave in the morn for we will celebrate Easter there and await news of your father's return. He hopes to join us later in the spring.'

My hand flew to my breastbone. All the treasures I owned lay beneath my gown, save one. I needed nothing more for my journey except the small pin in the shape of a boar, a badge of St Thomas and my psalter, inside which lay a dried and faded flower, as precious to me as the words of Our Lord it nestled between. Fine gowns and heavy headcresses I could do without, cloaks and gloves I would willingly do without, if only my treasures were safe.

'What ails you this time, child?' Mama's tone held its usual hint of disappointment.

'Nothing Mama, I am quite well.'

Clasping hold of my chin, she roughly turned my head from side to side. 'Your colour is good, better than I have seen it for some time, yet I do not understand why you should be so listless. Does this magnificent place not offer distraction enough for your young mind?'

Warwick Castle offered distraction aplenty and that was precisely what ailed me. I yearned for memories I could conjure up at any moment; a step I had sat upon with my friend, a spot in the yard where I had watched him practice, a seat in the solar he had occupied. I yearned for the moors, for skies so wide I could see to the ends of the world, not a land swathed in green, suffocated by the Forest of Arden advancing threateningly upon the horizon. I yearned for a memory that had substance instead of wistful dreaming. Though a village grew beside the great castle at Warwick, and the River Avon turned and twisted about us, I felt trapped in this place, as though I should never escape. But I could not say so to Mama, for she would think me ungrateful for the manner of my birth and the privilege it allowed.

As bluebells bloomed in the copses around the castle, early May brought news that Papa had returned to English shores. Mama prepared for his arrival but he was delayed in the south, having received word a certain Robin of Redesdale had recently sprung to arms in the north. Papa's younger brother John, Earl of Northumberland, hastily gathered men to put down the rising. It was only as I studied Mama's face as she read of this, did I understand our uncle was facing men Papa had stirred and recruited, men who were quite possibly his own retainers and kin – and who had rallied far earlier than intended - causing our Uncle John to perform duties that caused him much grief. This astonishing fact was confirmed as we received word the perpetrators had conveniently slipped away into Lancashire.

As Mama kept up the pretence of a quiet home life, she received letters and visitors almost continually. While Isobel and I had nothing to do with her endeavours, indeed, we were deliberately kept away, I suspected she must have been acting on behalf of Papa, for he now attended the king at Windsor and, while there, could only respond to the most benign of matters.

Shortly after, another 'Robin' appeared, this time on the east coast of Yorkshire, in Holderness. As Mama read of this from a letter, I wondered if our journey south to Warwick had been planned well beforehand, especially as Papa relayed how the king had taken some persuading not to ride north to address the situation. Papa had assured His Grace all was under control in the hands of our uncle, the Earl of Northumberland, and the king had no need to bestir himself for such minor matters. Indeed, the rebels had championed for the restoration of Henry Percy to the Earldom of Northumberland but I had been schooled well enough to know Papa would not tolerate Lancastrian threats – or such a strong rival in the north. Soon enough, we learned our uncle had met the rioters at the gates of York whereupon he beheaded their leader. The king must have been content with the outcome for he abandoned all thought of travelling north, deciding to visit the shrines of Bury St Edmunds and Our Lady of Walsingham instead, making his way into East Anglia at a leisurely pace. As Mama carelessly relayed how, besides His Grace's Wydville family, the retinue had composed of the king and his youngest brother, Dickon. My heart pounded at the mention of that name.

'Ah,' Mama mused as she scanned the next page of Papa's letter. 'We shall not remain here for much longer.'

'Do we go home?' I blurted out, desperate to be back in Wensleydale and the castle I held most dear.

The ice in Mama's eyes was cooler than ever. 'Indeed not, we ride south.'

As I looked away to hide my reddened cheeks, Isobel squealed in delight. 'London, shall we make for the city or for the court?'

'Neither, my sweet,' Mama cooed. 'Though we shall still pack your finest gowns, especially the pale-blue silk you have not yet worn.'

Isobel squealed again and I braved a glance at my mother. Her face was a picture of triumph but I could take no joy in this news for such vague tidings could only serve us ill.

How right I was. Our carriage was accompanied by a small party of Papa's best men-at-arms, and in such company, we left Warwick just before dawn the next day. Instead of heading towards the ancient Roman road of Watling Street as I hoped, we turned southwest, following another ancient road, The Fosse Way. On we went till the green of Warwick was a distant memory and the world ahead opened up into a wider and wilder vista. As the road before us rose and fell, traversing the higher ground made famous by wool from these rolling hills, I prayed and prayed we would turn and make for London. We did not, turning east instead and making, Mama informed us, for Oxford. I could not understand what business we could possibly have in that esteemed place of learning, unless it was to stop over at one of the many abbeys or priories.

Before we reached the city our party turned once more, the escorting sergeant-at-arms drawing level with our carriage to speak in hushed tones to Mama. Isobel and I were not allowed to converse with our escorts at any time, so unless my mother decided to divulge our destination, I had no choice but to wait to be informed. Fortunately for our patience, she soon deigned to disclose our lodgings for the night and my heart leapt once more. We were bound for Minster Lovell, the family seat of my friend, Francis, Viscount Lovell.

Yet as we arrived at this well-appointed manor house, all hope was dashed to the ground. Met by my sullen cousin, Ann, and her mother, my aunt, it was instantly clear Francis was not in residence. Though disappointed by his absence, I drew some comfort from the fact Dickon had visited this place more than once and that evening I wandered around the family rooms as if he might suddenly appear from the shadows. It was poor consolation but I sought it wherever I could.

Mama spent much of our time at the Minster shut away with my aunt and Isobel. It was clear to both Cousin Ann and myself they did not require our counsel and we both felt the ignominy of it. The situation did not draw us any closer despite our exclusion and the best part of a day and night was spent in uncomfortable silence as our elders discussed we knew not what.

Having rested at Minster Lovell, we resumed our journey, bypassing Oxford and heading south to Wallingford. Our baggage had been sent on beforehand, which surprised me until I learned we were to take boats downriver. After a night in lodgings, we began the next stage of our journey well before the dawn and I soon suspected our route had been carefully planned by Papa as it transpired the Watermen employed to transport us were not known to the locals thereabouts.

The day spent sailing the upper reaches of the Thames, though long, I enjoyed especially. Although we travelled in far less comfort than expected, open to the weather save for a canvas to shield us from the sun and sat amongst the men paid to row us, the day was bright and warm, the water smooth and though the river teemed with other folk in small craft, we passed quietly and unremarked upon. Isobel and Mama whispered between themselves for almost the entire journey but I cared not. Trailing my fingers in the cool water, the feast of green meadows and sweeping willows on either bank more than compensated for their petty secrets.

At Kingston, we alighted and were escorted by our men to lodgings already secured for the night. I saw nothing of the town, for next day we rose well before the dawn and taken back to the river, boarding a different boat, complete with small cabin and sail. When I questioned this, Mama remarked how we were upon the tidal reaches of the river and that before long I would prefer to be aboard a sturdier vessel. Forced to wait until the tide was right, it was some hours before we finally set sail.

'Where do we go?' I dared to ask, once the town faded from view.

Mama looked at me for a moment, as if deciding how much I should know. 'We go to Dartford, to the priory there.'

'Not to London?' I ventured. 'Or Westminster?'

'No,' she snapped, but then seemed to regret the terse tone. 'Your father thinks it best if we avoid the city. By travelling this way, we shall do exactly that.'

'Is there plague?' It was not unknown for plague to sweep the city in the summer months and many nobles, the king and queen too, stayed away till the weather cooled and the sickness subsided.

'Not that I am aware,' Mama revealed, eyeing me as she spoke. 'Your father has business in Kent and, though we go to join him, it is not always necessary to announce one's plans to the world.'

Wherever we were bound, Papa did not wish it to be known beyond the family. The little pleasure I had taken in our journey thus far, faded entirely. I barely noticed as we sailed past the royal palaces at Windsor, Shene and Westminster, unwilling to allow myself the pain of wondering in which of these my dear friend had so recently laid his head. Soon though, I was jolted from this melancholy as we were ordered to make ready to pass under the great bridge of London. At the command to brace and be calm, I protested loudly, having heard tales of horror as boats tried to shoot the bridge but were dashed to pieces upon the bulky starlings supporting the bridge above, the occupants drowned in the murky, unforgiving waters.

'Cease your fretting, child, and behave like the lady you are!' Mama's terse tones sounded over the rush of the river. 'All know the tale of the old Duke of Norfolk and how he escaped with his life by leaping onto a starling. For those very reasons, your father has engaged the most experienced Watermen money can buy. We must trust in them and in The Lord.'

These barbed comments told me not only that the king was not to learn of our presence – but that Papa was willing to risk our lives to keep this journey quiet. As the buildings on the bridge loomed dark and menacing, I clasped my hands and prayed like I had never prayed before, only breaking the tight hand-fast to touch the badge of St Thomas still fastened to my chemise, in the faint hope he would look kindly upon this fearful wretch.

The river widened as we left the city behind, its distant banks given over to meadows or mud-flats and marshes but I was in no state to notice. After negotiating the tricky waters beneath the bridge, I sat with eyes closed and hands clasped, unaware as we sailed smoother waters past marshland and wilderness until, at last, our small ship turned into the mouth of the River Darent and on towards the small town of Dartford. As we finally tied up at the small dock, I yearned to be at the priory. My legs were unsteady even upon firm ground, and the only comfort at my disposal was the fact Dickon had stayed in this place but a twelvemonth before. Though comforted greatly by this and the silvered boar still secured beneath my gown, I was in shock, eating little and sleeping even less. I took scant notice of my surroundings, the terrifying assault on London Bridge still vivid in my young mind. Thankful to see a carriage awaiting us the next morning, I climbed inside without complaint, relishing the security of being ashore, especially as my birth-month had seen us once again take to the road, my special day unremarked upon and forgotten.

From Dartford we joined the ancient road towards Canterbury. To my distress, we avoided the ancient city, despite my fervent wished to give thanks after surviving the river. My protests were ignored as we headed for the small coastal town of Sandwich, a place my sister and mother appeared unusually keen to reach.

'Richard,' Mama clasped my father's hands as he greeted us at journey's end. Pulling her into a swift embrace, they exchanged brief but quiet words.

'This is a most auspicious day,' Papa announced, turning to us. 'Refresh yourselves after such a long journey, and then I shall reveal all.'

In that moment, I stretched out my arms to him, exactly as I had done in the old days when he returned to us. After the ordeal of shooting under London Bridge, confidence had left me completely and I felt far younger than my thirteen years. But instead of the embrace I yearned for, Papa simply took my hands and held me at a distance.

'Anne,' he said in a low voice. 'I am relieved to see you but there is much to be done. We must away to give thanks to The Lord for delivering you all safely here.'

Though he spoke the words to my face, Papa's eyes revealed how his mind was already upon other matters, preoccupied with his next move, no doubt. I curtsied, hollow and empty inside, for my dear father had not the time or inclination to spare a moment to comfort me, so immersed was he in the game being played betwixt crown and earl.

We became quite the family party at Sandwich when our Uncle George, Archbishop of York, greeted us at our lodgings. Though the king had bid him go north to investigate the disturbances within his See, the wily archbishop had implied he would do so as soon as he had attended to a trivial matter demanding his time. By joining us at Sandwich, he had defied the king instead of doing his bidding, though it was clear from his whispered conversations with Papa, the archbishop had never intended travelling north. When another George, the Duke of Clarence, arrived shortly after, there soon appeared a distinct atmosphere of celebration. Unbeknown to the king, the duke was also party to the shroud of secrecy wrapped around our family these days. My heart sank for I knew full well no good could come of such underhand arrangements.

Papa was as much a man of the sea as he was a man of the land. Made Captain of Calais around the time of my birth, he had been given funds to protect the

125

garrison at Calais after the sacking of Sandwich ignited fears of a French invasion. Under orders, his ships sailed up and down the English Channel, patrolling the waters, conducting what was considered by some to be acts of piracy against the Castilian and Hanseatic fleets. Papa always said he did what he did for the realm and I never doubted him for a moment, for we were taught his reputation as a military leader with connections to the leading noblemen of France and Burgundy had brought England many benefits. As both a girl-child and obedient daughter, it would never have occurred to me to question why my father conducted himself so.

In the heat of a June day, we stood upon the quayside, overseeing the fruits of my father's reputation as a seaman and loyal protector of England's interests. Papa's flagship 'Trinity' had been refitted and now sat splendid in her berth. In all our finery, careful negotiation was needed to cross the gang-plank and board. We need not have worried, Papa's men were waiting with outstretched hands should one of us lose our footing. Once safely on deck, we assembled with others already waiting so the archbishop could bless the ship. High Mass would also be said, performed in the presence of my father, the Duke of Clarence, the Bishop of London and the Prior of Christ Church Abbey, Canterbury and a number of Papa's friends and retainers.

Though I ought to have taken joy in such a prestigious dedication, I could not. The mere presence of my uncle was enough to stir up concern, without that of the duke and other prelates. I shivered throughout the service despite a blazing summer sun. Far too frequently did my hand flick up to caress the trim of my gown, under which lay two of my most treasured possessions. As my fingertips grazed the silvered boar, I wondered what Dickon would make of such a gathering. Though justified by the blessing of the ship in the name of The Lord and King Edward, I knew he would see through the fragile veneer of propriety and see this charade for what it truly was.

In our lodgings at The Bell Inn, situated upon the quay and in view of Papa's fine ship, I retired to my chamber as soon as Mama would allow. Though displeased with my conduct, she clearly had other matters to occupy the time as I received no immediate chastisement. Only when Isobel crept into bed later did I discover what was afoot.

'I trust you will be in better spirits on the morrow, sister, for your face was a poor sight today.' Isobel was as unkind as ever.

'Pray what is to happen on the morrow that requires my enthusiasm?' I feigned interest but in truth had no desire to hear what my sister had to say lest it confirm my dark suspicions.

Giving a deep sigh, Isobel fingered the gown spread out over a chair. 'We set sail, sister.'

Clutching at the sheets, I drew a deep breath. 'And where are we bound?'

'You are such a simpleton, Anne, can you not guess?'

'Calais,' I murmured as my sister's eyes lit up.

'The Lord be praised!' she laughed. 'My little sister is not a lackwit after all.'

Perhaps would be better for us all if I were that foolish, and blind, too. My sister was about to be wed in Calais, directly against the king's wishes, hence the reason for all the secrecy. I wondered what my dearest friend would make of events, though I knew he, too, would disapprove of such scheming. The open disregard for His Grace's opinion was reason enough for

127

him to gainsay such an arrangement, whatever the justification behind it. The secrecy and deliberate concealment of the arrangements would only further sour his opinion of those involved. I tried with all my might to conjure up an image, but could no longer see Dickon's face in my mind. The silhouette was there, standing in the garden exactly as I had seen him on that June day last year but, as I thought and thought of him, the shadowy figure began to fade till there was no more than the arbour, rose petals blowing on the breeze and each snow-white bloom had been stripped bare.

'So you are to become a duchess,' I said, the words springing from my mouth before I had time to stop them.

'Of course I am, exactly as Papa said. Why should we take a ship otherwise?'

Why else indeed. After his refusal of the match, Edward would hardly allow use of St Stephen's chapel in Westminster Palace. Indeed, no chapel the length and breadth of the realm could host the ceremony without attracting a king's fury. I drew the coverlet back over my shoulders, but 'twas no more than a gesture to thwart conversation, for the night was ungodly hot. Though huddling down in the bed, I could scarcely sleep, for we were about to openly defy His Grace, King Edward. Dickon might not see my father's sins as mine, but only the Lord above knew what Edward would think when he learned of our conduct.

Mama, Isobel and I set sail upon the next tide, accompanied by our Uncle George and a small number of retainers I knew not. Papa and my new brother-in-law-to-be, George, stayed behind having business to do before they made for Calais. I later learned how they rode back to Canterbury, arriving just two days after the Duchess of York appeared at Christ Church Abbey, announcing she wished to see her son. I had no knowledge of what occurred betwixt the duchess and her son, was not told whether they met or if the duchess had somehow caught wind of her son's plans. Even if she had been privy to such knowledge, I did not want to imagine the resulting altercation.

Papa made directly for London, knowing the king was busy gathering his troops at Fotheringhay in Northamptonshire and no doubt accompanied by his most loyal of brothers: Dickon. I heard whispers of how Robin of Redesdale's men were moving south and how Papa, confident in his schemes, had made contact with this 'Robin', asking they head west around the king's forces and so block his route to London. Papa also wrote to friends and well-wishers in the city of Coventry announcing he was about to wed Isobel to George, Duke of Clarence, after which he intended to join the king. He then commanded the city to prepare armed men to accompany him.

And in such fashion the forbidden wedding was announced to the world. Though I was safely ensconced in the comfort of Calais Castle, Dickon drifted farther away from me with each passing hour.

'Gently, Anne!' Isobel snapped, snatching the comb from my hand. 'Or you will take the skin from my scalp.'

'And we cannot have that.' As Mama took over, I retreated to the back of the chamber, hiding in shadows. It was early July and the summer heat unbearable. Though every effort had been made to encourage cooler air into the chamber, with so many ladies crammed inside and so many candles lit, the heat seemed worse that it had earlier in the day as we watched my uncle perform a wedding forbidden by the King of England. Sitting beside the open window, I fanned my face, looking out into the darkness and wondering what my friend did this night.

My sister was being made ready for her husband and shortly we would put her to bed and leave the chamber. The thought of what was about to happen in the great bed beside us, to be left exposed and vulnerable before a man, made me quite ill. It was something I also must endure for we had been taught this was our Christian duty; to beget children, and to do so we must endure the marriage bed – and whatever demands our husbands might make upon us. Papa would never consider we should not marry, for it was the only way to secure inheritance and pass on titles and lands while hopefully acquiring more. Though he did not mention the lack of sons so much these days, I knew it still preyed upon his mind and was no doubt one of the reasons this particular match appealed so much.

As she laughed with Mama, Lady Wenlock and the other ladies, Isobel glowed. Her cheeks flushed with colour, incited by both wine and anticipation. Whatever instruction she had received about what awaited her this night, evidently distressed her not. Indeed, as I watched from the shadows, I thought she showed rather more excitement than a virgin-maid ought.

'There.' Mama stepped back to admire her work. 'You are a truly beautiful bride, Isobel, as I knew you would be. Your husband will not be disappointed.'

As Isobel lifted a silvered hand-mirror and inspected closely, I could not help but feel some small measure of envy. Bathed in the golden glow of

130

candlelight, my sister's fair hair gleamed and shone as though it belonged to the angels themselves. Hanging down past her waist, the silken locks were unadorned save for two tiny twists draped from her temples and lightly knotted at the back of her head. With blue eyes bright as a summer sky, she nodded approval at the women's work. Groomed, powdered and fragranced, Isobel wore nothing more than a light dressing-gown and the wedding band upon her hand.

I watched in silence as Mama and Lady Wenlock escorted her to the bed. Isobel slipped daintily between the sheets, removing the gown as she did so. As she re-arranged the sheet to protect her modesty, the ladies placed candles in the niches of the headboard and scattered more summer flowers across the cover. At last Mama leaned over to kiss her daughter.

'Remember what I told you,' she looked deep into Isobel's face. 'And all will be well. I bid you a goodnight daughter, and pray Our Lady of Heaven watches over you.'

Lady Wenlock also kissed Isobel, whispering words that made my sister both blush and laugh. The ladies then stepped towards the door.

'Come, Anne.' Mama's tone had regained its usual chill. 'The men will be here soon so we must depart.'

Turning towards the bed, I had every intention of kissing Isobel goodnight and giving her my heartfelt good wishes. Yet as she saw me, my dear sister gave a dismissive little wave as if I was a maid and not her flesh and blood.

'Run along, Anne, for Mama will want you to attend her in my absence . . . but in the morning, come directly, for no doubt you shall want to hear every detail.'

I had no desire to do any such thing and fled from the room without another word.

# Chapter Eight - When Knights and Kings Dance

## *1469*

Isobel was wedded and bedded with all the pomp and celebration she could have wished for. At least, that was how it had occurred according to Mama. I kept silent on the matter, knowing that had my sister been married with the blessing of His Grace, King Edward, not only would she have been wed in the grandeur of an English cathedral, but the highest and oldest blood of the land would have lauded and attended her upon that special day. She might have been joined by the queen herself, eager to ready a bride for bed. Instead, she made do with guests whose primary reason for an invitation was their contempt for the Wydvilles, growing dissatisfaction with the man sitting upon England's throne, or their loyalty to Papa above all others. The ladies attending my sisters were the spouses of such disenchanted men, and while most likely had little choice in their presence, were not those who should have attended Isobel.

Before my sister's marriage bed was even cold, Papa was sending messages back to his supporters, by means of an open letter attached to the petition of the troublesome Robin of Redesdale. Papa, my new brother-in-law, George, and our uncle, the smiling, conniving archbishop, announced they meant to lay this just complaint before the king and called upon men to join them at Canterbury forthwith.

Left in Calais with my mother and bereft sister, I knew little of Papa's movements other than he had sailed back to English shores, head held high and hope burning bright, just a few days after my sister's nuptials.

Mama clearly knew of Papa's intentions but was tight-lipped as the clams we so regularly ate as she waved her kerchief to those heading out into the waters beyond Calais. She was no less reticent for the following few days as we idled in our fine chambers, talking over the minutiae of the wedding yet again. Though I now had the luxury of sleeping alone at night, my sister pining for her husband in the finest bed our accommodation offered, I missed her company despite the condescension she so relentlessly used.

Papa, Clarence and the archbishop arrived safely upon the Kentish coast and made good time in reaching Canterbury, collecting many men along the way. Papa's summons had brought men in their throngs responding to his arms and soon there were hundreds marching upon London itself, under the Bear and Ragged Staff banner. Mama made their entrance into the city sound grand and as though the citizens had welcomed Papa's force with open arms, but I later heard her ladies talking and while the crowds cheered and waved, the mayor and aldermen had given my father little more than the polite welcome his position demanded.

Once Papa had reached London and settled there, King Edward still at a safe distance in Nottingham Castle, he gave out the impression he and Clarence still held every intention of joining the king. Yet my father remained in the south, travelling between the city and Westminster, watching carefully as the hapless councillors ran in circles, unable to get word to or from their king, who was still gathering troops in the counties of the midlands.

During this confusion, we quietly sailed back to England, avoiding Kent and London, and docking at a port somewhere farther west along the south coast. I know not where we landed, for my troubled mind had no interest in these matters, save that we were returned to England. Mama was too preoccupied attending to her duchess daughter to notice my malcontent, though no doubt she thought me envious of my sister's status and an ungrateful daughter, best ignored. But nothing was further from the truth. I knew in my heart Papa had done us an ill turn and fear gripped me almost constantly, for I could see no way to gain the king's forgiveness after such an open and obvious slight.

I asked nothing and, in return, was told nothing, other than we were to make for Warwick and await news from Papa there. Though I had no love for the fortress to which we returned, at least its walls offered security and I almost looked forward to the safety of its inner ward. Passing almost unnoticed after we disembarked, we soon retraced our steps of a few weeks earlier, arriving into the welcoming arms of my aunt and cousin at Minster Lovell where we would rest for a few days. Once more in a building where my dear friend had once laid his head, my spirits began to improve. And though often wandering the halls and passages alone, I took much solace in its stony embrace.

While the ladies fêted Isobel at every opportunity, Cousin Ann struggled to subdue the disdain lurking beneath her plump, pale face. One afternoon as the ladies discussed the wedding for the hundredth time, I watched her troubled visage and it occurred to me there might be an advantage to be gained from the situation.

'Cousin?' I whispered. 'Would you care to take a walk with me? I find the air in here stale and not to my liking.'

Her eyes lit up, though she said nothing. Taking that as a good sign, I rose from the settle, and was rewarded when Ann rose too.

Fresher after a night's rainfall, the gardens were fragrant and lush. We walked in silence for some time, past roses, lavenders, camomile and many other bright flowers of the summer months. At the far end of the path stood a stone bench, a twisted willow arbour above offering shelter. Ann indicated we should sit.

'Thank you, cousin,' I breathed. 'The air is far sweeter out here.'

'Indeed it is,' she said softly. 'I have grown heartily sick of hearing the same tales repeated, as I suspect have you. Better out here, than inside with those self-satisfied harpies.'

I stared at the girl beside me, shocked by the venom in her tone. 'I beg your pardon?'

She gave a snort and grinned. 'Ah, Anne, do not be coy with me, I know you have thoughts about this wedding that must not be spoken out loud.'

'Pray what makes you think that?' I cried, my heart pounding in fear at this unexpected unveiling.

Ann had the grace to stare deep into the garden. 'At first, 'twas no more than a suspicion, but coupled with comments Francis has made and, watching how you struggle to hide the unhappiness beneath your good manners, I must conclude this arrangement is not to your liking.'

Though these words were sharp, Ann's tone was not. It seemed my young cousin was not so thoughtless or foolish after all. I swiftly decided honesty would serve me well here.

'Rest assured I have no designs on becoming a duchess, so do not think me filled with envy for Isobel's position.   What weighs on my mind is the fear repercussions of this forbidden match will reach us all.'

She smiled and took my hand. 'I was less than kind to you last Christmas, Anne, something I beg pardon for. But I confess to fear as well, for your father writes to mine often and I hear his news from Mama, as well as gossip amongst the servants. What I also hear from Francis allows me to consider there is another side to events . . . '

My heart raced. 'And what does such knowledge allow you to conclude.'

Ann looked into my eyes. 'As my dear husband oft reminds me, Edward is our anointed king and whatever his faults, he is owed our loyalty because he was crowned in the sight of God. Moreover, Francis holds the virtue of loyalty in the highest regard and, in this matter, I am in full agreement. Where would this world be if no-one respected such things?'

I nodded, tears stinging my eyes. 'The Lord be thanked sense prevails, in this garden at least.'

She leaned closer. 'And inside the house too. Mama loves your father dear, he is her favourite of brothers, but she is not blinded by his greatness. Indeed, I think she sees his faults clearer than most, better even than your lady mother. Though Mama is careful to conceal it, she fears your father will overreach himself and, in doing so, bring suffering upon all his family.'

'I fear that too, Cousin, more than you can imagine.'

Ann turned to face me. 'Then we must put the past behind us, for a day may come when we need all the friends we can muster. Francis is far away from me at present but I reside in his house and, as his wife, may welcome those whom I choose. You are always welcome here.'

Her words were like a balm upon my poor, battered heart. Though she had not said as much directly, Ann was of the same mind as her husband, and having reconciled herself to my loyalties to Francis and his friends, was offering me shelter and friendship should I ever find myself in need of such.

More than one deep breath was necessary before I could answer such a generous and unexpected announcement. 'I shall remember your kindness with gratitude, Cousin Ann, for who knows what the future may bring.'

Ann took both my hands inside her own. 'You have a deep affection for my mother just as she holds great affection for you. She also worries for your welfare, knowing that unwed, you are at risk from your father's schemes and mother's less than kind hand. Mama fears for you more than your sister, and from what I have learned of late, so do I.'

I could not speak, could not answer. After the ice-cold reception Ann had offered previously, this seemed an unexpected turn-around. But in truth it was not, for Ann had been educated by her husband. Once her eyes and mind had been opened, Ann had recognised her mother's doubts over my family's ambitions. It was heartening to learn I was not alone in fearing for the future.

After my cousin's revealing smile, she seemed unable to return her features to their previous dour expression. I watched in wonderment as this simple action lit up her face almost beyond recognition and could not believe all these years I had thought her a plain girl. Seated in the verdant shade of the arbour, and with a newly-found friend beside me, I clasped hands and thanked The Lord above for this small light in a dark world.

Much occurred during late summer of that year as Mama, Isobel and I sat behind the high stone walls of Warwick Castle. Though I welcomed the scant news from Papa's infrequent letters, each time Mama summoned us, I was gripped by the cold hand of fear, dreading the news he had been captured or killed. Or, worse, hearing Papa's forces had killed someone I held dear.

Brimming with confidence after his easy ride into the city of London, Papa and Clarence had somehow persuaded the city to make loans of a considerable sum available to them, though Mama refused to say exactly how much. As this was occurring, two of the king's favourites, the Earls of Pembroke and Devon met at Banbury, accompanied by Welsh pikemen and archers from the counties of the west. As Robin of Redesdale and his army drew ever closer to Banbury, King Edward remained in Nottingham, awaiting the earls. When Papa and Clarence finally marched out of London, mounted men were sent ahead to support Robin's rebels, only to come upon Devon and Pembroke busy quarrelling amongst themselves. In a fit of pique, Devon withdrew his archers and at an obscure place named Edgecot Moor, just north of Banbury. Pembroke and his Welshmen were caught by surprise as the rebel Robin and his men also arrived. Without Devon's archers, the Welsh suffered losses, though they put up a fight of some note. The Earl of Pembroke, William Herbert, and his brother, Richard, were reported to have fought with great courage, believing Devon would still join them.

Papa's advance force had joined the field with Robin and his men and, in doing so, secured a victory. The Herbert brothers were taken captive and beheaded the next morn in Northampton. Mama relayed the news with such glee I was taken aback for a moment, unable to truly grasp what she was speaking of. My father had not only joined the rebels openly, he had also executed men whose only crime was to support the anointed king of the country. The grip of fear seized me once more; Papa was a military commander, one of the highest in the land, and to minister the king's justice was part of his duty – but not to put men to death when those men were nobles, and supporters of the king. My father had stepped over a line even I could see.

'So,' Mama murmured, the letter clutched tight in her hand and a hint of a smile lingering upon her lips. 'It seems the name Edgecot has struck more fear into the king's men than we could have imagined possible.'

'How so?' Isobel looked up from the table, Papa's beautiful playing cards spread out before her. I noticed she had laid out the picture cards – but as usual, only the lords and ladies.

'It seems when Edward's men heard what had happened, they abandoned the king forthwith.' At Mama's triumphant tone, I shivered despite the heat of the day.

'What has happened to His Grace?' Isobel whirled around, her eyes bright and alert. I bristled as I understood her query; as the king was still without an heir of his body, the heir to the throne was still Isobel's husband, George. I prayed my sister was not being led astray by sinful thoughts, for I feared she was perilously close to breaking the commandment of covetousness.

Mama laughed long and loud. 'Always the diplomat, your father sent his brother, the archbishop to greet Edward. The archbishop and his party soon discovered the king had been deserted by all but a few, his friend Hastings and youngest brother the only men of note left in his company.'

At mention of such a person, my heart began to pound. Praying with all my might the king and his brother had not been harmed, I could not stop shivering, chilled to the bone as I waited for the blow to fall.

'Though your uncle wore armour and not a mitre that day,' Mama continued her tale with relish. 'He soon discovered the king in a small place named Olney, where his silver tongue persuaded Edward it would be in his best interests to be taken to your father. They make their way to Warwick as I speak.'

She had said nothing of my dear friend but I needed to learn the worst of it. Somehow, I know not how, I summoned up courage and, one hand clutched to my breast feeling for that tiny silvered boar, asked what had become of the king's companions. Mama laughed again, staring at me as though I was a fool.

'William Hastings is family,' she sneered. 'How could you forget he wed your Neville aunt Katherine? Sometimes I wonder if you have any wits at all, girl!'

'But if our uncle has captured the king . . .' I spluttered, imagining swords clashing, bloodshed and much worse.

Mama let out a long sigh. 'Katherine would never forgive your father if harm came to her husband, but then, I rather think your father hopes to persuade him to see things as we do. The king's closest companion would make a useful ally.'

She made no mention of Dickon but I dared not ask, dared not draw attention to my interest. I clenched my hands and prayed again.

But the Lord had heard my prayers. Isobel's voice sounded from the settle where she lay surrounded by silk cushions. 'Will Dickon accompany Edward and Papa? I cannot imagine George enjoying entertaining both his brothers here under such circumstances.'

Mama did not look up from the letter, her eyes scanning a second page. 'Hastings was free to go and headed I know not where. I believe Gloucester rode away with him.'

She had referred to Dickon by his title, the first time I had ever heard her speak of him in so remote a manner. That single word told me that she and Papa now viewed my dearest friend as entirely the king's creature, and, I knew without glancing up, her face reflected this change towards the boy she had once welcomed with open arms.

I sat, still as a church carving, almost hoping she would forget I was here.

'Come, Anne.' The cool voice called as my mother rose from her chair. 'His Grace will arrive shortly and we must make ready to greet him in the manner he will expect.'

I did not see Edward arrive. Nor did I see Papa, for he did not accompany his captive into the castle. Confined to my chamber, I begged forgiveness for the sin of falsehood, lying to Mama about cramps in my stomach and the unexpected arrival of my menses. Whether she believed my lie, I cared not. I had no desire to be paraded before this unwilling guest, no desire to pretend all was well while hiding behind a screen of polite conversation and perfect manners. Most of all I had no desire to see a king put in such circumstance while my father played the most dangerous game I had ever known.

Though Edward was to be kept sweet by lavish surroundings, as well as being served the finest foods and entertainment available, Warwick Castle was nothing more than a gilded cage. And Edward knew it. But as I peeked at the man through cracks in the door or from behind the screen, he did not look like a captive to me. Bright honey-coloured hair curled down to his shoulders, while the eyes were as blue as the sky outside, flicking over everything thrice and thrice over again. There was an aura about Edward; it proclaimed him as a man of substance as well as a man with patience to spare. He knew from experience how one opportune move would unexpectedly present itself in the game of power and politics and, when it did, he would be ready to snatch it up. Languid on the settle, one long leg hooked over the arm, Edward gave out the impression he could wait as long as was necessary for that chance to appear, be that days, weeks or months. This languid disinterest was a veil, cleverly concealing opportunity itself, because my father was a man who could not bear to wait a moment longer than he had to – and Edward knew that.

'Anne,' Mama hissed as she made for the king's chamber. 'Get away from there. His Grace does not want you leering at him every hour of every day.'

I mumbled apologies, scurrying away before she could change her mind and insist I join Isobel, already sitting with Edward. Up until this day I had been spared the ordeal, though more by deliberate avoidance than chance, but still I thanked the Lord above for it. As I turned to make my escape, Isobel appeared in the passage, brushing past me and marching along as though something terrible had occurred.

'Whatever has happened?' I cried, snatching at my sister's gown to slow her down.

In defence of her finery, Isobel stopped at last, smoothing down the crumpled silk before pulling me into an alcove hosting a small, open window. We squeezed into the space, breathing in the warm, sweet air of a summer's day. There was not a sound coming from the chamber she had left, as though no-one used the room this day. Yet I knew full well Mama and the king both sat inside.

'The king has received unwelcome news.' Isobel spoke in such quiet tones I could barely hear her. 'Mama bade me leave them alone.'

Peering around the stone, I saw not only the steward leaving the chamber in haste but the guards at the door had stepped away, to stand well out of the king's sight. No one, it appeared, was allowed to be in the same place as this man. Quite what I expected, I did not know, but it seemed odd there was still no sound coming from the room beyond. At the very least I had expected to hear raised voices, perhaps the king voicing his displeasure loudly, or as Mama had been known to do, throw wine cups or other small objects at the wall or nearest servant. This convent-like silence unnerved me and, after a few moments, I dared another look. Mama was stepping out along the passage, her face dark and drawn.

Flattening myself against the wall, I prayed she would not notice but, this time, The Lord heard me not.

'Disobedient child!' she hissed, grasping a handful of gown and pulling me into the passage. 'You remained here, thinking it in order to listen in when the business is not yours to know.'

Dragged along in so rude a fashion, I stayed silent for Mama was in no mood to hear my protests. At the stairwell, she pushed me up against the wall, spitting words into my face.

'Perhaps you should know the king's business after all. Perhaps you should know how that witch still holds him in her spell, blinding him to all but the poison of her kin. He cannot see beyond her grasp, will not see what damage her family have done to this land. Your father has only done what he must, done what others dared not do . . . '

I shuddered at her words. 'Pray, what has Papa done?'

Mama looked at the stones behind my head. 'Along the banks of the River Severn, he came upon the queen's kin.'

An invisible, icy hand laid itself upon my shoulder and I shivered. Only The Lord knew where I found the courage but, driven on by some unseen thing, I needed to learn the truth about what had occurred.

'What happened then, Mama, what has been done?'

'It befell me to inform His Grace how his father-in-law, Earl Rivers, and John, younger son of the earl, were lately executed at Coventry.'

'Who dared to order their deaths?' I ventured to ask, aware if the men had committed no crime worthy of such treatment, the consequences would resonate throughout the land.

Mama spoke not a word, her ice-blue eyes fixed upon my face, while her expression was as still as a stone carving. The silence said everything I needed to know.

'Papa has killed the queen's father and brother?' My voice was inhuman, shrill and scared.

Mama looked down upon my fearful form, her eyes ablaze. 'What else was he to do, pray, let them go free to bring the wrath of that wretched family down upon us?'

I drew a deep breath. 'It will fall upon us for certes. If what you say of the queen is true, may God have mercy upon us, for she will spare none.'

Mama slapped my face. As the force of her hand pushed my head back against the wall she hissed words into my face. The spittle flew onto my cheeks and brow but I dared not move, dared not wipe it away.

'How dare you speak so. Your father does what he can to keep the realm from being bled dry by that family's greed. We are one of the foremost families of the land, our bloodlines are ancient and our houses noble. The queen is naught but a squire's daughter and should be thankful for all she has been given!'

The squire in question, father to the queen, had some years back taken it upon himself to wed the young widow of a duke, without permission from the king at the time. The deceased duke had been brother to a king, while his bride was descended from the noblest house in Luxemburg. Though much was made of their illicit marriage and that the bride was foreign, the widowed duchess traced her ancestors back to the kings of England. That surprised me not, for, as we had learned in our lessons, the royal houses of Europe married their offspring to each other to settle disagreements, close settlements and seal treaties. As we were all cousins in one form or another that no doubt went a long way in explaining the constant turmoil between the royal houses either side of the English Channel. Yet none of this was good enough for

146

Mama, or indeed Papa. The mother was deemed too foreign, the father naught but a lowly squire and the daughter lower-born than desirable for a queen of England. But what I suspected had truly inflamed the ire of older houses, was how the queen's siblings held the positions, titles and power usual y bestowed upon families such as mine. The Wydvilles had risen; their star shone brightly in the heavens because they had willingly taken what was offered, what the rest of the nobility saw as their right and their due. Envy was one of the Seven Deadly Sins but it was hardly an appropriate moment to remind my mother of it.

Still furious with the injustices done to her family, Mama stormed off, abandoning me in the passage. Bravely, I stepped closer to the chamber door. I knew not where such courage sprang from, but curiosity led me on far more than fear of the handsome man who once held me upon his lap. To the discomfiture of the guards, I peered through the door cracks once again. The king was still lounging upon Mama's fine settle. In his hand was an apple, red on one side, green on the other. With practised skill, he threw this apple into the air, catching it deftly with the other hand before it landed upon his chest. This he did many times over, his eye not leaving the fruit as it rose and fell.

Edward did not look like a prisoner. Nor did he look like a man who had just learned of the deaths of his wife's family. The handsome face was expressionless, serene almost, but the blue eyes blazed with an intensity that struck fear into my young heart. Up the apple went, and down it fell. Again and again the king caught it, never missing but, in the blink of an eye, the apple was thrust towards his mouth and he took a large bite. Juice running from the corners of his mouth, he laughed; a maniacal, almost wild sound, and I knew Papa's actions had cut a wound so deep it would never heal.

# Chapter Nine – A Horse to Water

*1469 - August*

My mother's voice echoed around the chamber but I did not move. I had no desire to be paraded before the king like a horse he may wish to purchase. I held my breath, praying she would not think to look behind the window shutters. After expelling a few furious words, Mama headed back down the passageway and I breathed a sigh of relief.

Waiting another moment or two to ensure she did not return, I slid down from my hiding place, confident she had no idea of where I had been.

'Should I tell on you?' a voice sounded from the settle.

I halted mid-room, my hands clenching into fists because I had forgotten that Isobel was there.

'Pray do not . . .' my voice sounded so feeble and terrified, I despised myself for showing such weakness.

'Perhaps it is just as well,' Isobel crooned. 'The king is displeased and with Papa away, Mama must deal with the brunt of his ire.'

Though I knew the king would not abuse my mother, least of all within her own home, for my sister to say such words meant this unnatural situation had only become worse.

'Has something happened?' My voice was even and confident at last.

Isobel laughed. 'Of a fashion, it has. Edward has learned Papa recently bestowed upon himself offices in Wales made vacant by the Herberts' executions, the positon of Chief Justice and Chamberlain of South Wales in particular. Papa has also made appointments to men he considers suitable for offices within the customs service, and appointed our uncle-by-marriage, Lord Hastings, to the positon of Chamberlain of North Wales . . .'

Mama's words about persuading Hastings to our side echoed in my mind. I wondered if the blustering, pleasure-seeking man my aunt had wed would turn his coat. I had heard much said of his firm friendship with the king and wondered who would serve my uncle-by-marriage best: King Edward or Papa.

Isobel had not finished, her murmurings dragging me from thoughts of betrayals. 'Though Papa has not returned The Great Seal to our uncle because Edward's chancellor remains with the council in London, Mama is certain he will do so soon. I hope he finds something for my dear husband as well, we cannot live on Papa's generosity forever.'

I drew a sharp breath; Papa's arm reached long indeed. Not only was he helping himself to offices of men he had executed, he was appointing his own supporters left, right and centre. For a brief moment, I wondered where Dickon would find himself in all of this. And as for Isobel and Clarence living on my father's purse, the young duke had lands and titles aplenty.

My brow creasing with concern, Isobel laughed once more. 'You do not understand, do you? Though the council tries to keep up the pretence of control, Edward signs everything Papa puts before him, even ordering Parliament to convene in York this September.'

I drew a second breath. My father was ensuring the next Parliament was held deep within a Neville stronghold. His grip upon England grew tighter with each passing day.

'Pray what does His Grace have to say of all this?'

150

'Very little, it seems.  He does not argue, does not question, simply doing whatever Papa asks.' Isobel shrieked with laughter. 'His might be the hand that holds the pen, but Papa holds the power of this land and Edward knows it well.'

And no doubt my father wished to receive some sort of confirmation of this great and terrible power — hence the Parliament next month.  Yet I could not stop the dark shadows grasping hold of my heart.  This did not feel right or appropriate; to hold a king captive and force him to sign away his name and quite possibly his life.

My dreams were dark at this time.  Dickon's face had faded completely from my mind and I could no longer conjure up an image of him, last seen upon that June day so many months ago.  Nor could I purge the worries for his safety.  Needless to say, my young mind was a maelstrom of unhappy thoughts.  Perhaps Papa meant him no harm, perhaps he would find a suitable office for the young duke he had once mentored, but thereto I wrestled with the fate of the Herbert brothers, steadfast Yorkist men with whom Mama had once danced and conversed at the court.

'Child, cease fiddling with your gown this instant!' My mother's keen eyes had noticed my hand flicking up to the spot where the secret boar was pinned.

'Of course, Mama.' I turned away, desperate she should not investigate and discover my treasure.

'Stand up straight and be still,' she hissed next. 'Your father and the king will arrive at any moment.'

I could not escape or hide this time. Papa was returning to Warwick and with him, came George, my sister's husband. We were to dine with the king in the great hall and, according to Mama, I would attend whether I wished it or no, even if she had to drag me there herself.

The hall was not only show of colour, but a display of our family's wealth and power. Splendid with Neville banners hung from the high roof-beams, it sang of our success with the finest tapestries workshops that Arras and Tournai could produce gracing each and every wall. As I looked upon their beauty, steps sounded in the passage outside. Servants threw open the heavy oak doors, and we ladies curtsied as the men entered. I glanced up to see Papa at the head of the party, the king behind him and a dour-looking Clarence at the rear. They halted before us and observed the formalities before we were guided to our seats. Papa escorted Mama, and George accompanied his wife. His Grace, King Edward, held out a hand towards me. Unprepared for such a situation, I swayed on the spot, silent and reluctant. As I delayed, uncertain what to do, the king winked.

Leaning forward, he whispered into my ear, 'Of all here, your company might prove the most enjoyable. Please accept my hand, Lady Anne, for I should not like to dine alone.'

At his gentle words and light tone, so reminiscent of his youngest brother at play, I could not hold back a smile. Taking his hand, we walked to the dais, whereupon Edward insisted I be seated beside him, much to Mama's displeasure.

The dinner passed without incident, though even one as young as I could tell the conversation was strained and false at times. But the minstrels in the gallery played well, the carver showed great skill at his craft, and the food was rich and varied enough for a king's table. Edward was politeness itself, insisting I eat from his plate, and encouraging me to try a morsel of every dish we were served. His manners were faultless, his conversation benign and slowly I began to lose my fear of this man and respond to his questions. As the final courses were brought out, sugared subtleties to delight and entertain, I found myself laughing at his jests and good-natured remarks. Even the marchepane subtlety, skilfully constructed from sugar and almond paste to represent the fine place in which we now dined, drew his compliments. Yet as I listened, these compliments were directed at the cooks and kitchen staff, not Papa or his hospitality.

As the minstrels struck up another tune, Edward turned to me. 'Would you care to dance, Lady Anne?'

The last thing on God's earth I wished to do was dance with the man my father held captive but I must do my duty as Mama constantly reminded. I accepted his hand, fighting to hide my reluctance and surprise at such a request. The king said not a word till we were upon the floor before the dais, and well away from other ears.

'I hope you do not mind being the one who all eyes are upon,' he murmured, gaze fixed directly ahead as we stepped out. 'Some might consider such exposure an ordeal.'

"Tis hardly an ordeal with so few eyes, Your Grace,' I whispered. 'We are such a small party, 'tis hardly more than a family dinner.'

My family, the king and a few of Papa's most loyal retainers and captains, along with those wives serving as Mama's ladies, were all that dined this day. The great hall was almost empty, leaving us outnumbered by servants and minstrels. In truth, it was a feeble show with such a magnificent hall and wondered if the king thought so too.

Edward gave a soft laugh and we stepped on through the dance but no one else came to join us and soon I forgot all watched the floor, keen to hear what he might say next.

'Your mother and sister visit my chambers every day, yet you have not been once since my arrival.'

'I have not,' I replied with care. 'And I beg forgiveness for such disrespect.'

He smiled. 'Forgiveness is unnecessary. I am not here on a royal visit.'

'More is the pity.' The words slipped out of my mouth but I had taken it into my head to let the king know I did not agree with my father's actions. This was an act of great disloyalty to my family but I cared not. The man beside me was a direct route to my dearest friend and I could not pass up the opportunity to nurture any channel of communication.

He smiled again. 'Do I understand you correctly, my Lady, this avoidance of my company is because I am held unwillingly and for no other reason?'

Though I kept silent, simply nodding my head to confirm the king's suspicions, something unseen drove me on. Bolstered by the king's interest, I became bolder by the second, smiling at the king as we danced. Mama would have had a seizure if she knew of my treacherous behaviour.

The steps of the dance did not allow for conversation. This was fortunate, for as I sensed Mama's gaze upon me, the fortitude I had so recently discovered, evaporated. This allowed time to reflect upon my last comment, leaving me in no doubt that I had said too much. But I did not agree with my father's actions and, though I could never say as much to either of my parents, the king himself had asked for my opinion. I must be brave and say what was in my heart. I must think of Dickon and hope a little kindness towards the House of York might enable me to see him once again.

As we drew together once more, Edward smiled. 'So, am I to presume you do not approve of recent events?'

'I do not, Your Grace,' I whispered, the urge to disclose my feelings as strong as before. ''Tis a shameful state of affairs when an anointed king is so poorly treated.'

He smiled again and this time it reached his eyes, lighting up the fair features till I was quite blinded by their handsomeness. In that moment, it seemed he had scarcely changed from that day I sat upon his lap as a small child.

'I heard loyalty was one of your finest virtues,' he murmured, as we drew close once more. 'Indeed, I have heard much of you, my Lady, and am delighted to see every word is true.'

Unable to respond, I stepped on through the dance, my mind in a whirl, my heart pounding. Who had spoken of me thus: Dickon, Francis? No other would, I was certain, for none knew me well enough to praise such a small, plain girl to the King of England. Except Papa, but he was too preoccupied to think of me.

No other words were exchanged as we danced and, when the chords ended, Edward signalled we should return to our seats. As I left the floor, others rose, my sister and brother-in-law included. I was relieved to see this, for I had no desire to discuss the dance with anyone, and certainly not Isobel. The king still remained in the centre of the floor, bent down as if adjusting the fastenings upon his shoes. Puzzled, I watched him for some moments but he soon rose and resumed his seat upon the dais.

Sipping my wine, I busied myself watching those around the table. Edward lazed back in his great chair, also observing, but rarely taking his eyes off Papa. As my gaze drifted across to my parents, I noticed the dark rings beneath Papa's eyes seemed far more prominent when observed from afar. As I looked closer, I thought he had never seemed so tired and strained, the lines creasing his brow and temples deeper with each passing day.

My gaze falling back upon the king, he winked once more and I knew he had observed the same.

'Perhaps your father finds governing a heavy burden,' Edward murmured into his wine cup. 'Perhaps he finds the country far more troublesome than expected. Power is the most fickle of mistresses.'

My father was most certainly discovering this was the case. While there were no signs of revolt against my father's government, demands were being made openly for the release of the king. Lawlessness had returned to the country, especially in London where many of the lower classes who had previously wished my father well, saw the situation as license to do as they pleased. Messengers arrived many times a day, each bringing reports of how the city magistrates and royal council were struggling to keep order. Though Mama kept her silence over such matters when Isobel and I attended her, I shamelessly listened to the servants' gossip, and was much disheartened by what I heard. The world was falling apart and even my clever, capable father could not keep it in one piece. Inevitably, my thoughts and prayers turned to Dickon, wondering if he was safe amongst the mayhem crippling the city and beyond.

Thinking on Edward's words, my hand raised unconsciously to my breastbone. As my fingers touched nothing, the one event I had long since dreaded became a reality. The room drifted in and out of focus, my body flushed with heat and almost instantly with such cold, I shivered in my seat.

'Anne, pray what ails you?' Edward, the anointed king of this country was whispering his concern into my ear, his large and well-manicured hand resting gently upon my arm.

Stunned by both my discovery and his reaction, I could barely speak. 'Nothing at all, Your Grace, I . . . I am quite well.'

He studied me closely. 'I think not. The colour has quite drained from your face - as though you have unexpectedly lost something dear to you.'

And so I had. A hand still resting upon my chest, I clutched at the empty space where the precious silver boar should now sit. After fussing so much before greeting the king, it must have become loose and tumbled from my gown as I danced.

Edward sat back in his chair, his thoughts masked but the vivid blue eyes studying my face. One of his hands was closed tightly and resting in his lap, while the other still lay upon my arm.

'Do not fret, my Lady. Your precious belonging might yet be found.'

I made to speak but tears filled my eyes and choked my throat. The king's grip upon me tightened a little.

'Hush, little Annie, I suspect your mother is unaware you possess something so treasured it must be hidden away, and would be wroth beyond forgiveness if she learned of it. Do not alert her to the fact now.'

Did this man have the second sight or was he mocking me? I did not know, swallowing over and over to keep from showing myself up in such company.

Passing his wine cup, Edward's eyes were still upon my unhappy face. I took the cup and though my hands trembled, I tried to take a sip. As I did so, he smiled and stretched out the closed hand beneath the table. 'Your father would see it as betrayal if he knew what you wore beneath that gown, but there is another who would bless you for it.'

In the king's outstretched palm sat my beloved boar. Edward must have picked it up as we left the floor. Though one small gasp escaped my lips, I sent silent prayers to the Lord above for such grace and kindness, trying not to snatch it from the king's hand and secure it inside my gown there and then.

'Keep it safe, little one,' he murmured. 'Let no one see or know of its existence. I am especially pleased to see loyalty to my house has not left this family entirely and shall remember it. Be assured this incident shall not be spoken of again – to anyone.'

My face must have reflected my disappointment, for though he appeared to have ceased speaking, as he rose, Edward murmured, 'Though as I think on it, perhaps the one whose interests are served by this device might like to hear of its whereabouts, should I ever be freed from this place.'

With that, the king indicated to my father he wished to leave. Though Edward might be captive in this castle, he could hardly be forced to remain at a feast when he did not want to.

'Your Grace . . . ' I mumbled, my mind blank with all that had happened but there was so much I wished to say, so many thanks I would offer if only my tongue was not dry and ineffectual.

He did not wait, stepping away from the table, his long legs covering more ground in one step than I could in many. Just as I thought he had no more to say, Edward turned back, bestowing a blinding smile upon me. 'Such delightful company was quite unexpected considering the circumstances.'

As Isobel and her husband stared at me with disdain and disbelief, the king headed to the door. My father, reluctant to allow his royal captive a moment's freedom, scurried behind him, more like an over-worked steward than the premier nobleman of the land.

To me, Edward was still the least likely captive imaginable. I had seen in his demeanour the best traits of a player; patience and resilience in abundance. Nor did he reveal his thoughts and thus, did not allow his brother, Clarence, or my father to see a hint of what hope he still held to. As chaos gripped the country, Edward behaved like the perfect house-guest; demanding nothing, troubling his hosts for nothing and entertaining himself well within the limits set upon him.

Much to our relief, the mobs of London soon subsided. Though this was good news, Papa's face did not reflect the respite. Each time I saw him, the shadows seemed darker, the lines more pronounced and the child in me could not understand why he would put himself through such suffering when he did not need to. Sometime later, I recalled the expression he wore each day was so like the one I had witnessed when he lost a game of tables or chess. Rarely had I seen such a thing occur, for Papa could not bear to lose, but the dark demeanour he sported afterwards was not easily forgotten.

'Daughters . . .' Mama called across the solar one fine afternoon towards the end of August. 'Come to me.'

We sat beside her upon the settle, exactly as she had indicated. Hands neatly folded in her lap, Mama began her tale as though we were infants at her feet, barely out of the nursery.

'Your father works tirelessly for our family, doing what he must to protect its interests. In this I am in agreement with all his decisions. Know he has left us, departing quietly some nights past, to escort the king north.'

It was clear from her expression, Isobel knew naught of this. Her new husband had not seen fit to inform her, if indeed he even knew of Papa's plans. I was not so surprised. The Parliament was shortly due to convene in York, it would hardly be prudent to move the king the day before.

'Do we travel north too?' I asked, trying to keep my enthusiasm for such a scheme quiet.

'We may, in time.' Mama did not even look at me as she spoke, watching my sister instead. 'Your father will send word when he feels it is safe for us to do so.'

'Is the king at Middleham?' I asked next. In my mind it made perfect sense to move Edward there. Our home sat in the centre of Papa's lands, a place where his power was unquestioned and unrivalled. Though I was no man, nor an expert on military matters, I knew the castle I loved was an easily-defended place to take a captive.

'What makes you say that?' Mama snapped. 'To whom have you been speaking?'

160

She leered over me, too close for comfort. I edged away but was trapped by the arm of the settle. My mother's face loomed large before me and I took a deep breath before answering.

'No-one, Mama. It . . . it seemed the most likely place for Papa to host such a guest.'

Her eyes blazed ice upon me for several moments but at last she turned away. 'He has indeed gone to Middleham. Your father will send for us in due course, once his guest is settled.'

So much she did not say. So much she kept to herself, but I had to be content with the little she had revealed. It was better than nothing. Moreover, I had learned we would be home-ward bound, albeit in due course.

The king remained in Wensleydale for some days, while Papa conducted his affairs from Sherriff Hutton, close to York and well within his power base but less than a day's ride from his precious captive. I had not expected to return home for some weeks, but a message arrived from Papa commanding us to set out forthwith, no doubt to soften the king's incarceration in such a wild place. I took great joy in returning to my home, even greater joy re-acquainting myself with all those precious places recalling memories of my dear friend. As my mind lingered on thoughts of Dickon, I wondered if Edward had enjoyed his stay in my home, or whether he saw it simply as another dark stronghold holding him captive. Yet Dickon must have spoken of his time there, spoken of hunting up on the moors, about the repair of the keep or height of the walls, perhaps of the families thereabouts whose company he had kept. At least, I hoped he had spoken if it, but the conversations of men were quite different from that of women.  Certainly, that was my experience within this family.

Though Mama, and occasionally my sister, attended the king, I shouldered no such burden.  As the days of late August were fine, with clear skies and light breezes, I insisted upon riding onto the moors whenever there were sufficient men to accompany me.  Though Mama was often reluctant to allow me such freedom, I suspect she preferred that I was out of the way and occupied.  I did not care, delighted to be out of the brittle atmosphere of the castle and, beneath the bluest of skies, my mind filled with the best of childhood memories.

With such poor company, and when I could not ride out, I oft wandered around the chambers and wards of Middleham, watching our servants and retainers going about their daily business.  This I found fascinating, not only because I must understand the running of a great household as part of my duty as a lady and, one day, a wife, but simply because I had begun to understand without these scores of people, our lives would be vastly different and far less comfortable.  One dull, grey afternoon when it rained too much to dare venture out even into the ward, I visited the sewing room with some particular instructions from Mama.  There I had come upon a plain-faced young woman, only a little older than my sister.

Recently engaged by the castle seamstress, Fridha was finding it especially hard to settle in her new role.  The daughter of a low-born washer woman, Fridha had spent her life in the service of my family.  She had worked hard, beginning in the laundry in the outer ward.  Showing herself more than capable, and willing to learn far more than just a task, she found work as a mender of the family's sheets and household linen. Indeed, so fine was her work and so improved were her manners, she soon secured a position within the main household itself. But life was not easy for Fridha, for even amongst the servants there was protocol and strict status. With such low origins, she soon discovered unexpected prejudices and often had to work alone, shunned by not only the other girls in the sewing room and at times, the seamstress herself. Finding her miserable and disconsolate, I offered what small comfort I could, and in the process recognised another isolated and unhappy soul. Soon, I drifted to the sewing room whenever I had a moment. In the relative calm and solitude of that small room, Fridha and I sewed together almost every day, chatting with an ease and familiarity the other girls and especially the seamstress found disconcerting.

My unhappy sister remained in the solar, spending her days moping upon Mama's fine settle and lamenting the fact her husband had been sent to London. Papa had instructed George to make for the capital to bolster the authority of the council, accompanied by our uncle, the archbishop. I was in no doubt George, Duke of Clarence, would relish an opportunity to flaunt his position, especially as I recalled his glee at such responsibility, crowing about how the council ought to cower before him. My uncle had been a little more wary, counselling caution and restraint but, to his wife, Mama and myself, George declared loudly how the council were naught but a gaggle of old men who should return to their homes and let those younger and quicker of mind decide what was best for England. Papa's letter recounting the arrogance of his son-in-law was filled with dark comments, hinting at his growing disappointment in

George.  Of course, Mama said nothing of it to Isobel and me, but as she left the solar to attend to another matter, the letter had fluttered from her lap, and, may God forgive me, as I retrieved it from the floor my eyes were drawn to Papa's words.  His tone was morose and deeply unhappy and he noted how none with any sense crossed him.

The discontent across the country continued.  Even the most loyal and high-born of nobles took the opportunity to settle grievances with their own hand and without the knowledge of king or my father.  When a distant Neville kinsman of Papa's somehow provoked a rising in the name of Lancaster, Papa called for men to put down this rising.  However, my father soon realised his friends and retainers would not so easily respond, confused by the ongoing captivity of their king, and would not risk their lives until they truly understood what was occurring.

In this matter, I wholly sympathised.  Though I endured Mama's fury as she read Papa's unhappy words out loud, if I, the daughter of the earl concerned, had no understanding of the situation, many others would not either.  To ask a man to lay down his life for something he holds dear, or believes fervently in, is one thing, but to risk injury or death for a scheme he does not understand, is another matter entirely.  My dear father had found himself surrounded by men asking such direct and pivotal questions.

As Mama waited nervously, Papa sent my recently-returned uncle to speak with the king.  Though still captive, Edward agreed to support my father's campaign against Humphrey Neville in return for a little more freedom.  As Mama relayed the king's assurances he harboured no ill-will towards our House, I saw her visage visibly relax, the features smoother and far more youthful than I had seen for weeks.

And so Papa allowed Edward to leave us, to enter York in a fashion befitting a king, and to speak freely with those waiting to pay him homage. From there, he took up residence at Pontefract Castle, in the comfort and splendour of an official residence. After his appearance before the City of York, the sight of their anointed king seemed to calm the inhabitants and diffuse the situation. As word of this timely appearance spread, England breathed once more.

Papa hastily rode north to put down the Lancastrian uprising once and for all, demonstrating to his king he had England's best interests at heart. Soon after, Edward rode once more into York to witness the execution of Papa's Neville kinsman. Naturally, the ladies did not attend the execution but gossip around the castle afterwards reported the king was in fine spirits and exceptionally good humour despite the severity of the day. The image of a patient game-player with his next move decided upon exploded back into my mind and what I learned occurred next came as no great surprise, at least to me.

Uninvited and seemingly without summons, there arrived in the north a party of the most noble and loyal lords of His Grace, riding forth with banners on display and a great party of men at their backs. Amongst others, Lord Hastings and my dearest friend, the young Duke of Gloucester, arrived to attend to their king. Even Papa's beloved brother, John, Earl of Northumberland, had sided with the king, much to the surprise and disdain of my mother. Somehow, during his captivity, Edward had got word to his supporters. Though at first it came as a great shock, in truth it was not so surprising. Papa's actions had confused a great many, and no doubt even amongst my father's own servants and retainers were those who saw their duty lay first to a king anointed in the sight of God, one treated poorly by their lord. Given Edward's easy nature and his ability to put the most awkward at ease, it was quite likely men had fallen over themselves to do their king's bidding, despite the fact it would see their lord betrayed. At the sight of England's finest, Papa was helpless to do anything. The great houses of the land milled politely around their king, all knowing, but not speaking of, the reason they had traversed half of the country. After greeting these lords and their men, Edward remarked in a casual manner he would be returning to Westminster forthwith, leaving Papa with no choice but to let him ride out unopposed and accompanied by the foremost lords of the land.

As I had observed the first time I set eyes upon him, Edward was the least likely captive imaginable. Now he was free and I feared for my father. I feared for us all.

# Chapter Ten – Jewels and Felons

## *1470*

'Be still, Anne!' My mother's scornful tones echoed around the solar. Though she had summoned me, she showed no haste to explain why. She crossed herself twice over before speaking again. 'Anyone would think you were showing signs of the falling sickness.'

I had once witnessed a villager suffering with this terrible condition. He had fallen to the ground before our riding party, writhing and twitching with no control of his limbs, his wits utterly gone. The Lord watched over him that day, for my father somehow halted his mount just before trampling the poor soul into the ground. He turned his horse on the spot, signalling for us all to stop also. In silence we watched the poor wretch writhing in the dirt and though he recovered enough to be helped to his feet soon after, the poor bewildered soul remembered naught of his strange fit. Only later did I discover there was no cure for such an affliction and those suffering oft died from injuries incurred during a seizure, or were cast out by loved ones believing they were possessed by the devil.

I became motionless instantly. 'What can I do for you, Mama? I have not yet completed my lessons.'

'That I know well,' she snapped. 'For these days you do not appear to complete any. Indeed, from what I hear, you are oft to be found in the servants' quarters instead of attending your family or your lessons.'

So, I had been discovered and must now face the wrath of a mother who deemed the acquaintance I had cultivated with Fridha to be well beneath the daughter of the earl.

'At all times, I have conducted myself as taught to do,' I protested, feeling the sting of this slight as well as concern for my newest friend's position.

'That may be so, but the fact you even choose such unsuitable company in the first place gives me much concern.' Mama spat the words with such force spittle flew across the small space separating us. 'As if there is not already enough to keep me awake at night, you choose to be contrary when I need you by my side.'

As usual, my mother was filled with concern for Papa. Since the king had ridden back to Westminster surrounded by his lords and leaving my father useless, the façade of friendship and loyalty had grown thin indeed. While outwardly, an air of civility was maintained, the reality was quite different. My uncle had followed the king south as a show of goodwill, joining the Earl of Oxford on the journey, but the king had sent a message, relaying in no uncertain terms how he would send for them when he wanted them. Edward's detachment from the House of Neville could not have been clearer. As October frosts settled in the north, the king was settled back in Westminster, surrounded by those he trusted.

Over the following months, Edward stripped Papa of the self-appointed offices, bestowing several upon my dear friend, Dickon. Now appointed Constable of England, I took great joy he was so trusted and honoured by the king. Alas, I dared not share my feelings on the matter and was forced to stay silent as Mama berated and decried the small, quiet boy she had once welcomed in her home. At the same time, I endured Isobel bemoaning how her poor husband was deserving of such high office while Dickon was hardly man enough to hold such position. It never occurred to my dear sister that perhaps loyalty had been the deciding factor, and had her husband not become so mired with my father's schemes and discontent, he might also hold such high offices. And so it continued, for Edward and my father seemed unable to govern with one another but equally, unable to govern without an accord of some sort.

Thankfully, an uneasy truce somehow came into being between my family and the king. Neither openly antagonised the other, yet each knew the other watched for the next move in this game of knights and kings. The intrigue was left to Isobel's husband. After a hollow and miserable Christmastide, Clarence, encouraged by my father, became the integral part of a scheme begun by a distant cousin, Lord Welles. Not wishing to become embroiled in this conspiracy by default, I removed myself from Mama's company whenever possible. Eschewing the constant need to provoke and challenge the authority of the land, I chose not to learn what occurred outside of these walls.

Isobel was weary and ailing at this time, her company even more miserable than Mama's, and not understanding why she should be cossetted so by Mama, I stayed from their company as oft as I dared. In a heartbeat, my world had become smaller and I risked much by cloistering myself in such a fashion, but my young heart bled with the betrayal my family condoned with such ease and no outward display of conscience. Inevitably, I learned nothing more of the scheming of Clarence, Lord Welles and others. Dickon's words about loyalty had never left my mind, and so I chose to be as loyal as possible given my own constrained circumstances. Perhaps I should have paid more attention to Mama's complaints, for then I might have been better prepared for what lay ahead. Perhaps too, I might have learned what occurred within my own family, as it was from servants' gossip I heard that my sister was with child.

As we sat in the solar, the fire burning bright to counteract the bitter February winds buffeting the castle, Mama's voice sounded out. 'Twas as cold as the day outside.

'I have a task for you, Anne, come this instant.'

Stepping across the room, I held my breath for something was afoot, I was certain.

'This girl, this servant . . .' she began, the ice-blue eyes looking deep into my face. 'She has a young child, I believe.'

The servant Mama spoke of in such disdainful tones had a young son, no more than eight at most. He was dear to her and the sole reason Fridha strove so hard to improve herself. Having lost her husband in the last months, the boy's only chance of a better life was dictated by what she could provide. I glanced up, wary of Mama.

'I believe that is true.'

'Good,' Mama smiled. 'Fetch her to me.'

I could scarcely believe my ears for, in my mother's opinion, the seamstress's assistant was hardly suitable company to attend us anywhere, let alone in the solar. Nerves on edge, I set off to find Fridha, recalling what had encouraged this unusual acquaintance. My sister was with child, due later in the spring, and had no time for me these days, coveting every moment Mama could spare. Though Isobel was hardly the first woman in the history of the world to be with child, it seemed that way in our home these days. Mama spoke to me only to chastise and it seemed she disapproved of my very existence, her attentions poured upon my sister without thought for my welfare. Though I harboured no envy towards Isobel, indeed, I was pleased she had fallen with child so soon, I was quite forgotten, finding my way to the sewing room and more welcoming company, at every opportunity. In truth, I ought to have known it was only a matter of time before suspicion brought the matter to Mama's attention.

Fridha smoothed her apron and skirts as we approached the solar door, asking for the tenth time, 'Why does the countess wish to see me?'

I could give no answer, as perplexed about this summons as Fridha. We appeared an odd couple; the young woman was at least a head taller than me and, with a sturdy, almost muscular build, her figure contrasted sharply with my small stature. Tucked away beneath a linen cap, Fridha's chestnut brown plaits were smoothed and tidy, unlike my unruly locks that seemed determined to escape the confines of the tightest headdresses in Christendom. Fridha's nose was sprinkled with freckles the colour of her braids, softening her wide features, whereas my complexion was pale in the extreme. Despite concern over this summons, hers was a kindly face, a face I would trust, even if I knew her not. As the brown eyes flashed across to me one last time, we stepped inside the solar. Mama sat in her great chair, surrounded by silken cushions and an open book in her hands. She glanced up as Fridha curtsied while I stood behind, nervous for myself as well as my friend.

'Pray what exactly do you hope to gain by my daughter's attentions?' Mama's tone was sharp and suspicious.

'Nothing, my . . . my Lady.' Shocked the countess had addressed her so directly, Fridha's voice was a whisper.

'So you do not hope to glean information from her, information you may sell on to those willing to pay for hearsay about this family?'

'By all that is holy, no!' Fridha's head shot up. 'My Lady, I have served this family all my life, indeed my family have worked here for generations. I . . . I wish no ill upon the House of Neville.'

'I do not believe you,' Mama's tone was cold and haughty. I braced, knowing worse was to come from her lips. 'And can see no other reason for you to cultivate an acquaintance with the Lady Anne, than to profit by it.'

The young woman was frightened, I could tell simply by the tension across her shoulders. But this was the way of our world; a duchess, countess or lady of any household could choose how she treated her servants. She could promote or discard as she saw fit, change lives with a single word and on whatever whim took her fancy. That was the bitter truth of it, and as a lowly maid, Fridha had no redress, even though the friendship had been at my instigation.

'I thank The Lord my husband is far from here,' Mama continued. 'For if he should hear of such an improper arrangement, he would be enraged beyond consolation and we all should suffer his wrath. Know that and think on it, girl.'

Though my mother knew Fridha's name, she resolutely refused to use it, endorsing the fact she was in charge. Fridha's head dropped lower and lower and I knew I must speak out, for the situation was of my own doing.

I dashed forward to stand beside the chair. 'Mama, please do not blame Fridha, she is not at fault here, it is I . . . '

'Silence.' Mama did not even look at me, simply holding a hand up to my face. 'When I want your opinion I shall ask for it. I am already aware at whose feet the blame lies, but that does not alter the fact this girl should know her place, no matter what.'

Beckoning for Fridha to come closer still, ice-cold eyes glared at the girl. 'You are a widow, I believe?'

'Yes, my Lady.'

'And how did your husband die?'

'He . . . he was in the earl's service and went as ordered to Edgecot. He did not return.'

'Ah, yes. May he rest in peace.' As Mama's thoughts drifted away, I recalled Fridha saying how my mother had gifted a coin for masses to be said for her husband's soul. Mama had gifted a number of coins that day.

'Thank you, my Lady.'

My mother's eyes still flashed ice. 'You may once have been a respectable married woman but I hear that is no longer the case.'

Fridha's gasp resonated around the chamber. 'My . . . my Lady, I am still in mourning and keep myself tidy as a good widow should. But, even if the appropriate time had passed, I have a child to think of and would never behave in an unbecoming manner lest he think ill of me . . . '

'That is not how I hear it.' Rising from the chair, Mama's book slid to the floor but she did not notice, so busy was she walking around Fridha, scrutinising her from top to toe. Pulling at the plain gown, linen apron and kerchief, Mama inspected every inch. Leaning into the young woman's face, she hissed, 'Know also I have heard your young son helps himself from the kitchens when he thinks no one watches.'

There was nothing Fridha could say and nothing she could do to counteract Mama for, as countess and employer, her word was final. No doubt the young woman saw herself and her child thrown out into the world, reputation ruined and with nothing to her name. For certes, I imagined that all too clearly.

Returning to her seat, my mother made herself comfortable once more, rearranging cushions while we waited. At last she murmured, 'You are fortunate I am a benevolent employer, and have no desire to see you turned out of the castle this day.'

Though her head shot up and mouth opened as if to offer thanks, Fridha snapped it shut as if comprehending there would be a price to pay for this reprieve. As the silence hung heavy in the chamber, I watched as she pulled her shoulders back and stood upright, bracing before the blow fell. The only assistance I could offer was to pray my mother found the grace and humility to treat this young woman better than she had thus far.

'I have a task for you, one demanding the utmost secrecy and discretion.'

'I will do it, my Lady, rest assured.' So desperate was Fridha, she agreed without knowing the task in hand. I braced again, fearing the worst.

'Indeed you shall, girl, and do it well or I will see you sent to a brothel, your boy left on the streets to fend for himself.'

Fridha stifled a sob as my mother watched, studying the young woman's face with such intent I could not imagine what was in her mind. At last she leaned back into the cushions and graced us both with a smile. 'I have seen the quality of your stitching and it is

174

a little better than most. Such skills are useful to me at present.'

Though appalled my mother would treat any servant in so careless a manner, I noticed the young woman's relief that sewing was her task and nothing more arduous.

'Pray what would you have me sew, my Lady?' Fridha did not dare look at her lady.

'Some small repairs, nothing of note.' Mama retrieved her book from the floor, studying it with intent as she spoke. 'However every piece of your work must be undertaken with the utmost care.'

The depth of Fridha's relief left her swaying. I reached out, putting my palm between her shoulder blades. It was just enough to steady her without attracting attention.

'Come along,' Mama departed in a swish of silk. 'You too, Anne, for this continued disobedience and wilfulness shall be redeemed by work.'

Standing in Mama's chamber, I presumed Fridha and I must ready my mother's garments, for we often moved from one residence to another at short notice. This was nothing unusual and I could not imagine the need for secrecy.

'We must be ready to leave at a moment's notice,' Mama noted, sorting through her coffer.

I stayed silent, shocked to see Mama doing such a task herself. There were ladies aplenty to fold and clean clothing for the countess, and I had never witnessed her lift a finger before.

'There is much to be done,' she said next, reaching for her jewel box. 'When the time comes, we must travel light.'

As Mama explained our task further, my heart sank as never before. I had heard sewing jewels into the hems of clothing or travelling cloaks was a well-known means of safe-guarding valuables but, to actually be given this instruction and be sworn to secrecy about it, meant our position was far more perilous than I knew. Never, in all the times of uncertainty had we behaved in this manner; like felons avoiding the law of the land. That we could soon be a family on the run, fleeing from place to place, seemed like a nightmare. Mama refused to be drawn further on the matter, so I was forced to conclude we could do nothing else until such time as my father was in a position to rebuild his eroded status and influence. In my heart I knew he would deal and scheme, beg and claw at the smallest shred of hope to regain his power and influence, or he would die trying. But that could take months, even years, and I shuddered to think what that would mean for us all.

My mother had laid out a selection of clothing upon her great bed. Though Fridha gave the garments a respectful but cursory glance, her eyes were drawn to the room itself and she gazed in bewilderment at the fine tapestries, drapes and coverlets. Her eyes then turned towards Mama's dressing table, whereupon lay an array of pots and phials, all filled with scented powders and oils from far across the Continent, each more exotic than the last. I too, looked around, taking a moment to drink in the splendour of the chamber for, if my fears proved true, we would not see the like of for some time to come.

'Where shall we start?' Fridha whispered, her fingers poised above the finest woollen cloak money could buy. 'I durst not touch this finery, lest I spoil it.'

'Here,' I said, passing over a linen underdress. 'Begin with this.'

We gathered up the clothing and carried it all to my bedchamber. In this seclusion, we spent the following days stitching and sewing until our fingers were raw, our eyes bleary and our conversations exhausted. To maintain the secrecy of our task, food was oft delivered to us and we ate where we worked, only leaving the chamber for prayers. Fridha even slept on a hurdle at the foot of my bed to ensure her silence. Though pleased to have my companion so close, this task served only to confirm my worst fears about the situation. Silence was my only comfort, for Mama expected me to do my duty and not to question. Her current mood was so severe, she snapped and shouted at the most trivial of matters. Like many of our household servants, I avoided her as much as possible.

Carefully, we hid jewels, rosaries, coins, rings and all manner of fine things inside the seams and hems of under garments, outer garments and cloaks until I began to wonder how we should stand upright under such weight. One morning, just as we thought the end was in sight, we were sent a number of items locked in Mama's jewel box, with explicit instructions these must be concealed with haste. As soon as I lifted the lid, Fridha gasped, pointing to one particular item.

'What is this?'

I reached for the beautiful, shining jewel. 'I have always been told it was a part of Mama's Beauchamp inheritance . . . '

Handing it to Fridha, she was reluctant to touch such a magnificent piece but I insisted. Though

177

cautious, she turned it over and over, its golden glow reflected in her eyes.

'But what is it?' Fridha asked in bewilderment.

'I know not exactly, but when younger, Mama used to wear it tied round her throat most every day. I had forgotten how beautiful it is.'

A diamond-shaped pendant, the jewel was larger than anything Fridha had seen before, yet still small enough to be worn comfortably around the neck. Engraved with the most intricate designs, it was clear Fridha would have liked nothing better than to gaze at the Christ child, his mother and the saints surrounding them in golden, shining glory. She was in awe, never having looked upon anything so fine in her life before. She watched the light play on its many sides, glinting as though it had its own source of light. Memories flooded back into my mind, recalling how I too had been enraptured by the beauty of this jewel.

The outside of the pendant was finished with jewels but Fridha's eye was drawn to a particularly fine sapphire adorning the front, almost eclipsing the finely detailed image of the Trinity. This bewitching stone was as blue as a summer sky and Fridha stroked the sapphire, as if it would somehow offer peace or solace against the unhappiness permeating each day.

At that moment, Mama arrived in my bedchamber. Snapped out of her daze, Fridha clambered to her feet, causing the jewel to tumble to the floor. I rose also, bobbing a swift curtsey while praying Mama had not seen her precious jewel fall in so careless a manner.

'Are you not yet finished?' Mama glared at Fridha until the young woman trembled in fear.

'My Lady, we have only just received these items to secure . . .' Fridha's voice was barely audible and though I stepped towards Mama, she held up her hand to silence me.

'You agreed to do my bidding, did you not?' she demanded, glaring at my poor friend.

Fridha's response was little more than a mumble. Her life and that of her young son depended upon my mother's goodwill, or lack thereof. I prayed to The Lord above Mama might find some compassion, despite the severity of our situation. Yet as I looked, my mother seemed like a madwoman, eyes wild and demeanour unpredictable. The strain of these last days had worn her nerves quite away. I stepped back, for as her moods had become less predictable, Mama had become increasingly free with her hands and I had no desire to feel the smart of one upon my arm or cheek again this day.

'I have received word, and we shall depart shortly. First, we must pray for a safe journey and prepare away from prying eyes. Anne, bring your belongings to the chapel, we shall make ready after the priest sings Sext.'

My hand flew to my breastbone where the silvered boar and saint's pins sat hidden from all eyes but mine. They were safely concealed, but I must fetch my psalter and the faded rose kept safe within.

Mama pointed at the last few items inside her jewel box then at Fridha. 'You have till we have finished our prayers but not a moment longer.'

As my mother left in a swirl of silk, Fridha looked at me with wide, uncertain eyes, but there were no words of comfort to be found.

'We must work quickly, though it is a little while till the noon bell,' I said, even though we both knew time was not our friend.

'Your lady mother will have me thrown out into the streets for certes,' Fridha panted, fear distorting her face.

I clasped the young woman's wrist. 'She will not, I shall ensure you and your boy are safe.'

Fridha breathed thanks but I knew my power to ensure her safety was small indeed. Any instruction from Mama would counteract my words in a heartbeat. I could only pray there was so much to occupy my mother's mind, the fate of one maid-servant would not be her foremost consideration.

After retrieving the jewel from the floor, we stitched and sewed like the devil stood behind us. The fine golden case was left till last, for I had decided it should be inserted into Mam's clothing, as I considered it unfair that I or my heavily pregnant sister should be expected to carry more.

I held out the blue jewel to Fridha. 'You must secure this inside the countess's cloak, for she expects me in the chapel.'

Numbed by the task in hand, she stared at me. 'I cannot, Lady Anne, I am not worthy to handle such a treasure.'

'You must.' I made for the door, fearful of my mother's impatience. 'I trust you to do this.'

But glancing across to the bed, I saw the dark blue cloak was gone. Mama must have taken it when she left. These days, Mama slept in the privy chamber high up in the keep, giving up her own luxurious quarters in the south range for Isobel's comfort. I knew Fridha would need the speed of angels behind her if she was to complete this task before prayers ended. Yet, as she fled through the door, I was unexpectedly engulfed with guilt. There was no need to put this young woman's future any more at risk than it already was and if we were about to leave, I must protect my companion by ensuring this final task was done. Gathering up my skirts, I made as much haste as I dared without breaking into a run. The inner courtyard seemed unusually busy, but I kept moving, weaving my way through the bodies stepping into my path with what seemed like deliberate intent. It was more than Fridha's life was worth to risk crossing the wooden bridge linking the grand rooms of the south range and the keep, for even in her current position, she would not be allowed access to the family's private walkway. In my mind, I tried to picture where she might walk, while fearing the precious item would be lost along the way. I prayed she had sense enough to clutch it to her chest, out of sight of others, while making her way up the keep's many stone stairs. She must then cross the great hall, trying not to draw attention before reaching the stair up to the chamber. I stepped out across the bridge, hoping against hope to meet her there before anyone could question her presence amongst such grandeur.

As I reached the last stairwell, a voice sounded out ahead of me. It did not speak kindly. Hitching up my skirts once more, I took the steps two at a time, arriving to see Mama standing in the doorway. I crept up behind my mother, spying Fridha in the room beyond. The young woman was sitting upon the floor before the great bed. In one hand she held the cloak, in the other Mama's beautiful jewel, while her features were a picture of terror. Before I could do anything my mother was beside Fridha in two strides. Grasping Fridha's arm, she dragged her away across the room, throwing her against the furniture.

'What do you have to say girl, repaying kindness by stealing from your Lord and Lady in their darkest hour?'

Dazed and half-blinded by blood trickling into her eyes, Fridha was only vaguely aware she had hit a small table, glass phials of oils and fragrances spewing all around.

My mother's hand reached out to the side, her fingers wrapping themselves around an iron poker, sitting benignly beside the fireplace. I had to stop her, had to prevent this anxious, hysterical woman from behaving as a brawling fish-wife.

'Mama,' I called, praying my voice stayed calm enough to conceal I had witnessed her vile fury. 'There are still repairs needed upon your cloak. Fridha will be here forthwith to complete your instructions . . . '

The poker fell from Mama's hand, clattering onto the floorboards but she did not turn around. 'Ah, Anne, still you try my patience when there is none to spare. Clearly you have not yet learned to knock before entering my bedchamber. 'Tis a failing you should have grown out of long since.'

I ignored her open insult, once more finding my sweetest voice. 'May I assist with the repair?'

Still she did not turn around. 'Away to the chapel as I have instructed. The girl will do what is necessary.'

Such contempt rang from my mother's tone, combined with the image of the poker clenched in her hand, I grew suddenly fearful. I would not let her treat a dog with such thoughtlessness, less so a young woman who was guilty of no more than showing kindness to a lonely girl. Prepared to take punishment for my insolence and disobedience, I refused to move.

Yet I was ignored completely, as though my unexpected appearance had shattered something.

Sighing, Mama looked down upon a dishevelled and forlorn Fridha. 'Despite my forbearance and generosity, you have still proved unequal to the smallest of tasks. '

She held the jewel under Fridha's nose, 'A few things in this world are irreplaceable and you should remember that. A reputation perhaps, or a child's life; such great treasures, once lost, can never be regained.'

My mother was going mad, I was certain. Thrusting the beautiful jewel further towards Fridha's face, she hissed, 'I should be very loath to lose this, for it is precious to me. Do your duty, girl, and complete the work you were set before I have the sergeant take you away!'

She tossed the jewel onto her cloak, turning away in a swirl of skirts. Still she did not speak to me, simply clicking her fingers for me to follow as if I were the servant. Wilfulness once more overtook me and I did not move. Though I glanced into my mother's dark and thunderous face, the stunned and still bleeding girl upon the floor needed my assistance. Moreover, for reasons I would need to seek forgiveness for later, I had no desire to obey a mother who showed such little compassion.

Once certain Mama had descended the stairs, I raced across the room, trying with all my might to lift Fridha. Sitting her upright, I applied a napkin to her forehead to staunch the bleeding. Then I retrieved the cloak and jewel and began to work. Both Mama and the seamstress would have been horrified at the standard of my stitches but there was no time to waste; I was expected in the chapel forthwith.

After prayers, as I trailed through the keep and about to leave my beloved home for what might be the last time, I did not look about. I dared not. To drink in those precious places still brimming with memories was too cruel a pastime for me this day. I walked, with head bowed, behind my mother and sister. As I lingered at the top of the steps to the ward, a hand shot out of the shadows. Clasping onto mine, it was warm and soft, not what I expected at that moment. My head jerked up to see Fridha, pressed against the wall and deep in shadow.

She whispered, 'My Lady, I must thank you before I depart, if it had not been for your kindness, I would have gone mad these last months.'

I clasped both her hands. 'I will say the same, Fridha, and shall not forget all you have done.'

'Where might you be bound, Lady Anne?'

'Mama would not say but I think most likely we go to Warwick, for she did not seem displeased.'

'Go with God,' Fridha choked, urging me towards the great door. 'Be brave through whatever trials The Lord or your Lady Mother may put you through. I shall pray you might return home one day.'

Though I nodded at her hopeful words, Fridha's expression told me she believed nothing of the sort. But then, neither did I. The world had gone quite mad and I knew not what to expect next. We shared a swift, wordless embrace, both of us fearful for the future.

Soon after, our small party rode out of the bailey and onto the track behind the castle. Just a few men accompanied us, those most trusted by Mama. We would be heading up into the dale, towards the great abbey at Jervaulx but there would be no time or mind to take in the views, for it had been impressed upon us how we must be careful, while making as much haste as reasonable. I set my mind to concentrate upon the journey ahead, not allowing a moment to wonder or fear where we were bound. To throw off any watchful eyes, we avoided the village and inevitable scrutiny of the vassals, giving the impression we were simply off riding for an afternoon's distraction.

Isobel was in great discomfort but that could not be helped. In these later months of pregnancy, she should have been preparing for her confinement, or at least travelling slowly and in short stages, within the comfort of a carriage. Bearing it as best she could, my sister had no choice but to sit before one of Mama's men-at-arms and be held upon the horse, dressed in clothing made heavy by our treasures. I knew just by the grim set of her mouth the journey ahead would be far from easy but I also knew my sister would endure it without complaint, for she was a duchess and wed to the heir to the throne, even though that heir was busy making mischief behind the king's back. Moreover, the child in her womb could be the boy-child that had eluded Mama, and, so far, the queen. If, God willing, it was a boy, as nephew to an heir-less king, this child could be of the utmost importance to a great many people - but especially to my father and his son-in-law.

Mama paid little attention to anyone as we left Middleham. Riding out of the bailey, she made no backward glance, giving the distinct impression this was simply an afternoon's jaunt. But in her haste and determination, my mother did not realise the heel of her riding boot had caught in her cloak. Though I called out for her to take care, fearful my work would not withstand rough treatment, she heard me not, tugging the garment away while taking out her frustrations on the cloth. As she did so, a small line of stitches unravelled and unbeknown to my mother, the seam opened up like a wound. Once more I tried to call out, tried to alert Mama to the danger of her actions but my mouth was dry, my tongue paralysed. I could only watch in despair as something fell, tumbling down to be claimed by the earth over which she so frantically rode. For a brief moment, its golden beauty flashed in the sun but was then extinguished as pounding hooves trampled the jewel into the sod, as though it was worth naught in the world.

# Chapter Eleven – Perilous Times

## 1470 – April

We made Warwick in good time, and, for the first time in my life, I felt some measure of joy as its towers appeared before us, assuring a weary party of comfort and safety. Isobel had survived the ordeal of travelling in early spring far better than any of our party expected, but, harbouring grave concerns for her health, Mama insisted she begin her lying-in forthwith despite it being early to do so. Maintaining a façade of doting grandmother-to-be, Mama organised everything for Isobel with the efficiency she was renowned for. Yet I saw through the mask, saw how the strain of the last weeks was taking its toll, hollowing her cheeks, dulling her eyes and shortening her already quick temper. The unkind treatment of Fridha was only the beginning and, as the days wore on, my mother's behaviour became more and more unbecoming of a great lady. The servants kept their distance and only those of braver dispositions or without a choice attended Mama. There was no comfort I could offer. My mother sunned my company yet expected absolute obedience at all times, no matter how strange or outlandish her demands. This madness seemed to consume her more with each passing day.

'Come to me, Anne, I have need of you.' My sister's voice came from behind the drapes.

Emerging from the shadows, I took a moment or two to cross the bedchamber, uncertain why Isobel should deign to speak to me now. As I stepped on, the spring storm outside continued to unleash its fury upon the stone walls, rain hitting the glass windows with such force I feared they might shatter. My thoughts lingered upon the primroses blooming at the base of the walls, their pretty, pale faces fighting to withstand such wild weather. But the shutters were drawn and the room in darkness for Isobel's lying-in, and would remain so till after the birth of her child.

'What may I fetch for you, sister?'

'Nothing,' Isobel croaked, the gloom serving only to highlight the shadows on her face. 'I desire your company, if you have time enough to spare.'

Only then, for the first time in many weeks, did I truly look at my sister. Surrounded by cushions, she half-sat, half-lay upon her finely carved bed, the coverlets thrown off, for the fire blazed bright. In this stuffy and airless gloom, Isobel had discarded her dressing gown and was clad only in a linen underdress, much like a nightgown. Her bright hair loose, it trailed down over one shoulder and onto the great mound of her belly. She appeared the epitome of impending motherhood, but her face was a picture of misery. The eyes were red and puffed, while wet streaks trailed down her cheeks.

'Are you in pain, should I call for Mama?'

Isobel reached out for my hand. 'I am not, so do not summon her. Indeed, if she should come, tell her I am sleeping.'

I gasped. 'You would lie openly to keep her away?'

'Do not think badly of me, Anne. There are things we must speak of outside of her hearing.'

Throughout the years of our childhood, my sister had rarely made time to talk to me and had not done so once since she had wed the king's brother. Wondering what she was about to demand, I busied myself straightening the coverlets lest I give uncharitable thoughts away.

'You must think it odd, little sister, that I desire your company now,' she spoke softly as if uncertain she even wanted to speak at all. 'But in truth, I am more fearful than I have ever been before - and your presence comforts me.'

I sat beside her, concealing my surprise at such conciliatory and honest words. 'It is only to be expected you are fearful, childbirth cannot be easy.'

'I did not mean the travail of labour.' Isobel clasped both of my hands. 'I meant the look upon Mama's face, the words she does not say. Surely you have seen it too?'

I nodded. 'Of course I have.'

Isobel clung to me. 'She is going quite mad with worry. Indeed, I have heard her weeping when she thinks I sleep.'

'What concerns her so deeply she is driven to melancholy?' I had also reached the conclusion my mother was given to madness, though I had yet to see her shed so much as a tear.

'It is more than concern, she fears deeply for Papa. Forgive me, Anne but I need to speak openly for grave worries also flood my mind.'

Perhaps this was partially my own fault for refusing to hear of Mama's news but, if matters distressed my sister so, perhaps it was time to learn of them.

'Pray what has occurred?'

My sister drew a long, loud breath. 'Ah, Anne, even I have seen how you withdraw when news arrives and make every effort not to hear it, but so much has happened of late, you ought to learn the worst.'

A chill washed through my body. I had withdrawn for good reason but perhaps that had not been the wisest thing to do. Clenching my hands as she

189

made to speak, I sensed the tidings Isobel was about to impart were far from good.

'The king will see us incarcerated and stripped of all we own in this world.'

Such dark words, I took a breath or two before answering. 'Pray how do you know this?'

She began to sob. 'I scarcely know where to begin.   Suffice to say, the king caught wind of Lord Welles' dealings, fetching him and his brother-in-law, Sir Thomas Dymmock, to London.   Once there, he threatened them unless they submitted.'

I did not understand. 'What does that mean for Papa and George?'

She pulled me closer. 'It means he knows. Edward is somehow privy to Papa's plans and the depth of George's involvement with Welles.  Most likely he has information, or at least suspects, Papa's desire to see another on the throne.'

There was nothing I could add, Isobel's fear was contagious.

Isobel still wept. 'Unless George and Papa can persuade the king of their innocence, we shall all pay for their missteps.   When she thinks I cannot hear, Mama cries how The Lord has forsaken us all, and we are surely doomed.'

Darker words still.  Though I had suspected for some time my father's intentions were to see another upon the throne, one he might have some chance of controlling, to finally hear those words spoken out loud somehow made it real.   My grip upon Isobel's hand tightened.

'Has Mama spoken of this matter to you directly?'

'She would not dare speak openly of such things.' Isobel shook her head, the bright hair swirling

190

around her forlorn face like a golden cloud. 'But I knew of their plans some while ago, well before I was wed. Indeed, I was encouraged to think of becoming a duchess as simply the beginning.'

My heart sank. If Edward had proof of Papa's involvement then Isobel's prediction of doom was all too real. In that moment I saw myself and Isobel incarcerated within convents, a life of cloistered penance; suitable punishment for daughters of a traitor.

'After the wedding,' Isobel murmured. 'Little mention was made, at least within my hearing, and I began to wonder if Papa had dismissed the idea . . . '

Most likely because George was not showing as much promise as my father had hoped. Though my brother-in-law could probably be controlled by one wiser and more intelligent than he, in his role as king's brother and so far, the heir, George was given to arrogance rather than eloquence and humility. His first thought was always himself, how he could improve his situation and especially how others perceived him. This, combined with far less intelligence than Edward, and, in my humble opinion, Dickon also, suggested Papa had realised some time back George was not the kingly material he had hoped for. The brother who showed the most promise had chosen loyalty above vanity and greed.

Isobel continued as if I was not there beside her. 'George was desperate to prove himself, to be of use and show his worth. Papa had a hard time reining him in lest he acted in haste, often bemoaning his behaviour and tactlessness to Mama, yet once they knew about the babe, everything seemed to change.'

Of course it had. No doubt my father had intended to see his plan through despite the failings of George's character, but the possibility of a male child gave him yet another option, another move in his great game. Papa was ever the game-player.

I tried to steer the conversation away from this delicate matter. 'How do you know so much if Mama will not speak of it?'

'I gleaned what I could from Papa's letters, despite Mama's reticence. When possible, I sent my maid to speak to George's steward, for she could sometimes wheedle a snippet or two from him.' Isobel could not look at me. 'In between, I resorted to eavesdropping upon the servants' gossip.'

Hardly a sin; I too, had been forced to resort to such methods when no other sources were forthcoming. I gently caressed her hand.

'Ah, Annie,' Isobel's voice was raw, bitter. 'This is hardly the life I imagined as duchess . . . '

It was not the life any of us had imagined. I shuffled closer, wrapping my arms about her shoulders. As the bones dug into my arms, I feared she had not been eating properly. No doubt my sister was frightened; childbirth alone was enough to remind any woman of her mortality, but, combined with all she had just spoken of, it was surprising she too was not giving into the hysteria overtaking our mother.

'Hush Isobel, things will improve, I am certain. At present, there is naught we can do except pray and await word from Papa. We must think only of the birth of your child and look forward to welcoming a new life into the family.'

Though she nodded, Isobel was not placated by my words. I tried once more. 'As I said, we must await word from Papa. He will have a plan and know what to do . . . '

Snatching her hands away, Isobel cried, 'Our father can do nothing! The king caught up with the

192

rebels near Stamford, routing them all. As the men fled, Edward captured Welles and his commander and now they are dead, but only after naming George and Papa as their partners in the rebellion. Soon after, an esquire of the royal household delivered letters to our menfolk desiring they dismiss their men and join the king at once.'

I gasped. 'Do they attend him, is that where they head now?'

'Oh, Anne, after all that has occurred, should they truly risk their heads?' Isobel's arms flailed around as she shouted. 'They made towards Derby, knowing the Earl of Shrewsbury had joined the royal army, while our Uncle John of Northumberland broke up the northern rising. Papa tried to bargain with the king while at Chesterfield.'

I neither knew nor cared where these places were. All I could think of was how we would lose everything should Papa take a step beyond redemption or forgiveness. I scarcely heard my sister's next words.

'Our men demanded safe passages but Edward refused. My poor husband and Papa then rode hard towards Stanley lands, where they hoped to secure promised assistance from Lord Thomas.'

'Are they safely there?' I breathed, praying it was so.

Isobel gave a shrill laugh. 'Alas no, the last we heard Lord Stanley had declared himself powerless to assist. I know not where my father and husband are now.'

This was too much to take in. I took her hand, stroking the palm. My action was meant to comfort and console but, strangely, it did no such thing. While I shivered at the thought of my father fleeing from those he thought were friends, Isobel grew increasingly distressed.

Tears spotting onto her linen gown, Isobel hissed, 'Mama feigns all is well but I know it is not. She says nothing at all, refusing to speak of Papa. When she attends me, she just wanders around the chamber muttering under her breath. Oh, Anne, what can I do confined in this manner?'

'Nothing,' I said, praying my voice did not waver, for I was chilled to the bone by these revelations. 'And for that reason you must not trouble yourself with such nonsense. If what you say is true, 'tis only because Mama is worried for Papa and, no doubt, want to keep it from you. Stay calm, sister, for you will only distress the babe.'

'George tells me nothing!' she sobbed as if I had not spoken. 'He writes rarely, and then says nothing of note. It is as if it does not occur to him I might wish to share his concerns and to support him. I had hopes our marriage might be like Mama and Papa's, where troubles are shared and difficulties overcome together, but it is not at all like that . . . '

My sister must have spent her life in a cloud of delusion, for our parents' marriage was not as she had described. Mama was like all other women of her age and status. She did her duty as expected by Papa, obeying him in all things as she had been educated to do and, indeed, as my sister and I had also been taught. Our mother might have reigned when Papa was absent but she deferred the instant he returned. Quite what Isobel had expected of marriage, I could not imagine, but now was hardly the time for such discussion.

'Hush, Isobel, do not distress yourself so.'

'But what if Edward is on his way here as Papa flees? What if he has an army at his back and they besiege the castle, thinking him here?'

My mind was a maelstrom of thoughts; wild untamed fears. Isobel's words were a knife into my heart, for we were only women and could do little to prevent such devastation. I took a deep breath before speaking. 'You know as well as I do Edward will not wage war upon women and unborn children, he is not that kind of man . . . '

'How can you be so certain?' Isobel was verging on the hysterical, her eyes as wild as Mama's had been. 'He will most assuredly wage war upon our husbands and fathers, and should we be widowed, he will spare no pity for us!'

Edward might well behave in that manner. He was no shy violet in matters of warfare but I could not think on that now lest I give in to hysteria. I must think of my sister's unborn child and nothing else.

'If we could get a message to the king, he may allow us to remain here in safety. His Grace was kindness itself when I attended him in the great hall.' I was desperate, turning on the spot, trying to find a way to help my sister. 'If I write, he might recall the dancing, our light-hearted conversations and how he enjoyed the company . . . '

'The king has no thought other than to thwart us,' Mama's cold tones sounded at the doorway. 'Nothing we say will make a difference. Your father and George make for Warwick as I speak and we are to leave forthwith. Isobel must rise from her lying-in so we can ride south.

'Where do we head?' I cried, clutching my poor sister's hand.

Mama did not want to answer at first but, as she looked at her daughters huddled together upon the bed, she relented. Lips drawn into a thin line, she spat, 'We make for the coast. There we shall board a ship and leave this accursed land.'

'No!' Isobel and I cried out together.

'We have no choice. Let us pray for Godspeed and that Our Lady of Heaven watches over the babe in the womb.' Mama stood over us, her face dark and menacing, even in the shadow of the room. 'May The Lord forgive Edward for the strife he now forces upon our family.'

I stopped. Tipping my head to one side, I tried to make sense of it all. The strife Edward had forced upon us? This was the result of Papa's shadowy dealings and resentment towards both Edward and his wife, no one else could take the blame for our situation. Could my mother and sister not see this? I made to speak but Mama gave me such a dark look I dared not question her further. Instead I pleaded for instruction and soon was running the length of the castle to retrieve clothing lined with our wealth. Yet all I could think about was securing my own meagre treasures, more valuable to me than gold or precious jewels.

Our ship had been buffeted continually by the wind and waves. The crew were used to the unsettled, unpredictable weather that so often coursed up and down the channel and the stalwart men bore the conditions with grim defiance, but those of us uncomfortably crammed into the hold and captain's quarters, fared far less well.

As we approached Calais, an additional horror offered its welcome as fire and gunpowder descended from all sides. This was shocking to say the least and not at all what we had expected – or had hoped – to find. A message from the king had somehow arrived before we had even sighted land, spurring the garrison into action. Though my father harboured suspicions the Deputy Captain of Calais, his old friend and ally, Lord Wenlock, might be simply making a show instead of intentionally trying to sink us, from where we sat below the rolling decks, it felt like the world was about to end.

To myself, Isobel and Mama, huddled in fear in the captain's cabin, this was one surprise we were unprepared for. Sick of the constant motion, I sought in vain to comfort my sister, suffering intolerably as a result of another unexpected and most unwelcome surprise. Isobel had begun her labour on board the grimy ship as guns pounded all around. There were no midwives to attend to her, no tinctures or concoctions to ease her pain; just the incessant rolling of the boat, the howl of wind and the aroma of salt, vomit and gunpowder. Not a place to welcome a child into the world.

Mama, though doubtless doing her best, had scant with sympathy for my poor sister. I could only watch from the shadows, fetching what little clean water we had left and wringing out small-cloths to wipe my sister's brow. As the pangs of her labour grew closer together and Isobel cried out in pain almost without ceasing, I prayed The Lord would hear her and send succour of some kind. I had never witnessed a birth, though I had heard tales both joyous and horrific. I knew, as a woman, it was my duty by God and the husband I would undoubtedly wed to bear children. Yet seeing Isobel struggle, not only under such terrible

197

conditions but in so great and constant pain she seemed to fade before my eyes, left me wondering if that cloistered life of a nun might not be so bad after all. Utterly helpless, and terrified that one day I, too, must travail and endure so much, I could do naught but watch as my sister fought for her life and that of her unborn child.

Though only bearing two daughters herself, Mama had oft assisted in a birthing chamber. Indeed, over the years she had made it her duty to attend births wherever and whenever possible, giving the benefit of her wisdom to both midwives and mothers-to-be. Whether these midwives and mothers had wanted her assistance was another matter but, as a countess and lady of status, Mama had felt it her Christian duty to assist. An Agnus Dei, the beautiful jewel I had sewn into her cloak, was an integral part of the custom and ritual of childbirth amongst ladies of high status and Mama had oft produced it to assist with a birth, its religious significance giving succour and comfort to the mother-to-be.

But there was no Agnus Dei present at this delivery. Nor were there any midwives, relics for the mother to clutch while praying for a safe delivery, tinctures, or any of the comforts a woman of Isobel's status could expect. There was no soft bed, linen sheets, hot water or warmed wine to ease her travail. As the timbers above us creaked and groaned, and blood bloomed across Isobel's linen shift like thunderclouds on a summer's eve, it was as though God had forsaken us in our hour of need. It could not have been worse if my sister had been abandoned to give birth in the gutters, with nothing but a frightened girl and her hysterical mother to aid her.

198

At last, the bombardment ceased with no damage sustained to our ship, thanks be to God. In the calm, messages were hastily exchanged. Although Wenlock was polite in the extreme, he made it clear he had no intention of allowing my father's ship to make port and so openly defy the king. Calais was closed to us. As my sister's travail grew more difficult and Mama could do naught but hold her hand and pray, I was sent to beg Papa for help. Breathing in deep, I relished the sting of sea air in my throat but dared not linger, even for a moment. Clutching the top of the ladder, I scanned the deck for signs of life. My father stood some feet ahead, deep in discussion with the captain and Isobel's husband. As I approached, George frowned, waving me away as if he did not wish to learn the outcome of his wife's efforts below. Papa ceased speaking but did not acknowledge me till the captain politely stepped away to give us a moment's privacy.

'Anne.' Papa's tone gave nothing away though his eyes scanned every inch of my face.

I gave a low curtsey. 'Papa, we need your assistance; Isobel must have aid or comfort of some kind for she labours hard but the babe does not yet come. Our prayers to The Virgin go unanswered and Mama begs you to find a way. . . '

Papa scowled, less than impressed the birthing was not yet done. 'Look around you daughter, what would you have me do, ask for midwives to be rowed out to us?'

That would be a miracle of the most welcome kind but I knew no such comfort would be forthcoming. Head bowed, I spoke with the utmost respect. 'I know not, Papa, but Isobel needs something to assist with the birth. Mama fears for both mother and child.'

Turning away, he whispered urgently in George's ear. My brother-in-law nodded in agreement, though he did not seem overly concerned by his wife's predicament, walking away after. Papa clasped my shoulder and pushed me towards the doorway. As he spoke, his voice was firm and in full control; a voice one dare not contradict.

'Go back below, child, and pray harder still that The Lord looks kindly upon your sister.'

Stunned by his lack of interest, I took a step forward. 'Papa, please help her . . . '

He stared as though seeing me for the first time. 'They are in God's hands for I can do nothing trapped out here.'

Such cold words did not console. Yet after I returned below, Papa managed to send a message ashore, with promises of our gold. His efforts negotiated a single barrel of wine to ease my sister's discomfort.

There was no respite for Isobel. Trapped in one small, fetid room, Mama did what she could but with so little at her disposal the outcome looked bleak. My heart bled for poor Isobel, still engulfed by pain and fading hope that no amount of French wine would console. And so I prayed until I wept, for there was no other comfort to be found.

Mama had already stepped out onto the deck, leaving the sleeping Isobel in my charge. I watched the rhythmic rise and fall of her chest for a moment or two but could bear it no longer. Making one last check to ensure she was indeed asleep, I crept from the chamber, desperate for cooler, fresher air. As I climbed the ladder to the deck above, my nausea eased as the bracing air hit hard. I breathed in deep, once more savouring the clean, acrid scent before clambering out onto the deck. Almost instantly I was forced to hide, my parents standing together but a few feet from the doorway.

'Madame?' Papa greeted my mother with a bluntness that surprised me. But then, even in the half-light of dusk, the stresses of the last months were evident on his features. 'How goes the birthing?'

My mother looked away for an instant, and I realised he did not know the outcome of Isobel's travail. Crouched behind a barrel, I was trapped and would be forced to watch a meeting I ought not to. Clenching my hands together, I prayed for forgiveness – and that I should not be discovered.

'Alas, my Lord, the babe was stillborn,' Mama announced, her tone as chill as the evening air. She too, appeared on the verge of exhaustion, gripping the side of the ship to steady herself. 'The outcome was not so surprising considering all your daughter has endured. No woman on this earth, duchess or otherwise, should be forced to deliver in such poor circumstances.'

There was silence, broken only by the creak of timber and distant cry of a gull. Side by side they stood, staring across the waves to the faraway lights of Calais, the feeble flickers as weak as the hope we clung to.

'And Isobel?' my father eventually asked. Though his voice had cracked as he spoke, the delay of his enquiry led me to believe Isobel's welfare was not his most pressing concern. My mother was of that mind also.

'Weak,' she replied with equal detachment. 'I fear she will also be lost if we do not get off this wretched boat. I must to speak to the Captain, arrange disposal of the body.'

More silence. And though they stood looking directly at each other, it was as if they were strangers.

'It is as I thought,' My father said at last, his voice as steely as the blade by his side. 'You blame me for this unfortunate turn of events.'

Mama's head shot up. 'Yes, husband, I most certainly do.'

I watched as my father raised himself up to full height, glaring at Mama. It was clear, even in the gloom he cared not to be spoken to in such manner by anyone – and especially not a woman. Behind the barrel, I braced, preparing for the fury to follow. Papa made a half-turn, staring out to sea before answering in a voice full of scorn.

'Perhaps I do not care what you think, wife. You purport to be proficient in the ways of childbirth, attending any woman's confinement you can find, you graciously bestow the benefit of your experiences and religious trinkets to all and sundry in their birthing chambers, yet cannot save your own grandchild. Pray, does your famed Agnus Dei no longer work? Did the mystical family jewel fail you this day?'

'It is gone,' Mama threw herself at Papa, beating fists upon his chest. 'Along with the rest of my Beauchamp inheritance. Lost to my daughters because we were forced to flee like thieves in the night because you would not let him be, could not stand graciously beside the throne! '

The madness affecting Mama held her tight in its grip, for she could not stop, could not hold her tongue like the good wife she should be, all the frustrations of the last few years flooding out in one long howl. Though my father grasped her wrists and held her at arm's length, she did not stop the tirade.

'Oh, no, my Lord, you must persist with your foolish envy and all that we had, all that we fought so hard for, is lost because of your vanity and eternal lust for power. All has been wasted on a fool's dream; as hollow and empty as that craven, strutting peacock you wed our daughter to. We are outcasts, we are ruined and 'tis your actions that have brought us to this.' She whipped her head around, the veil catching across Papa's face. 'Did you ever stop to think what such scheming would mean for your family?'

He slapped her so hard she staggered backwards several steps. As my mother wiped the blood from her lip, the shadows on my father's face were so dark they might have belonged to the devil himself. Never had I seen him so consumed by anger.

'Do not speak to me so,' he hissed into her face. 'You seem to think it is simple; that these matters are easily resolved. What little you know. I have not done what I have done to thwart Edward per se, I have done it to rid England of the leeches that cling to him and bleed the country dry. Pray tell me, how would you have done things? How differently would you have dealt with the subtleties of statecraft, or more pertinently, the witch's spawn tainting the blood of our land?'

There was nothing Mama could say in reply. She hung her head to hide both reddening cheek and humiliation. I prayed for an end to such awfulness, for I had not witnessed a scene like this before, revealing my parents to be so petty-minded and quarrelsome. I prayed Mama would step away, that Papa would let her go and end this horror, for no child should see their parents in such strife. Mama did not move a muscle. It

203

was as if she knew he was not finished yet.  She waited, head still bowed, hands clenched until my father leaned in closer.

'What do you know of family, Ann?  If you had delivered me a son as was your duty, perhaps none of this would have been necessary.  Perhaps the blame should lie at your feet . . . '

So, even after all these years, my father still had not accepted the lack of a son.  My heart went out to Mama over the cruelty of such a remark; she had indeed failed to provide an heir, and even in all this chaos, perhaps Papa's hurt was not entirely misplaced on that count.  Yet we are taught what occurs to us in this life is the will of The Lord and, huddled behind the barrel, it became clear to me The Lord did not wish my father to have a son.  My father had no such vision, and as I looked upon the misery before me, for the first time in my life I pitied Mama.

She moved to walk away, clearly hurt by his last rebuke, but he grabbed her arm, pulling her roughly back.

'I did not give you leave to depart.'

Head still bowed in defiant deference, my mother waited for more wounding words.  I closed my eyes, sickened by what was playing out before me but Mama still had one weapon at her disposal, one she was not afraid to use.

'The babe . . . ?' Papa stopped almost as soon as he had begun, as though he did not know how to ask the very question he needed answered.

This was Mama's reprieve and no doubt the reason she had endured his ire thus far.  Pulling herself up straight, she glared at her husband but did not answer him awhile.  Perhaps as her lip stung with the cold and the force of her husband's hand, she was overwhelmed with desire to see him feel the anguish of our predicament.

'This babe was born of the great houses of England,' she said at last, her voice cold and haughty, her head held high. 'Descended from the finest blood in the land, this babe should have been swaddled in the finest linen and bestowed with gifts. Alas, that is not to be. He . . . yes, my Lord, he . . . was a fine boy, beautiful and perfect in every way except for the small fact he lived not. He is as dead as your dreams of a crown, dreams that should also be consigned to a watery grave.'

She lied. My God-fearing, devout mother lied openly and blatantly to her husband, for I had seen the babe was a girl-child. Mama had wept as she held its pitiful form but said not a word of its sex to Isobel. My sister seemed to be under the impression 'twas a boy and Mama said naught to contradict, comforting her for the loss most deeply but no more. I had stayed quiet, consumed with grief and the horror of it all, pretending not to see or know. Perhaps I lied too, but in truth I could not bear to think of the sheer waste of it all.

Drawn back to the scene on deck, I glanced back up and held my breath. For one awful moment I believed Papa was about to hit my mother again. Although his hand hovered betwixt them for some time, he did not touch her as if some unseen thing held him back. Silently thanking God for this reprieve, I soon realised my fortitude was premature. A wild and maniacal look in his eye, Papa once more leaned in close, spitting his words into her face.

'Once more you underestimate me. You may have failed utterly to fulfil your purpose but my daughter did not. Mayhap she will have another son, mayhap her sister will. As I have said, you understand little of the ways of the world, for there is always an alternative, always another route to be considered.'

There was only impatience revealed in my father's features. Realisation dawned that he had already considered this, anticipated it even and was nowhere near as shocked as either my mother or I had hoped.

Mama considered for a moment, delaying once more. 'You are right, husband, as you always are, for there is indeed an alternative.'

Papa frowned, his gaze still fixed upon her unhappy visage but to my surprise he waited to hear her out.

'The Queen is again with child . . .' Mama's voice wavered as she spoke, and I knew she gambled much on her next words. 'Mayhap she will produce a son, mayhap she will not, but if she does so, before our family has another opportunity, pray what alternative will be open to you then?'

My father laughed out loud. It was a deep, resonating laugh that I felt as well as heard. 'There is always another route, Ann, always.'

As he turned and walked away I knew he had already found that other route; identified yet another way to chase his dream. I shuddered, wondering where this next move would lead.

The tide turned and we set sail, leaving Calais behind. I knew not where we were bound, for Papa would not say but behind we left all hope and, far beneath the waves, the tiny body of a child.

# Chapter Twelve – Turn and Turn Again

## Normandy - 1470

Our ship made port at Honfleur, in Normandy, the territory of King Louis of France, and a man who purported to be my father's friend. There, we were greeted by men Papa knew well, the Archbishop of Narbonne and the Admiral of France. At first this seemed in order and I was much relieved we had come ashore in a part of the world where our family was not about to be brought down and destroyed. My relief quickly soured, for soon after our arrival the remaining ships in Papa's fleet made berth in the harbour, and their presence caused great issue.

Of greater issue was the discovery of Papa's next move. In communications with King Louis, my father had revealed his intention to restore poor old King Henry to the throne of England. This was even more of a shock than the cannon-fire at Calais had been, and I could not believe my ears when the news was relayed. As a dutiful daughter I stayed silent, but, as I heard those words, my heart turned to ice. Papa had supported Edward and the House of York to remove this feeble man from the throne. His own father, my grandfather, had died at the hands of Queen Margaret's army and yet Papa was somehow able to put that all behind him in pursuit of power. Quite what my brother-in-law, George, thought about this turn of coat, I had no clue, for his scant words to me were only ever enquiries about Isobel's health.

I tended to my weak sister for as many hours of the day as I could manage. Still languid and feeble after the stillbirth, my sister seemed to have little will to recover.  Whether she suffered an illness of the mind as well as of the body, I could not be certain, but a melancholic cloud had hung over her since that dark day aboard ship.  Mama was too preoccupied with worries of her own to offer much sympathy or support, often appearing in my sister's bedchamber only to scold and chide that she was still abed.  Each day I read and prayed with Isobel, often just sitting beside her, our hands clasped together as she stared through the window.  Despite my efforts, her misery would not be moved.  Inevitably, I, too, was touched by that dark cloud, for my mind churned with possibilities both good and bad over Papa's unexpected change of mind, especially as the unpredictable Duke of Burgundy was reported to be much concerned by it, demanding the arrest of my father.

But King Louis did not dismiss the idea of restoring an enfeebled king so hastily. Careful not to break treaties the he had sworn to uphold, the French admiral and archbishop liaised with my father, careful not to break treaties King Louis had sworn to uphold. Negotiations progressed while all around us, Papa's ships and seamen remained visible; especially to those who spied on behalf of the Burgundian court.  King Louis insisted my father remove his ships to less obvious berths before any formal discussions could commence but, in his usual manner, my father stood firm, for he would speak with the king before doing anything. These were dark days, spent avoiding the grim mood of my father, my short-tempered mother, and the increasingly irritable and disconsolate George, Duke of Clarence.

Yet by month's end Papa's steadfastness had paid off.  Much to our relief, my father and George were summoned by King Louis to ride south into the Loire valley, to Chateau D'Amboise. The ships, however, had not moved.

The days of August grew increasingly stuffy and airless. As each day dawned, it seemed more oppressive than the last and I yearned for a cool breeze upon my face. Thunder rumbled in the distance and, though the chamber was in sore need of fresh air, I thought better of loosening the shutters, joining Isobel upon the settle instead. As the storm reverberated around, we sat close together, stitching in comfortable silence.

'Anne, why must you always hide when I have need of you?' Like a ghost in the night, Mama had appeared without a sound, her ashen features completing the ghoulish scene. Clutched in her hand was a letter, crumpled and much-read.

Looking upon her strained visage, I held a faint hope we might have been summoned elsewhere, be able to leave our lodgings. Though comfortable enough, the rooms were small and cramped and we had nowhere to walk or safely take the air. Papa had been gone from us for some time, the most trustworthy of his men alongside. I yearned for the wide, open skies of the moors, yearned to be able to breathe again. A small part of me even wished we could have ridden out to join Papa on his business.

"Tis as I feared, we are lost!' Mama announced in a fractured voice. She seemed bewildered, wringing her hands as she spoke.

'What ails you, Mama?' Isobel asked, continuing to stitch as though she humoured a simpleton.

Mama shuffled across the space between us. 'There is a . . . a fleet, attacking your father's ships this very moment!  It is made up of Burgundian and English ships and now fires upon the port.  Houses have been destroyed, men killed and some of your father's ships burned.  It seems our presence has caused much grief to King Edward and Duke Charles of Burgundy.  King Louis will be most displeased, especially after he counselled your father to remove his ships.'

I clasped hold of the settle, barely comprehending 'twas not a storm disturbing this afternoon's peace.  We were in peril from men, not nature.  This was grave news; we needed no further strife, weakened as we were.  Breathing deep, I sought to regain some control for, once more, there was naught to be done but wait it out and pray.

'I cannot think, daughters, cannot rest.' Still wringing her hands, Mama's plaintive tones pleaded for succour and comfort. 'What if the French king turns upon us also, who will help us then?  Come to that, what if we are captured?  Edward will have no mercy.'

'Let us pray The Lord looks kindly on us.' My beautiful embroidery fell to the floor as I clasped hands together.  Each dawn seemed to bring a new crisis and, like my mother, I existed in a nervous state, fearful of the next onslaught.

'But this is our doing, this we have brought upon ourselves!'  Mama looked into my face with the wide terrified eyes of a child.  Poor comfort could I offer, when little more than a child myself.

Yet The Lord works in mysterious ways.  Within days, the Burgundian ships had reputedly drawn away to refit.  Earl River's fleet had also sailed, off to deal with another situation threatening England, or so we were led to believe.  For reasons unfathomable to us trapped in these chambers, a reprieve had been granted. Needless to say we spent considerable time upon our knees thanking Our Father for his mercy.

Though the threat had passed, alongside the summer storms, my mother was not consoled in any way. As though she marked time until the next blow fell, the skin seemed stretched too thin across her cheekbones, dark circles spreading ever-wider beneath her eyes. Even her tongue had been dulled and I received far less chastisement than ever before in my short life. One morn, she glided into the bedchamber, only to stare vacantly at the bed until I touched her arm. Turning towards to me with unseeing eyes, it was only after I called her name over and over did she finally respond.

'Ah, yes. Anne.' She halted, staring at the tapestry ahead, her mind blank once more. 'You . . . you must help Isobel to rise and dress for I have at last received word from your father.'

Both Isobel and I demanded to know more. Yet Mama seemed unmoved by our keenness.

'He returns to us, this evening, I believe.' Her voice was utterly without expression, and more importantly, the joy usually expressed upon our father's return.

Though Isobel had shown the first real interest in anything for a long time, we said nothing more, watching our mother walk around the room, muttering as she stepped on.

'Did Papa write much of his reception with the king?' I prompted her again and again, such was Mama's distraction, but in truth I was curious, having little else to divert me these days. Whilst there were memories and dreams aplenty whirling in my mind, I refused to think on them lest they send me mad, so far from England and the one who was the reason for those memories.

She continued to stare at nothing. 'A little, but no doubt he will furnish us with every detail after he has rested.'

Mama had barely registered my interest. Something was not right, something had distracted her to the point of catatonia, for she was as a wraith walking between worlds, not the firebrand of a mother I was used to.

'What is it?' I stepped directly into her path. But at the sight of her face, I began to tremble.

She did not halt, did not cease following the circle trodden since entering the chamber. Her eyes were wide but unseeing as she muttered to herself. 'After meeting with King Louis, my dearest husband travelled to Angers. The deposed Queen Margaret also attended. At the behest of the king, he entered her company, begging pardon for the wrongs he had done her. After kneeling before her for some considerable time, and using great patience and considered words, he . . . he . . . oh, may The Lord forgive our sins, he has paid homage to the House of Lancaster!'

'No . . . !' Isobel and I cried out simultaneously.

Mama's eyes shone bright with the truth. Fear, confusion and panic consumed her too. Isobel reached for my hand as she also understood Mama was on the verge of hysteria. Together we guided the bewildered woman to the settle, feeding her sip after sip of wine till her eyelids began to close. After ensuring she was comfortable, Isobel and I sat in silence, stunned by the latest twist of events.

'Do not ask me to do this, I beg of you!'

Papa stood over me, his fingers tap-tapping upon the table. 'You must do your duty, daughter, and that is to obey.'

Caught in a nightmare, a horror of the most fiendish kind, there was no escape. The man before me looked like my father, spoke like my father, but it could not be, for such a kind and loving man would never have made such demands. Yet this man had done exactly that. He could not be my sire; he must be a changeling, for he appeared as a complete stranger. Tapping irritably upon the table, this stranger had somehow come to terms with Queen Margaret, agreed to support her cause to place King Henry back upon the throne of England. And worse still this unnatural, abhorrent arrangement was to be sealed with my marriage to their son, Prince Edward.

Safe in his palace, King Louis must have been delighted securing this accord, especially after my father had spent so long decrying the Frenchwoman, cursing her to Hell everlasting. I, on the other hand, was desolate. To hear what had been done, and to hear it from my father's own lips was as though he had sold his soul to the devil once and for all. And as he stood over me, face thunderous and eyes ablaze, it was as if he had sold mine as well. I did not try to stop the tears. Burning hot, they flowed in rivers down my face and onto the silken gown, spotting and spoiling its finery. Perhaps if Papa saw how truly unhappy I was he would reconsider, realise how wrong this unholy arrangement was, especially after all that had occurred.

'There is no question over the matter, daughter, the marriage has been settled and cannot now be undone.' Papa's voice was utterly devoid of emotion. Any fury he felt at my outburst was well concealed. But that made my father's request all the more terrifying, for while it was impossible to know his thoughts, I had learned enough to know he was implacable when in this frame of mind.

Still I cried, the tears unfeigned and unstopping. My heart beat violently inside my ribcage as heat flushed through my young body. 'I cannot wed that boy. Pray, do you recall what his mother did to our family, to King Edward's family . . .?'

'*Silence!*' Papa's face was stone, revealing not a flicker of emotion. 'You will marry Prince Edward to secure our arrangement and that is final. The French king agrees it is to be so and will support you all while I endeavour to reclaim England. Some gratitude for the king's generosity would be appropriate instead of this unnecessary hysteria.'

As he made to leave, I crumpled at his feet, his beloved daughter distraught beyond consolation. A deep frown creased his brow as he looked down, the eyes harsh and unrelenting.

'But why must it be this way?' I pleaded. 'Can I not marry Dickon as we once hoped?'

Papa's eyebrows bowed so much they almost touched. As I looked into his face it was as though I had spoken the name of a demon, such was his fury.

'You could never have married that boy, the king would have seen to that. Even so, Gloucester's choice was made years ago when he walked away from our family.' As the eyes still glared, he snorted. 'Such childish notions ought to have been forgotten long since.'

'But I have not forgotten!' Though still upon the floor, the wilfulness I could not quite expunge bubbled out once more. 'He is still in my thoughts and if you had not strayed so far from the king's side, perhaps a marriage might have been negotiated!'

For one terrible moment I thought the man I loved would strike me as he had Mama. As I cowered, with hands ready to shield my head, the moments dragged on. At last, I dared a glance. The arm was suspended above and poised to strike, but motionless as though 'twas carved in stone.

'Forgive me, Papa,' the voice I found was barely more than a whisper. 'I should not have spoken so but this is all so hard for me to understand. I thought you despised Queen Margaret . . . '

If I sought refuge in the obedient daughter he demanded, there might be room for negotiation. Perhaps he would explain his actions to me and in doing so, reconsider. 'Twas a small hope but the only hope I had at this moment. The hand fell away and I breathed again, daring another glance at his face. The eyes chilled me to the bone, for these were not the eyes of the father I loved.

'Your place is not to understand, daughter, it is to obey as you have been taught to do. You are to be betrothed forthwith. Then, once the dispensation is received, the wedding will be performed. I will hear no more on the matter, for it is settled.'

I lurched forward, grasping handfuls of his tunic. 'I beg of you, Papa, if you love me at all, please do not make me do this.'

But Papa was utterly unmoved by my words. The man who had raised me, the man I looked up to, adored and trusted beyond question was impervious to my misery.

'And if you loved me, daughter, you would do my bidding without question.'

I had been bought and sold completely. My hands fell from his tunic and Papa turned away, striding across the chamber, his fury weighing down each step. As he snatched the door open, Mama appeared, face pale and features wary. Pale-blue eyes flicked from my father to me and back again while her fingers were raised to her lips as if she could scarcely believe what had occurred.

'Madame,' Papa's tone was pure ice. 'Your daughter's education is severely lacking, for she cannot grasp the concepts of obedience and duty. See she does so directly.'

With that he was gone, the rhythmic click of his boots sounding upon the passage floor for some moments after. I remained crumpled upon the floor, the sky falling in on top of me.

Today had seen another birthday pass, but this year, my thirteenth, had bestowed the most despicable gift imaginable.

'Why must you remain so defiant?' Isobel whispered as we huddled beside the fire. 'You are already betrothed and the wedding will go ahead whether you like it or not. You cannot defy our father and the King of France.'

Outside, wild December weather beat against the walls of our lodging. Almost six months had passed since I was told I would wed the Lancastrian prince. Though the seasons had changed, and changed again, I had not come to terms with such an abhorrent arrangement and doubted I ever would. Pleas and protestations had fallen upon deaf ears, my father furious at such rebellion within his family, while Mama treated me with icy politeness, her disdain barely concealed. Attending to my sister was the only solace I found during those bleak months, and with George in England with Papa, the chill between us began to thaw at last.

Although Isobel continually counselled restraint, I refused to submit meekly and would not accept my fate. In my heart I felt this was the wrong of all wrongs. After all, had I not been brought up hearing tales of the devastation Queen Margaret and her troops had wrought upon England? Had I not heard how her son was described as a blood-lusting, bastard-whelp, sired by someone other than pious, feeble King Henry? Long after Margaret's men had killed my grandfather and uncle at Wakefield alongside Dickon's father and brother, grisly accounts of their deaths relayed by Papa's wards had made me tremble long into the night. Thereto had I heard the grim tale of how the Frenchwoman had ordered a paper crown to be placed upon the Duke of York's severed head as it stood upon Micklegate Bar in the city of York. Yet my father had made peace with this harpy and sealed it with a marriage. In my young mind, it passed all understanding.

'I should rather die than wed that arrogant cur.' Still clad in my nightgown, I could not stop shivering. 'Let me go outside, Isobel, for then I shall catch cold within moments and be stricken with a fever and, God willing, be struck down beyond saving. . .'

Isobel clamped a hand over my mouth. 'Anne, do not speak so! Not only are such thoughts a mortal sin, but this wedding will happen, even if you are ailing. Accept it, for there is no other way.'

'I cannot, will not, wed him!' Papa's angry words aboard ship echoed through my mind. 'There must be an alternative, there must.'

'His name is Edward and he is a Prince of Wales,' Isobel's weary voice sounded above the wind. 'He may even be King of England one day. With a crown upon your head, you will be thankful there was no alternative.'

'The prince will only become king if Papa prevails.'

'He will.' Isobel's tone changed. 'Can you recall when Papa did not succeed? He finds a way no matter what.'

So my sister was more observant than I had given her credit for. Perhaps she also had come to realise she held no control over her own life. As my father's ambitious words sounded once more in my mind, I turned and clasped hold of Isobel, pulling her into an embrace. She stiffened at such unexpected attention but did not pull away. However, I had taken a liberty she did not care for, so dropped my arms. Though I was sorely in need of comfort and reassurance, the look upon Isobel's face served as a reminder her affection towards me had only thawed, not warmed.

'Ah, Isobel, you have not deserved such poor treatment.' I offered an olive branch. 'Once you believed Papa would set George upon the throne with you beside him, but then . . . '

'But then he changed his mind and sold you for men and arms, finding another way to pursue his ambitions.' She sighed. 'Perhaps Edward will make a better king than George.'

Or perhaps not; the boy had a ruthless streak that made George look like a lapdog. I kept my lips

218

clamped together lest words slip out I might later regret. Isobel was my sole ally in this terrible affair and, though I cared little for George, I ought not to insult her husband. The young duke might be deeply flawed in character but George was still a link to Dickon.

'Perhaps George is not the stuff of kings but it is not so bad being wed to him. Marriage held no great surprises for me.' Isobel stared ahead, lost in thought. 'Even so, our lessons do not prepare us for what to expect.'

'How so?'

'As daughters of Eve it is our place to endure and suffer, but sometimes I think our menfolk add to this burden without thinking, for they never seem to consider how their actions might affect us.'

Poor Isobel. A dead babe, a husband who had not lived up to expectations and a life in exile were all she had to show for her trouble. Not what she had expected as a duchess.

My sister's troubles were not foremost on my mind. I tried my best to keep a clear head, but 'twas impossible to escape thoughts of my forthcoming wedding. As if he knew of my strife and desperation, Dickon crept into my dreams upon many a night. Though I had not seen his face clearly for more than a year, in the depths of the darkness his handsome features came hauntingly close. Each time his expression was one of bemusement, as if he questioned why I was even trying to resist. Yet I could not give up all hope, my heart belonged to him and always would, I could not in all conscience go willingly to the altar with another, though 'twas my duty to do so. A small part of me rejoiced to see Dickon's face once more but it served only to remind me what was about to happen and what I had lost. As his crooked grin loomed large in my mind, I could almost hear the words he said to me that day in London, reminding how we must do as bidden. He would understand my situation, would acknowledge this decision had not been mine to make, but it was not nearly enough to console my shattered heart.

Each night, after braiding my hair before bed, I caressed the bodice of my nightgown, feeling for the tiny silver pin hidden beneath. The comfort it gave lessened with each passing day but I hoarded my meagre treasures like an old miser, ensuring their whereabouts each morn as I rose and each evening as I prepared for bed. The pilgrim badge was securely pinned on the underside of my best chemise tucked away in my coffer, while the faded rose lay pressed between the pages of my psalter. I had grown especially careful after Papa's announcement of the arrangement between myself and the young Prince of Wales, fearing discovery of my treasures. In the darkness as Isobel slept, I oft sought out that tiny silvered boar, caressing it as if it could make everything right. But it could not. My world had turned upside down and there was naught I could do to put it right. Most nights, silent tears ran sideways into my hair and pillow as I waited for sleep's embrace, clinging to the hope Dickon would step into my dreams.

And so on a bleak, December morn, Prince Edward and I were wed, to our mutual dissatisfaction. Perhaps the church was a fine example, but I took no notice. Perhaps the priest singing the mass was kind and well-educated, but I did not hear. Even though Mama and Queen Margaret could barely conceal their contempt for each other, I did not see.    Trembling beneath my finery, fighting the burn in my throat and the sting of tears in my eyes, I was consumed by the fact my father had not deemed it necessary to witness the arrangement he had sold his soul to procure.  Declaring there was much business to attend to, the men had gone by August's end, George and Papa heading north to prepare the fleet for sailing for England.  News was scarce over the coming weeks, though Mama and Isobel both received letters from their husbands.    Neither shared much with me.  However, eavesdropping upon conversations, I once caught wind of trouble stirring amongst Papa's men over what his intentions were after arriving back across the channel.  But nothing else of note was forthcoming until the month of September, when we heard they had set sail for ports in the West Country.  Apart from brief news the ships had safely made land at Dartmouth and Plymouth, I heard no more throughout the autumn.  With no word received counteracting my father's schemes, the dreaded wedding went ahead as planned.

Papa's absence had wounded me as deeply as his volte-face.    During the dark months between betrothal and marriage, I held to the hope that if there was no possibility of breaking the arrangement then he would support me upon the day, offer the encouragement showered upon me as a child.  It was not to be, and the wound cut by this despicable arrangement was ripped open as I learned he had not even sent word to bless our union.

There were few enough guests at our wedding ceremony; Queen Margaret, Mama and Isobel, and two of the queen's ladies.  Throughout the ceremony, the queen sat upon a throne-like seat, the dark eyes fixed upon my unworthy form while her lips were pursed up

221

in perpetual distaste. Her petite figure was lost in the vastness of the episcopal seat and, despite being in the sight of God, she made no effort to pretend this match was to her liking. My hand was accepted because she needed my father, and for no other reason. As I had spoken those despicable vows, binding me to a man I could never like, let alone love or respect, my voice faltered more than once. In response, the priest scowled while my dear mother kicked my ankle to prompt a more dignified response, hissing her contempt as she did so. The burn in my throat grew as the moments passed, those around frowning as though this lapse proved my unworthiness beyond contestation rather than revealing the child I still was. I had never felt so alone or desolate since arriving upon God's earth. My heart bled for the lack of care or pity my family showed at this time, its shattered pieces broken beyond repair knowing Dickon was utterly lost to me.

I had disliked Edward from the first moment I set eyes upon him and the day of our wedding proved no different. Seventeen, tall and handsome with fine, chiselled features, I ought to have been pleased by this match, but in truth, I feared him from the moment he had entered the chamber. As dark and sultry in complexion as his mother, Edward's brown eyes showed not a scrap of care, only darkness I feared to drown in. His welcome offered no warmth, only scorn and derision as he said the fewest words possible. When he did speak out, it was only to his mother and in her native French. They spoke so fast I could scarcely make out a single word, despite having been schooled in the language myself. Though I did not understand their conversation, right from the beginning it seemed to me Prince Edward resented the match almost as much as me. Each time our company was forced upon the other,

222

he wilfully reminded his mother of his feelings as if I was not present. Each time the fury of her reply brought only silence from my intended and, as she looked over my pitiful form once more, I saw the same disdain in her eyes, the same reluctance that her prince must make do with a second-best bride.

Using every skill at my disposal, I had tried to make a good impression, fearful of my father's ire should he witness the disdain in which I was held. At every meeting I was politeness itself, behaving as a lady of the finest breeding and education ought to do, yet still the prince and his mother looked down upon me as though I had been dragged from the gutter that morn.

The feast for our wedding was even more of a paltry affair than the ceremony. Almost as soon as she stepped into the solar, Queen Margaret declared she had a headache and left without so much as raising a cup of wine to her son, taking her ladies with her. Prince Edward said not a word, sipping from his cup as if he wished to be anywhere other than here, while an exhausted Isobel sat in the corner, pale and quiet. As Edward emptied his cup, he thrust it at a servant and left the room without a word or backward glance. I retreated to the window seat, hurt beyond words over this vile arrangement and how no-one but I seemed to care much about the ignominy of it all.

Mama glided across the room, settling herself beside me. 'So daughter, you are wed at last, and to a prince, no less.'

Though I looked up, I said nothing. Edward may have been a prince but his conduct was far from regal. As she shifted the cushions around to make herself comfortable, I knew Mama was about to tell me something I had no desire to hear.

'As you know, the queen has demanded there be no consummation of this marriage until your father has accomplished all he needs to in England.'

I nodded, thankful beyond words for this small reprieve.

'However, your father has directed otherwise.'

My wine cup fell to the floor earning only a look of disgust from my mother. 'But if the queen has said it should not happen then surely it will not . . . '

'Your father wishes to secure this arrangement beyond breaking and, though you will not be formally bedded this evening,' Mama sniffed as if this decree was not to her liking. 'Should Edward find his way into your bed, you will do your duty as a wife ought.'

'But Edward likes me not at all, and so surely will take heed of his mother's instruction . . .' only after I had finished speaking did I comprehend how truly desperate I must have sounded. I bowed my head, not daring to look at Mama.

'Whether he likes you or not is irrelevant. He is a young man, and will take his pleasure whenever he may. You are his wife and, as such, must do his will. Though Edward might exercise restraint for the moment, a night will come when no serving-maid or other bed-mate can be found. Then he will remember his wife.'

It was as though she had slapped my face. I fell to my knees, pleading for respite from a situation I dreaded. 'I cannot be alone with him, Mama, I fear it so!'

'Get up this instant,' Mama hissed. 'Do not show yourself up in such a poor manner. You will do your duty without question, Anne, for this is how it has always been done. A girl weds where her family decide, for she cannot possibly know what is best. If you would take my advice, find some patience and humility, for these virtues will allow your husband to see you in a favourable light. This way, you might secure his respect and, given time, perhaps even affection.'

My last hope had lain with Mama, in that she disapproved of the match and would somehow protect me until it was no longer possible to do so. Though I tried, the sobs simply would not be silenced.

'I too, had no choice where I was wed,' she stared out of the window, trying to ignore my distress. 'And it has not always been easy, for I was not much older than you but, by demonstrating virtues whenever I could, your father came to love me in his way. I have been more fortunate than most, but this is the way of our world, and no exception will be made for an ungrateful girl who does not know her place.'

'But you might have prepared me for this part of marriage, might have spoken of it before!' I cried, uncaring if those left in the chamber heard my distress.

'Duty and obedience,' Mama's voice had no warmth whatsoever. She still did not look at me. 'For a woman, these virtues are of the utmost importance alongside those already mentioned. Live your life by these, Anne, for that is the best advice I can give a new wife. Indeed, you ought to have grasped a good understanding of this long since.'

In that moment I knew whatever my mother's thoughts on this diabolical arrangement, she held no sway in my father's eyes. Her opinion was never sought, her objections never considered – if indeed she had ever raised any. Perhaps the friction I had witnessed between my parents on that awful day aboard ship had continued ever since, or had never ceased throughout the long years of their marriage, invisible to Isobel and me until recently. Mama was truly as much subject to Papa's will as I was, and if I sought escape, she could no more help me than I could help myself. Clasping my hands, I silently begged Our Lady of Heaven to look kindly upon me for there was no-one else upon this earth able to offer aid.

'Am I to be abandoned in this way, to endure bedding without the blessing of a priest or a mother's care and guidance?' The words fell from my mouth for I had not the will to stop them.

My mother sighed. 'Anne, I am too weary to discuss this matter now. Let us pray it will not be necessary for a while, but in the meantime, if it eases your concern, speak to Isobel. She will instruct you on what to expect.'

Even my own mother had forsaken me.

# Chapter Thirteen – An Inconvenient Bride

*Normandy - 1471*

'My Lady.' A sturdy, middle-aged woman with bright, watchful eyes bobbed a curtsey as we passed in the entrance to Isobel's chamber.

I closed the door. 'Who is that woman?'

Isobel barely looked up from her book. 'Alys is my lady-in-waiting. I cannot believe you do not know that, sister.'

'Since when?' I halted mid-step, convinced I was going mad. 'Papa engaged all our servants when we first arrived from England so he could ensure they were not in the pay of another. She was not amongst them.'

Still reading, Isobel murmured with impatience, 'She has been here some time, though perhaps you have been too preoccupied to notice.'

Though fretful about my marriage I had not missed the arrival of a stranger in our midst. 'But she is English, how did she . . .?'

Isobel heaved an impatient sigh. 'She travelled across the sea to care for me, though it took her some while to reach us.'

'But how . . . why?' This was an unexpected development. No one had visited or attended us since fleeing from Warwick apart from those encouraged or directed to by King Louis. A woman appearing from nowhere only raised suspicion.

'Alys has served in my household before.' Isobel turned another page of her book. 'When she heard of the loss of my babe aboard that dreadful ship, she knew I would be in need of comfort and care, so made it her business to seek me out.'

227

'I do not believe you.' I was defiant – and frightened. Alys, whatever her true identity might be, could be in the pay of any number of interested parties, even my new mother-in-law. And the more I thought on it, could recall no such woman attending my sister at any time.

Isobel put the book aside, then beckoned to me. 'Pour a cup of wine, I am in need of refreshment.'

As I held out the cup, Isobel grasped my arm causing wine to slosh over her gown. I gasped but she put a hand over my mouth.

'Make no mind of the gown and listen,' she whispered. 'Alys Winterbourne came directly from His Grace, King Edward, no less. She departed England months ago, passing through Calais on her way to find me. Mama must not learn any of this, for she believes Alys has been in Lady Wenlock's service until recently.'

'Did she not see her when you were wed in Calais?'

Isobel shook her head. 'Alys hinted she was in England, attending to her ailing mother.'

Lies and yet more lies. 'Should I assume Alys is not her real name?'

Though glancing up at me, my sister said nothing.

I did not enjoy subterfuge in any shape or form. 'And am I also to assume you will never reveal her name, even to me?'

My sister smiled. 'You are far too suspicious for your own good, Anne, but you are also correct.'

I took that as a compliment. 'I do not care about your new woman but whatever can the king have to say that he must do so by means of a lady's maid?'

'Nothing, apart from wishing me a swift recovery.' Isobel leaned so close, her lips touched my ears. 'However, he has much to say to my husband.'

I jumped back, my brow creasing deeply. 'Does he seek to arrest him?'

She gave a quiet laugh, 'Quite the opposite!'

All became clear. The lady, for she was clearly a lady and not a commoner, had been despatched to reconcile the House of York by securing the return of a prodigal son, through his wife. King Edward had made another clever move, for if he could reunite the family, he could also thwart Papa. George was being offered an olive branch by his brother, the king, and if he chose to accept it he would be forgiven and welcomed with open arms. Papa would receive no such offer.

My throat burning, I sought to keep my voice even. 'So you will soon be gone, leaving me alone with that wretched boy.'

She pulled me into an embrace, the cup of wine tumbling from her hand, its contents splattering the floor with blood-coloured droplets.

'I shall be here by your side for some time to come, sister,' she whispered into my hair. 'Everything remains in place until we return to England.'

Though I pulled Isobel closer still, and thanked her for such reassurance, in my heart I knew I was alone and at my husband's mercy from the moment she set foot on English soil.

Mama retreated more and more into a world of her own. Though she often sat with Isobel and me, listening as we read together, our time at the small court of Queen Margaret seemed to diminish her more with each passing day. I, too, would have given all I owned to be far from here – both in mind and body, but I could not. I was joined in matrimony to the arrogant youth who ignored me as we walked, prayed and ate, belittling my manners, countenance and breeding when he thought I could not hear. I envied my mother's withdrawal from the world.

The chateau at Amboise was impressive and comfortable but I cared not for its views or finely furnished chambers. I cared not that King Louis was fond of its gardens and I cared nothing for the musicians and minstrels engaged to entertain. I cared only that I was trapped, cornered in a war not of my making and my sister had been thrown a lifeline while I had been left to sink below the murky waters of politics and power.

Since our miserable wedding day, Prince Edward had avoided my company whenever possible. Indeed, as we had celebrated Christmas at Chateau D'Amboise, we spoke no more than ten words directly to each other. His mother, Queen Margaret, spoke even less. During this time I was thankful beyond words Mama and Isobel were here and I could not bring myself to imagine how miserable my life would be once they left. As January lingered, grey and despondent, Isobel and Mama both succumbed to chest colds. They remained separate to the rest of us, so as to prevent the queen from contracting such a wretched ailment, and often at this time I was alone. Though I hid away whenever possible, I was still required to eat and pray with my new family. Inevitably perhaps, shortly after Twelfth Night, my mother was proved right when Edward found his way to my chamber. Already abed, the bed-drapes closed and the fire burned down low, I was almost asleep. No candles burned and the embers from the dying fire threw out so little light it cut no path through the darkness. In such a drowsy state, I was barely aware of another stumbling around the bedchamber and pulling back the drapes, my subconscious no doubt reminded of the numerous times Isobel had sought out my chamber. Yet as I turned over, a shadow loomed tall, darker than the night around. 'Twas a silent, menacing shadow, reeking of wine and though shuffled towards the far edge of the bed, I could not gainsay the strength and determination of a beast so fired. In the darkness of a winter's night I was forced to yield, for, as I had been informed, there was no choice in this matter. Supposedly, this violent act was no crime because I now belonged to this monster of the darkness. His actions would not bring the wrath of one house down upon another; this was his right and his duty, expected and even encouraged, though I was allowed no say in any of it. Hot, silent tears ran sideways into my hair while the virtues of duty and obedience echoed in my mind. According to my elders and betters, these virtues were all that mattered, nothing else, and especially not the wishes of a terrified fourteen-year-old girl.

In the morn it seemed no more than a terrible dream, sleep's interruption of the darkest kind. For one brief moment upon waking, I believed only a hideous nightmare had occurred but, as I rose from the bed, the blood-stained sheet brought everything back with clarity. Muscles aching after the resistance I had somehow found, I fled to the prie-dieu in the corner of my chamber. Tears streaming down my cheeks, I begged for forgiveness and absolution. I was a maid no more and, though the sin might not be mine, 'twas still a sin to be paid for in whatever ways The Lord saw fit.

'What is it, Annie?' Isobel's eyes narrowed as she saw my face. I had expected no sympathy or comfort from her but she reached for my hands.

I could not speak, clutching at her. But she knew, somehow she saw the sin I carried and pulled me into her arms. 'Hush, little sister. 'Tis done, 'tis over for now.'

For now. One day soon I would be Edward's wife in every way, acknowledged openly as such and forced to endure his attentions whenever he felt the need. This burden weighed heavily indeed but, as I lay in my sister's arms, I received a small gift in the guise of her ire.

'You deserved far better than this, sister, with no preparation or care from our mother. I am truly sorry for it, Anne, and wish I could have served you better as a sister.'

I reached for her hand, pulling it to my cheek. I had no words but needed her to know I was grateful, even for the thought of help.

She pulled me tighter still. 'Knowing Edward, I suspect he was neither patient nor gentle and, for that alone, I shall not forgive his behaviour towards you.'

Edward would not care whether he had Isobel's forgiveness or not but her consolation was some balm for my hurts.

'The queen was right to insist the marriage ought not to be consummated,' Isobel sighed, running her hands around my hips. 'For you are still too small to risk childbirth. A year or so will make all the difference and our lady mother knows this. She especially has failed in her duty to you.'

'Say naught to Mama of this, she only does Papa's will . . .' I croaked, still clinging to Isobel. It was a moment or two before the truth of the situation dawned upon her.

'How could she do that to you?' Isobel shook her head. 'She should put your welfare first, whatever Papa might say. If men had to bear the resulting babes, their thoughts on such matters might be quite different. Let us pray to Our Lady of Heaven your menses come swiftly and you are able to put this dark deed behind you. I shall let it slip to the queen's ladies how Prince Edward was seen skulking in the corridor outside your door. That should curb his interest for the present.'

'Pray, how will that help?' To me, the situation seemed utterly hopeless, misery still fogging my mind to the exclusion of all rational thought.

'Though you could bar the door, or sleep with your maids ever-present, these efforts can be easily deflected, for Edward is your husband and you must obey him in all.' My sister gave a smile so wide it lit up her eyes. 'However, the queen does not want you with child, sweet sister, for though a babe would be a blessing in most marriages, 'twould be a curse upon her house if Papa cannot deliver all he has promised – and we are yet to learn of what, if anything, he has accomplished in England. If Queen Margaret suspects Edward is paying the slightest attention to you, she will be furious. That fury is your friend, Anne, for she will not acquiesce until certain Papa has prevailed.'

I prayed hard that night. I prayed Edward would not insist I unbar my chamber door, I prayed for my menses to arrive forthwith, ensuring I did not carry a child of Lancaster and I also prayed for my sister. Though her company and care had given me great solace, one day she would be gone – and may Our Lady of Heaven help me then.

Queen Margaret was on edge, knowing her best hope for her husband's safety and crown were now far across the sea. Mama and Isobel fretted also, desperate for their menfolk to avoid the wrath of King Edward and his army. My concerns were closer to home, increasingly so as we travelled north back towards the Normandy coast. I knew, one day soon, we should set sail for England – and then the devil would be unleashed.

Settled into lodgings at Barfleur this time, I breathed again. Not only had my menses arrived exactly when expected, but our rooms were small and cramped, forcing Isobel and me to share a bed once again. For one dark moment I had thought the queen would insist I take my position as her son's wife, but as she scrutinized my small and feeble form, dark eyes flicking to Edward and then back to me, it was clear the thought was fleeting. Moments later, the queen, her ladies and Prince Edward left, escorted to their chambers by the servants. Isobel, Mama and I were left with the least-comfortable rooms in our lodgings, not that I minded. Needless to say, I spent the following hour upon my knees, giving thanks for The Lord's Divine Mercy.

'What news, Isobel?' I demanded, upon returning to our chamber.

'Very little.' Isobel screwed up her face as she looked around the room. After the opulence of Amboise, the chamber was austere and almost convent-like.

'Someone must know something.'

Alys entered the chamber bringing wine for Isobel. As she poured a cup, Isobel said nothing, simply indicating she should pour wine for me also. As Alys left, Isobel patted the seat beside her.

'There is news, Anne, but I fear you will not like it.'

Stepping across the small space between us, my feet seemed made of lead, so heavy did they weigh. I sat down, clutching at the cup Isobel offered but I did not drink. I could not drink.

'Pray tell me Isobel, for I would know the worst.'

She finished her wine, placing the cup aside before smoothing out her skirts. 'I have charged Alys with gathering what news she can. Some days past she heard from a servant who had spoken with a merchant. He brought news of what the last months have held for our menfolk.'

I held my breath.

'As you already know, Papa landed in Plymouth a few days after leaving Normandy. At that time, King Edward lingered in Yorkshire and so would not learn of the landing for some days. Papa used the delay to his advantage. The Lancastrian lords King Louis had housed hoisted their banners and went off to raise men, while Papa marched for Exeter, raising many men along the way. From there, he headed north-eastwards intending to counter King Edward, while still collecting more men and nobles along the way. 'Tis said when he arrived at Coventry, the townsfolk numbered them at thirty thousand strong.'

A great number indeed, but I could not rejoice for fear clutched my heart, its grip tightening with each passing moment. Those I cared for were caught in the chaos Isobel spoke of – caught on both sides.

'When King Edward was alerted to Papa's arrival, he gathered his forces, summoning our Uncle John to join him. John set out but, before he reached the royal encampment at Doncaster, he halted, declaring King Edward had forfeited his allegiance by taking away his earldom and replacing it with the paltry rank of Marquis.'

I gasped.   King Edward had returned the Earldom of Northumberland to Henry Percy some months past, after Percy had finally sworn fealty to Edward.   Though the king had placated my uncle with other titles, 'twas not nearly enough, as our uncle had declared to his men.   Yet my Uncle John was not like Papa, was not always seeking new ways to attain power and wealth.   In truth, I was greatly surprised by this action, especially when Isobel revealed he had then urged his men to follow Papa.   John was no Lancastrian, his father had died at the hands of Queen Margaret's army, and while Papa might have been blinded by King Louis' silvered tongue and guile, John had never been so easily swayed.   But he was a Neville, and Papa would not let him forget that fact, even unto death.

'What then?' I whispered.

'After much unrest in London - prisoners released, Flemings and Dutchmen harangued and attacked - Queen Elizabeth, her mother and daughters fled to sanctuary in Westminster Abbey while the king's chancellor sought refuge elsewhere.   The Tower was delivered up to the mayor and King Henry led from his confinement.   Our other Neville uncle, the archbishop, thereupon installed himself in The Tower.'

'Where was Papa in all of this?' I could not shake the feeling something terrible had occurred, clutching at Isobel for comfort.

She wrapped an arm around me. 'Papa and my husband then rode into London, their army alongside. Papa escorted King Henry to St Paul's where he made offerings, before being placed in the Bishop's palace.

George was given a great house once belonging to our Neville grandfather, and there he remained while Papa lodged with the king.'

This was far too much to take in. But then, this had not happened all at once, occurring over many weeks, albeit long before the winter had set in. Other names swirled around in my mind, other men we cared for, others we loved. 'What . . . what has become of King Edward?'

'As our Uncle John was encouraging his men to support Papa and the Lancastrian cause, word reached Edward of how close our uncle's forces were. Somehow, he, Hastings, Earl Rivers, Dickon and a few others fled for their lives with naught but the clothes they wore.'

I fainted dead away.

# Chapter Fourteen – Time and Tide

*April - 1471*

The month of February had passed me utterly by. Lost inside a fog of despair, I spoke little, ate little, prayed constantly and, in doing so, withdrew from my family. Each day blurred into the next. There was little enough to occupy us but given my increasing worries for Papa, my uncles, Francis and especially Dickon, I simply existed at this time, the feelings of dread never leaving my mind. My husband and mother-in-law hardly acknowledged my presence on any given day, so this change in my behaviour caused them little concern. Mama did not register my distress, or, if she did, had no inclination to console me for she battled enough demons of her own. Only Isobel held concerns for my welfare, but, after the ordeal I had suffered weeks before, she left me alone, believing I needed quiet and rest to recover my spirits.

In truth, nothing but the appearance of my dearest friend could have restored me to health. Yet I held no hope to ever set eyes upon him again in this life. In the autumn of the previous year, as I had fretted over my forthcoming marriage, he had fled in fear of his life. Tales had reached us of how ships were taken across the sea to the Low Countries where King Edward was forced to exist on the charity of his sister Margaret. Her husband, the Duke of Burgundy, who was under pressure from King Louis and others, deliberated whether to aid Edward or not. No word was spoken of Dickon. Rumour was all I had to cling to, rumour that spoke of a small number of English lords surviving on the generosity of the duchess and other friends in those domains, but of the truth I had no clue. Dickon might be hale and hearty, enjoying the company of a Flemish maid with high hemlines and low morals, but he could just as easily lie beneath the waves, lost to the sea like the stillborn babe we had been forced to abandon.

Neither Isobel nor I knew when we were to sail for England. We had been informed it would be in February but tide after tide had turned while Queen Margaret waited, steadfastly refusing to give the word to depart. What information she was privy to, or what awaited us in England, she divulged not a word, leastways nothing to Mama, Isobel or me. News was in scarce supply for no direct messages came our way. It was said our father worked tirelessly for England's benefit, but he did not write so we knew naught of his actions, thoughts or health. Queen Margaret was oft locked away in discussions with her personal advisors or the occasional emissary from King Louis, as the web of intrigue between this deposed Queen of England, the current King of France, the exiled King of England and the Dukes of Brittany and Burgundy grew more complex than I could ever hope to understand. All I could comprehend was that my father risked everything, while the king he had deposed would shortly wage war to regain his crown. Betwixt and between sat Isobel, Mama and me, a man I despised but was bound to, and, of course, my beloved Dickon. There was naught to do but pray Our Father would guide us home, wherever that might be.

'A whisper is abound the queen delays because she has word Edward sails for England,' Isobel murmured as she searched through her coffer.

'Is it true?' As thoughts lingered upon Dickon, my fingers touched the silvered boar beneath my chemise. I sent a silent prayer to The Virgin my friend was still alive.

'I cannot tell.' My sister glanced at our sleeping mother before whispering, 'The queen's ladies merely say it will be when she chooses and not a moment before.'

'Then 'tis no news at all.' I turned away, clutching at the pin above my breast. I could not bear this ignorance about the fates of those I loved, but to sail and set foot upon England's shores would see those fates revealed – and perhaps that could prove too much.

As February turned to March, violent winds descended from all four corners of God's earth. The weather was too severe to be out of doors at any hour, let alone take to the seas, yet Queen Margaret's mind changed. Though the captains and their men argued the conditions were hardly the best for taking to sea, she insisted we must do so without delay. The men began to make ready our ships and as March turned to April, I knew the time for departure drew close. Barely a week later, I watched Mama and Isobel preparing to board their vessel. It was all I could do to stop myself screaming out to them, imploring that I be allowed to accompany their party and not the queen's.

But my place was beside my husband – duty and obedience above all else. Choking back tears, my throat on fire, I waved a kerchief, blowing kisses to my sister who responded in kind as she stepped aboard. Mama made no such gesture. Head bent low, she put all her effort into negotiating the gang-plank with no thought to spare for her disconsolate daughter left behind upon the quay.

240

Up until this day, there had been few truly dark moments in my short life. The night in January was one, Dickon's departure from Middleham another, but the day I watched my sister and mother sail out of the harbour was a day well-deserved of such description. Every facet of the weather reflected my mood exactly. From threatening skies and wild wind, to the tumultuous seas, I could not imagine a worse day to sail and prayed with all my might those I loved might prevail in such dangerous waters.

Nor did I escape the fearful conditions. The queen ordered her ship be made ready and we sailed upon the next tide – and directly into the storm. Our ship carried upon it the hopes and dreams of Lancaster, and a frightened young woman who thought each wind-battered day to be her last. The Lord above surely looked elsewhere, for a crossing that should take no more than a few days at most, took thrice as long and thrice again. Though I did not suffer the sickness affecting so many aboard, the ghosts of previous sailings were relentless in their haunting. Each time I closed my eyes, the pounding of cannon and cries of my sister in her travail flooded back to mind. I ate little and slept even less, fearful I should see the watery image of my love, confirming the awful suspicion Dickon had died upon the treacherous seas.

I lost count of the days before our battered craft at last made port. Exhausted, sickened and desperate to be upon firm ground, my mind was incapable of any rational thought. Tossed and buffeted by the weather, we had made poor progress, oft finding we must sail back before we could sail forth. I grew heartily sick of the rolling boat, but was not stricken with the sickness like the queen's ladies, their moaning and retching as constant as the pounding of the waves. Though I spent as much time above deck as I could, the weather was so rough, and the captain and crew were so concerned for their passengers, I was forced below. There, I sat in silence while Queen Margaret and Edward bemoaned the situation in such rapid French I could not keep up – as they knew full well. I would be lying if I said there was not a day when I wished The Lord to send a wave and take us all below. Though a grave sin to think such things, I knew our landing would be far worse than what had beset us at sea. What I did not know was how such misery would manifest itself.

As Easter Sunday dawned, it seemed the resurrection of Our Lord Jesus Christ brought respite for us all, as land was sighted. Though it took a good part of the day to negotiate the still-violent waters, we finally landed at Weymouth, travelling onto the abbey at Cerne in time to hear Compline.

Hungry and exhausted, I heard little of the Mass, my mind filled with thoughts of what our arrival would bring. As we left the abbey church, a tall man wrapped up in a fine cloak stood outside in the darkness. It was clear he had been waiting for some time. Bowing to Queen Margaret, he spoke low and urgently. As she heard his words, the queen faltered but the man grasped her elbow, pulling her upright. Almost carrying her across to the guest house, the man beckoned to the ladies and Edward to accompany the queen. I was ignored and left utterly alone in the centre of the courtyard. With no idea where to head, nor whom I should attend, I stayed quite still, lost and forlorn in the hope someone would guide me in the right direction.

'My Lady?'

A soft voice sounded behind. I turned to see one of the monks looking at me, a quizzical expression upon his face.

'You do not go with the queen?'

'I was not asked to accompany her.'

He gasped, clearly stunned by my words. 'Come. You cannot remain here, for the night is bitterly cold.'

Within moments I was shown into the abbot's lodgings and through to his private chamber. Abbot John Vanne was a frail, elderly man with a kind face. He did not rise as I entered, confined to his chair beside the fire because of a chest-cold that made his reddened nose appear twice its size. The brother accompanying me knelt down beside the old man, and whispered urgently. The abbot stared at the brother, barely acknowledging his words. The brother stood back, turning towards me as the old abbot nodded and beckoned me inside. After ensuring I was made comfortable in another chair close beside the fire, and served warmed, spiced wine, the abbot bade the hosteller return to his duties, reminding him the queen also needed refreshment.

'My dear child.' Abbot Vanne peered at me, his eyes rheumy in the firelight. 'Is it true the queen did not require you to attend her?'

'No, Father, she did not, leastways she did not think of me once she had spoken with her visitor.'

'I see.' Abbot Vanne stared thoughtfully into the flames. 'Then am I to presume you have received no news?'

I shook my head. 'I am desperate to learn if the other ships made port, especially the one carrying my mother and sister. Have you heard, Father?'

The abbot turned his gaze back towards the fire. He seemed strangely distant and the cold hand of fear

243

gripped my heart. Then he nodded. 'The Lord saw to it I also heard.'

Something was amiss and though I tried to suppress the sob, I failed utterly. 'Then they are gone, lost beneath the waves!'

Abbot Vanne started, clutching at the rug across his ancient knees. 'No one is lost beneath the waves, child, cease your tears, for Our Father in His Mercy has guided them home. Your mother and sister are safe, reaching these shores some days past.'

I clasped my hands together as if in prayer. The abbot nodded his approval, but in truth 'twas only now did I realise how cold I had become whilst in the yard. As the fire burned bright, slowly thawing my chilled limbs, I thought over the abbot's words. For one moment the world was right again and I sat, hands still clasped trying to find words of thanks for God. Then I glanced across to the old man. Struggling from his chair, the abbot teetered across the space between us whereupon he took my hand inside his own. As I stared down at the gnarled, spotted knuckles deformed by age and hard work, his voice cut through the air, soft and kind yet bearing words to change my world.

'Child, 'twas your father called unto The Lord. This morn, a great battle was fought at a place named Barnet, just north of the city of London. King Edward prevailed. The man you saw outside the church was Edmund, Duke of Somerset, come to tell the queen.'

I could not take this in, staring at the old man who swayed beside me as a coughing fit took him. Numbed by his words, I could only watch as the ancient abbot groped his way back to the chair, gasping for breath between the spasms. After a few moments, he breathed easier, dabbing at the corners of his mouth with a large linen kerchief.

'I shall pray for your father's soul.' He spoke softly as if fearful the cough would return. 'And when you are ready, a brother will show you to a private chapel where you may do so too.'

Though I murmured appreciation of his kindness, inside I was hollow. My Papa, my beloved, dearest father was no more. He had died pursuing a desperate, unholy cause and I would be lying if I did not admit I considered his actions and death utterly unnecessary. Questions beat against the sides of my mind – how did he die and was his body despoiled as are so many in battle? Where did he lie now, in a hastily-dug grave or cleaned and tenderly laid out in a place of God? Though no comfort to me at the time, I could only think how my father would have preferred such an end, for he was not a man who wished to die in his bed.

The abbot still watched my expression, waiting for what, I did not know. At last I looked up. 'My mother, the countess, does she know?'

He nodded. 'According to the Duke of Somerset she does, and has this very day fled to Beaulieu Abbey, seeking sanctuary there.'

Stunned by these tidings, I told myself this was nothing more than a dream, albeit a dark and terrible one. But no, as I looked upon his face, the gentle abbot's expression confirmed this was the truth. It was several moments before I could think straight. In silence, I sipped the fine wine and tried hard to make sense of it all. At first I thought Mama must have been so overcome with grief and quite out of her mind, she could do naught else. But darker thoughts soon crept into my mind. Most likely Mama had done the only thing she could to protect herself and her wealth. All women of noble birth had heard tales of unfortunate heiresses and wealthy widows stolen away to be bedded and wedded before their families, and oft the king, could prevent it. But my own mother? Yet as I thought upon it, she was an attractive, accomplished and high-born woman in her middling years, not some old hag without teeth in her head. And though it sounded a self-serving and impossibly selfish thing to do, the threat both to Mama and her wealth was real, one perhaps my parents had discussed at some length should the worst come to pass.

As I thought upon this, the practicalities of this matter became clearer. At best, my dear Papa might easily be attainted after his death, indeed, it was highly likely given the depth of his betrayals. Mama, Isobel and I could lose everything – our lands, titles and inheritance all taken by the king because of my father's treason. I knew my parents had fought hard and long to ensure the vast Beauchamp and Warwick inheritances remained with Mama after her niece's death so many years ago. Papa would have done what he could to ensure such hard-earned gains, however entitled, were not snatched away at the first opportunity should events go awry. Moreover, my mother was a shrewd woman, and though suffering under the strains of recent weeks, would not allow something as even devastating as my father's death to deprive her of her birth right. In the glow of firelight, I eventually came to an understanding for her flight into the abbey. Once there, she would have protection until such time as she could appeal directly to the king. Yet the child inside me felt cheated, and more pertinently, abandoned by her actions.

My hand flicked to my breastbone, searching almost desperately for the pin hidden beneath. In my mind, thoughts turned to the only man under the sun who might help me now. But I was in the presence of a man of the cloth, and indeed, The Lord our God. A married woman should not think about another. Ever. And though Dickon was always in my thoughts, consciously or otherwise, he too, might already have been called unto The Lord. Those I could turn to were few indeed.

'My sister?' I whispered. 'Is there news of her too?'

Abbot Vanne shook his head. 'Though she disembarked with your mother, she is not at Beaulieu.'

'No.' I remembered Alys Winterbourne. 'She will have gone home. No doubt her husband had men waiting to escort her.'

'No doubt,' the abbot agreed. 'But what shall be done with you, my Lady?'

'I must join the queen. She might have need of me after such news.'

Yet as I bid a goodnight to the kindly abbot, his eyes reflected the stark and dreadful truth; the queen did not want me. She had never wanted me and, now my father was dead, I held no value for her cause. She would want nothing more to do with me. Until word could be sent to Isobel, wherever she might be, perhaps I would fare better to seek sanctuary like Mama. Then I remembered. I had a husband, one who would expect me to be by his side, whether I was to his liking or not. Sanctuary was not an option.

Hours passed and still I did not see my husband or the queen. Neither sent for me, nor to the best of my knowledge did they enquire after my health or send condolences for the loss of my father nor, I subsequently discovered, my Uncle John. Both had died facing the king but deep down I suspected my uncle had been broken by this split between the Nevilles and the House of York, for there were whispers within the brotherhood of how my uncle had died wearing the colours of York beneath his armour. Such tragic waste could not be truly comprehended by a bereft girl, one who found it easier to shed tears for an uncle she saw infrequently, than a father she had loved dear.

Though residing in the guest house with the queen's party, I was still very much alone, save for the occasional passing word with the queen's ladies. They did not seek me out, nor enquire if I needed aught, kept busy attending their queen and if they thought of me at all, 'twas only because I happened to be right before their eyes and in their way. The abbot, understanding the situation far better than me, and knowing far more than I could hope to, had given discreet instruction I was to be taken care of. The monks ensured I was brought food, there was a fire lit in my chamber, I heard the Mass and took confession. Oft I would encounter a brother as I walked the cloisters and would subsequently find myself given a guided tour of the herb-gardens, infirmary and even the orchards. The brothers also arranged for me to light candles and pray for my father and uncle in the private chapel, just as the abbot had promised. Despite my misery and the deep hurt I felt at my father's unnecessary death, for these small mercies I was most grateful.

The queen shut herself away with her son and the duke. Though she left her chambers long enough to hear Mass, she neither looked at nor spoke to me. In her eyes I was no longer of use and therefore not worth wasting a moment upon. Such brief sightings gave no clue as to the discussions but, given the number of messengers arriving and leaving the abbey, it was clear the queen and her favoured lords and captains plotted the next move. Somewhere, far across the country perhaps, King Edward most likely did the same. The situation grew more intolerable with each passing hour. No one gave any hint of what might happen to us or where we might be bound next. I had become invisible, and if not for the kindness and generosity of the monks, I should have believed myself to be dead.

Summoned to the abbot's quarters once more, I was delighted to find he wished me to take a cup of wine with him. This was an honour indeed, and, though I suspected it was to discover more of my circumstance, I did not care. The simple act of conversing in company reminded me I still belonged to the world.

'I have word of your sister,' the abbot revealed, as we sat beside the fire once more. 'Would it please you to learn of her?'

I jumped at the chance, expressing my eagerness before recalling manners were everything. The abbot gave a smile, one an indulgent father might make to his child.

'She is well and content, I am told, reunited with her husband and nursing him back to health after injuries sustained during the fighting.'

I gasped. 'Is he sorely wounded?'

The abbot grimaced, clearly regretting his candour. 'I do not believe so.'

'Thanks be to God,' I breathed but there were still many unanswered questions and I seized this rare opportunity. 'Did His Grace, King Edward treat him kindly afterwards? For my sister's sake I pray he showed mercy.'

Abbot Vanne frowned. 'Surely you knew of the reunion?'

249

As I shook my head, the abbot's frown deepened. 'You know nothing? May The Lord forgive Her Grace, Queen Margaret, this lack of care. Sins of omission are still sins in The Lord's eyes!'

I gripped the arms of the great chair, unable to imagine what treachery was about to be revealed. Yet The Lord had a surprise for me too, though I had to wait for another of the abbot's coughing fits to subside before I discovered the joy of it.

'Upon the third day of this month, long before your ship reached these shores, the Duke of Clarence was reconciled with his brothers.'

'His brothers?'

'Indeed.' The abbot's tone reflected that of one speaking to a simpleton. 'Their Graces, King Edward, and the Duke of Gloucester, received their prodigal brother with open arms. I beg pardon if this is painful for you, child, but it seems the Duke of Clarence has been forgiven his . . . *indiscretions*, and is returned to the bosom of his family, fighting for the king at Barnet. His Grace has shown his worth in this matter, setting an example for us all.'

I did not hear the abbot's last words, nor did I care what he had said of George, or indeed my father. The fact he described Dickon as being with the king told me everything I needed to know. Oh, how my heart leapt, how my soul rejoiced. My dearest friend was still beside the king and most important of all, alive! All was not lost.

# Chapter Fifteen – Aftermath

## *May 1471*

The joy of this discovery, though more welcome than I could have imagined, was short-lived. I could say nothing, celebrate nothing, save silently thanking God for Dickon's deliverance. I was a wife and as such ought not to think of any other man apart from my husband, Edward, Prince of Wales; a youth who still refused to speak to me but who argued with his mother and the experienced Duke of Somerset over their situation.

Queen Margaret, so the abbot informed me, had counselled a return to France, from where she could reassess Lancastrian forces and plan a counter-attack once new leadership was established. The prince refused. Arrogant, impetuous and filled with his own self-importance, he insisted this was their one chance to defeat King Edward and the rewards made it worth the risk. It appeared the queen and her loyal duke agreed, for all too soon we departed the abbey.

Of course, none of this reached my ears first-hand. Still reliant upon the kindly abbot, I learned nothing until the day of our departure. Though I could not confirm it, I suspected if it were not for the abbot, no word of their departure would have reached me and I could well have been left behind. However, suspicions also abounded that the abbot had no desire to shelter this unwanted wife, and in doing so, risk incurring the displeasure of whoever won the battle-to-come.

Assembled in the abbey yard, we made final preparations. Abbot Vanne had risen from his sickbed to see off our party, and, though heavily supported by two of the monks, insisted on speaking to each one of us. Needless to say, I was the last.

'May The Lord watch over you, child.' His voice was barely audible and I feared he would collapse at any moment.

'Thank you for the kindness shown to a lost and bereaved girl.' Though my own situation was grave indeed, as I looked upon the old man before me, I saw the true frailty of humankind. The gentle abbot was not long for this world. 'May The Lord watch over you also, Father.'

He forced a smile. 'Ah, Lady Anne, do not concern yourself with an old man nearing the end of his life. Save your prayers for those who will need them in the days to come.'

Abbot Vanne's words chilled me to the bone for he was right insofar as death and bloodshed lay ahead. Only Our Father knew to whom those deaths might belong and so I must save my prayers, for there were a great many in need not least of whom was my dearest friend.

And so we set out to join the army raised by the Duke of Somerset and Earl of Devon. Confined to a stuffy carriage with the queen's ladies, I discovered from their incessant chatter we were making for the west country, hoping to join forces with Lancastrians in Wales. Terrified to the point of paralysis, I could take interest in nothing other than to note each step we took westward put me farther away from Isobel and Dickon, and closer to a day when my husband might claim me again.

The queen's army made good time, headed by the Duke of Somerset and, much to my surprise, Papa's deputy at Calais, Lord Wenlock. Not that either of these men spoke a word to me. Stuck inside the carriage, I was once again all but invisible. I did catch Lord Wenlock's eye as we halted at our lodgings in the ancient town of Bath, but he made no effort to speak and, indeed, seemed to deliberately avoid me after that. Perhaps the death of my father was too painful for him, perhaps the blatant changing of sides made the situation too awkward for either of us to make satisfactory conversation. Either way, I was still alone, shunned by the queen and ignored by her son, and though one or two of her ladies might have sympathised with my plight, they made no effort to acknowledge me in any way.

The queen and her army turned briefly toward the city of Bristol where they somehow procured guns, reinforcements and money. Only by keeping my ears open did I learn of this, for not one spoke a word to me in all that time. Each night, I cried myself to sleep. I was utterly alone at this time, fearful of a great many things, and with no one but The Lord to share my burdens with.

Upon the third day of May, we approached the city of Gloucester. The mere name of the place was enough to make my heart skip a beat, though I knew full well my beloved duke would not be there – he rode beside the king and at the head of an army pursuing us at this very moment. Lost in my musings, and the scare-mongering tales of King Edward's battle-field prowess and merciless manner, I took little notice of our progress or whereabouts. Only as confusion reigned up ahead, did I sit up and take note of what was occurring outside of the cramped carriage. As I listened to the shouts of men and orders of their sergeants, it became apparent King Edward knew Queen Margaret made for Gloucester – and the only crossing of the River Severn hereabouts.  Ever the game-player, the wily king had sent word to the Governor to bar the city's gates and man its defences.  We arrived to find our way barred and the surrounding roads deserted.  'Twas as though all were prepared for our arrival and waited to see what awfulness might follow.  A ghostly sight, I could scarcely take in the view of a city so quiet it might have been deserted.

The queen's fury was unleashed as she comprehended what had occurred and, while screaming orders to her commanders, she became a wild woman, making outlandish and dangerous demands even I knew could not possibly be fulfilled.  But the Governor of Gloucester, Sir Richard Beauchamp, was under orders from the king, and it appeared, was not a man for turning.  Not intimidated by the appearance of Margaret's army, he refused to capitulate.  With Edward's army swiftly closing in behind us, there was no time to storm the city and, as the queen screamed at her commanders, for once I was thankful to be invisible.

The commanders decided to march on towards Tewkesbury in the hope they might cross at the next bridge, a short way upriver at a place named Upton.  Already weary, for the sun beat down upon us all that day, it seemed we must swelter a little longer.  Inside the carriage we endured more discomfort, though nearly fainting from the heat.  Though the ladies complained unceasingly, I said nothing, knowing the queen rode ahead with her men and would take no pity upon us, just as she had no pity for her forces trudging ahead under the merciless sun.

Arriving at Tewkesbury that evening, we halted at last.  Though blessed with a fine abbey, I saw nothing of the town's beauty nor received any welcome from

254

the abbot. With the Lancastrian army spread across a wide field before the abbey, and with a great number of the soldiers wandering through the town, nowhere was safe for us to walk and stretch our cramped limbs. Along with the queen, we were despatched to a well-built and ancient farmhouse nearby; one, Somerset protested, he could defend should needs be. Queen Margaret disagreed loudly, her heavily-accented words carrying far on the still evening air, but the duke was insistent, and so into the hall we did go. 'Twas pointless perhaps, for none of us slept that night. Knowing everything depended upon what occurred at dawn, the queen spent the night upon her knees, praying out loud. Though her women bemoaned the lack of comfort, I took much solace in the homely place and, like the queen, spent the night upon my knees. My coffer and belongings were lost amongst the baggage train of the army but I cared not for the lack of comfort. The only things I truly cared about had been kept upon my person since the day I had boarded the ship. The silvered boar and pilgrim badge were both stitched into my clothing and so secreted about my person, while the frail rose still lay safely within my psalter. Placing one hand upon the boar, the other reached into the leather bag suspended from my belt to touch the small book therein. Though a grave sin, my thoughts were consumed with Dickon. The morn would decide his fate – along with that of hundreds of men. Indeed, the morn would decide my fate too, but, at that moment, I cared only to pray for those I loved.

If she saw my devotions, the queen gave no indication, but then she was much occupied, praying for the life of her only and most-beloved son and perhaps also her feeble husband, still in the city of London. I, on the other hand, prayed for the king and his retinue, my sister's husband and a certain dark-haired duke fighting for the king. 'Twas wrong that my thoughts were not with my husband, and I begged The Lord's forgiveness for so grave a transgression, but my heart was heavy. Death would claim many men upon the morn, whichever side they fought for and I did not dare dwell upon who might or might not survive.

We were roused long before the dawn. Demanding his queen take refuge farther away, Somerset knew the battle would most likely take place within sight of the abbey and would not have the queen so close. Queen Margaret once again protested at such an outrageous suggestion, proclaiming as her only son was in the field, she would stand and watch him fight. But the gruff Somerset stood his ground and, as the eastern horizon began to show signs of grey, we were put astride horses and led away from the small town to seek shelter, before the fighting commenced.

A few short miles from Tewkesbury, the queen, her ladies and I sought refuge in a church. 'Twas a poor place and certainly not one that could offer us sanctuary should the day go ill, but the men clearly hoped this small place would be safe enough till commanders brought news of the battle. While the other women wailed and moaned, I knelt before the altar as if in prayer. Though I tried with all my might to speak to The Lord above, in truth my mind was empty. Whatever the outcome of this day, I was still in great peril. If the queen's forces won, I was a wife unwanted by my husband, for if victorious, Prince Edward would not want me by his side. If, however, the king prevailed,

256

then I was nothing more than a Lancastrian widow –
and an unwanted reminder of my father's turn of coat.

Closing my eyes, I prayed for The Lord's will to
be done. I prayed for mercy and forgiveness, especially
for those souls who would be taken during these
desperate hours. Throughout my devotions, noise
disturbed the peace of the chapel, carried along on the
morning breeze, though we were many miles from the
battlefield. Like a distant rumble of thunder on a
summer's eve, we all knew 'twas the sound of death
and destruction. What we did not know was to whom
those deaths belonged. My mind was filled with images
too dreadful to describe, and, though they were terrible
indeed, a small part of me knew I could not begin to
imagine the worst of battle.

Kneeling before an altar once more, my hands
were clasped so tightly I feared the blood might cease
to flow. Once more, I tried to pray but my mind was
blank and, though I needed comfort, the words of Our
Father did not come easily. The last few days had been
dreadful indeed, and though I now enjoyed the relative
comfort of a priory guest-house in the city of Coventry,
my mind was in turmoil as I feared for the future. In the
aftermath of battle, the reality of my situation was a
stark and uncaring friend as I waited to hear of my fate.

A voice whispered behind me, and I started in
surprise, halting in my devotions. It sounded familiar -
yet it could not be. The Lord above could not have
heard my prayers, for I had sinned so gravely of late I
did not deserve such bounteous gifts.

The voice called once more and, though I
yearned with all my battered heart to turn and see who

disturbed the peace of this chapel, I dared not. Certain my troubled mind played tricks, I stubbornly remained, convinced only the emptiness of the nave lay behind, lit by flickering candles. I could not have risen from the altar rail even had I wished it, for the ghosts of my past haunted relentlessly.

Yet 'twas no ghost, for the owner of the voice stepped forwards, the click of his heels upon the tiles causing me to tremble all the more. As he knelt beside me at the rail, no breath entered or left my poor body, for I was utterly numbed. But as his deep tones gave thanks to The Lord, I thought I had died and gone to heaven. Tears fell from my eyes, splashing upon my clenched hands and, though trying to join in the responses I knew so well, my mouth was dry and throat tight.

Our prayers finished at last, a hand reached across to cover mine. In that moment I knew whatever followed I would bear willingly, for no ghost or apparition had such warmth of touch, no adversary of mine showed such gentleness.

'Anne,' the voice said again. 'Forgive this intrusion but the king insisted I speak with you.'

This time, I turned to look at the man. His gaze was already fixed upon me and, as our eyes met, he smiled. 'Twas a bright, beautiful smile, and one I had thought never to look upon again in this life.

Still unable to speak, I nodded to acknowledge this handsome messenger, this duke of the realm, and my oldest, dearest, most beloved friend. Grateful for the kindness of King Edward, whatever news was to be bestowed I would receive gracefully, for not only had the king deigned to send Dickon to me, The Lord our God had seen fit to spare him.

He rose, and though there was barely strength enough in my limbs to move, I took his hand, refusing to fret over what words might come from his mouth. This single moment was enough, and, if I was to spend the rest of my days inside a convent paying for the sins of my father, this gesture of kindness would remain with me.

We left the chapel and walked in silence towards the gardens. Still holding my hand, Dickon led me along the gravel paths, winding our way through fragrant herbs and leafy vegetables until he found a place that pleased him. In a far corner lay a wooden bench, around and above it a neatly-woven willow arbour, not dissimilar to the arbour of roses we had once sat beneath in London. Dickon indicated I should make myself comfortable and 'twas only then I noticed a tray with wine jug and cups already waiting.

'Is this your doing?' I gasped.

The lop-sided grin flashed briefly. 'I thought you might enjoy the gardens on such a beautiful morning.'

'Twas all I could do to keep the tears from spilling down my cheeks at this thoughtfulness. Lips clamped together lest I cry out to The Lord above for this great mercy, I held my cup out for Dickon to fill. We sat for a moment or two, supping fine wine while the warmth of a late spring day thawed our minds and bodies.

'Your lodgings are comfortable?' Dickon had finished his wine and was already pouring another cup. 'And you have all you need?'

It took a moment for me to understand the confident nineteen-year-old man beside me was not confident at all, and had resorted to innocuous enquiries to fill the void. He was clearly struggling to begin what was about to be a difficult conversation.

Such discomfort was contagious and though dreading what he might have to say, I somehow forced a smile.

'After the past weeks, I have all the comfort I could wish for and more besides, and heartily thank Our Father and, of course, the king, for such grace.'

The dark blue eyes flicked over my face as though I had revealed far more than expected. Only as I thought upon those words did I realise they could be interpreted quite differently. Yet in truth I was not unduly concerned nor ashamed, I did indeed have all the comfort I could wish for, The Lord had taken the soul of my husband, Prince Edward, into his keeping instead of this dear, dear man.

I thought back to the morning of the battle. The king's men had found us at the church, no doubt directed by those who had nothing left to fight for. Bursting inside with swords drawn while we cowered in fear, they yelled out for the queen. Announcing in loud tones how her son had died upon the field, they spared no thought for a mother's grief. She crumpled to the floor as the men thought it fit to describe the last breaths of her prince, repeating the lurid details till the queen's ladies and the impoverished priest whose poor church this was, cried out for mercy. I might not have liked Prince Edward, might not have wanted to be his wife, might not have mourned for the loss of a husband, but in those pitiless and cruel moments, my heart went out to the defeated queen and heart-broken mother. Soon after, we were taken away, the queen escorted separately, while her ladies and I once again took to a carriage. Long was the journey to Coventry, for though I knew the king was victorious, naught was said of my dear friend. Our guards were too busy describing how the king had broken down the door to the abbey to seek out the men claiming sanctuary within, and especially the Duke of Somerset. Needless to say, he was executed soon after. The women around me had decried the ungodly behaviour towards men seeking sanctuary in a house of The Lord but, in truth, I was not so surprised by King Edward's actions. I had observed the ruthless streak beneath the conviviality, and knew, as a player, he would do what was needed to end the game once and for all.

'Anne?' Dickon's voice rang with concern. 'You are still mourning and I ought to have known better. Come, let me escort you back to the guest-house.'

'No!' The last place I wished to be was imprisoned in that room. 'Ah, Dickon, I have no desire to be alone and after all this time, 'tis such delight to have a friend's company.'

Dickon's expression eased and he sat back upon the bench. That small action told me much, told me how he had feared I might find his attentions inappropriate. I did not. Of all things under God's sun, the company of this man was all I needed.

'Might I ask your favour, Anne?' he was still lying back upon the bench, looking comfortable and relaxed.

'Of course.' I smiled at my friend.

'I am a man grown and, as such, have proved myself both in battle and before the king. He has rewarded me most generously for such loyalty and endeavours, so let us dispense with this nursery reminder of Dickon and use my given name henceforth.'

A perfectly reasonable request for he was indeed a man, proven, bloodied and even injured in battle. Thankfully, the wounds Dickon had sustained at Barnet were not severe, healing well enough for him to fight at Tewkesbury and I was gladdened not to have learned of the injuries before seeing him with my own eyes. This duke, this most loyal of brothers, had been at the side of the king throughout all that had beset the throne of late, and had been well-rewarded for his labours. But man or not, I was being chided for misdemeanours as though little more than child, despite the veil of widowhood. Dickon was behaving like my father, not my friend.

I stared at the ground, misery seeping through every pore. Though kind and gentle, it was clear my friend saw me as little more than a childhood companion remembered with fondness rather than with any deeper regard. Perhaps I should ask what most worried me, and forget childish nonsense of holding his regard.

'What is to be done with me?' My voice cracked as I spoke, wanting only to have this over and done, the worst of it out in the open.

Richard reached for my hand but halted, clearly thinking better of such an intimate gesture. After his pointed words, I was thankful for the respite.

'You are to be sent somewhere safe. Edward still has much to do before the country is truly peaceful and does not wish you to be in any danger.'

Certainly, if the threats to Mama's person were as real as she suspected, then I also needed to be kept safe. But perhaps more pertinently, whispers abounded of risings both in the northern counties as well as in Kent. The king would need his most trustworthy and capable commanders to quell such disturbances. No doubt this capable duke was about to depart, while an inconvenient widow was quietly disposed of.

Fear loomed large in my mind but somehow I formed the dreaded words. 'Am I to be sent to a convent, forced to take vows?'

'By the Rood, no!' Richard jumped back, his brow creasing as he looked at me. 'What makes you think such harsh treatment might be necessary?'

I swallowed. 'Because I am the widow of one rebellious Lancastrian and daughter of another. The king does not need to be reminded of that each time he sees my face.'

Twisting his hands together as if searching for the right words, Richard stared across the garden. I held my breath, waiting for the axe to fall.

'The king is aware of your enduring loyalty to the House of York and understands you had no choice in matters.'

'His Grace is most kind, but it changes nothing.' Desperate words leapt from my mouth. 'If I learned one thing from Papa, 'tis to anticipate what might later become a problem, and that is my situation exactly. Should I expect marriage to a foreign noble, be shipped off to distant countries and out of sight? Or perhaps be wedded to an obscure and impoverished knight, lost in the farthest reaches of the realm where I shall never again attend the court?'

Slowly Richard shifted around to face me. Taking my hand in his, he paused, once more choosing his words with care. I stared at our fingers, intertwined as though we were lovers about to be wed. That was my heart's desire but it could not be – all because of my father's treachery.

'He will insist you wed again, Anne,' Richard's voice was quiet, leaving me in dread of the words to follow. 'Be in no doubt about that, for you are a great heiress and cannot be disposed of lightly nor hidden away in the manner you fear.'

Of course. The fear overwhelming me these last weeks had wiped much from my mind and in truth, I

263

had thought little about this matter, living day-to-day only. I was a daughter of a noble house, and the offspring of a family with vast wealth, no doubt coveted by many. Isobel was already wed, which gave George much to be thankful for, but even with my mother still in sanctuary and complicating the situation further, there was no doubt as to my worth in terms of marriage.

'Then what is to be done?'

'Once the appropriate mourning has been observed, the king will find you a suitable husband for certes.'

Fear once again clutched at my heart, rendering me silent.

'Your sister married a duke,' he murmured. 'Perhaps you wish for such a match also?'

I sighed. 'I doubt the king would allow it, not after my father's actions.'

'He might be persuaded.'

I could not believe my ears. 'Who . . . who would persuade him?'

Richard gave a bright smile. 'I shall. The king will need to approve any match I suggest, but after the loyalty I have shown and service done him these past months, he might be more amenable than previously.'

Though the king had wed where he would, 'twas not for others to do so, especially not when it involved great swathes of land and a traitorous family name. Moreover, to have the man I loved choose my husband seemed the greatest punishment of all, one I would struggle to bear. Seeing these fears upon my face, Richard tightened his clasp upon my hand. Given my feelings for this man and questions over my future, I would have preferred he did not touch me so, but that would seem churlish after his kindness. As the silence lengthened between us, I tried not to think upon the warmth of his skin against mine.

'Anne,' he said at last. 'If the king were to agree, would it please you to wed this duke?'

My mouth dropped open. 'Do I understand you wish to marry *me*?'

He smiled. 'Indeed I do. Throughout these years and despite all that has occurred, you have never been far from my thoughts.'

This was too much. As the gardens swirled before my eyes, disbelief whirled around in my mind, I thought how The Lord must have a strange sense of amusement. One moment all is lost, then in a heartbeat, the world is right once more. But my world was not right – it was tarnished.

'You must wed a maiden, one worthy of your status.'

Richard shrugged. 'Perhaps, but if there are no maidens of good birth to be found then I must look elsewhere, perhaps to those who have been widowed but are still suitable brides. And so I look towards you, my dearest friend, but if such thoughts are painful for you, I will say no more.'

'Dickon,' I protested, before remembering his terse request. 'Richard, my reputation has been damaged, made worthless by events . . .'

I could not finish. Despite the treachery within my family, there lay a matter far more serious. How could I tell the man I loved that I was not whole and the bride he deserved? He would surely despise me, for I despised myself.

'I told you once before how I did not consider you responsible for what has occurred.' Richard shifted round on the seat to face me. 'That still holds true, Anne, especially since I have spoken with Isobel.'

The conversation was deteriorating with each passing moment. I could not imagine what my dear sister might have revealed. Fearful, I said nothing, freeing my hands from his and clasping them together in the vain hope God would look kindly upon this poor lamb.

Richard watched every action I made. 'We spoke of a great many things, but of your father especially. Though I asked nothing directly, she told me of that despicable marriage and how you fought it until you could do so no longer. After hearing of such wilfulness, I dared to hope the match was not to your liking.'

I did not want to taint this special morning with thoughts of Prince Edward, yet I could not hold back the tears. The hurts and frustrations of the past months escaped and once again, as tears streamed down my cheeks, I was weak before my love when I desired only to be strong.

'Ah, sweet girl,' he murmured. 'Do not distress yourself. I know how difficult it must have been to gainsay a man as determined as your father. For even attempting such a thing, you are far braver than I am.'

'But I am spoiled!' I sobbed, uncaring if this behaviour demeaned me. 'I am not a worthy bride for any man, leastways you, my beloved Dickon.'

He did not react to the misuse of his name, or to the revelation I cared so deeply for him. Instead, he took my poor face between his hands and leaned in close. 'Anne. I could say much about your position and fortune, protesting it mattered not at all, but that is not the truth of the matter, for marriage would not be a possibility if you were of lesser birth, nor indeed, without wealth. But I shall also say, long have I feared you would be treated ill. When your father betrayed my brother he also betrayed you, sweet girl, and I have not been able to clear my mind of treachery towards an innocent. You deserved far better than you received.'

'Such kindness,' I sobbed, unable to halt my tears. 'But as a daughter I was always to wed where my father decided. Your sisters expected no less from your father and would not have dared question him as I did Papa, nor been so disrespectful and disobedient.'

Richard wiped away my tears, his touch gentleness itself. 'We were taught it would be so, and, from the day I left Middleham, I expected to receive news of your betrothal sooner or later. As time passed and naught was heard, I held to hope we might rekindle our friendship one day. But when Edward refused George to wed your sister, that hope shrivelled away.'

Hope had dwindled for me at that time also, but I said nothing, waiting to hear what else my beloved had to impart on this vital matter.

'As your father's schemes deepened, and he secured your sister's marriage by less honest means, my fears for your situation worsened. Though I tried, 'twas impossible to put you from my mind, imagining how unsettled and fearful you must have been. It seemed I was right to fear, especially when events led to your family's flight across the sea. Despite problems enough of my own during those desperate months in Burgundy, you crept into my dreams, and would not be banished no matter what I did to distract myself.' He did not look up, did not acknowledge me as though he wished to conceal something. 'Whilst in exile, Edward and I talked more intimately than ever before and once, when the wine was upon him, he asked who I would care to marry should we ever reclaim England. Spurred on by those dreams, I gave him your name and much to my surprise, he behaved as though he had known it all along.'

267

'In truth?' This was music to my ears, balm for my broken and battered heart.

My beloved smiled, causing my heart to pound so fiercely it must have been loud enough to hear. 'Ah, Anne, the worst day of my life was when I heard you had been wed to that Lancastrian whelp. When Edward relayed the unhappy news, he was kind, so kind I knew he had seen how much your plight had affected me. His gentle manner also revealed he had discovered more of your character and, though he spoke naught of it, I sensed you had pleased him in some way.'

It was my turn to smile. ''Twas because he learned how I kept your silvered boar secured beneath my gown. Except upon one particular day, when it became loose as we danced. Edward found it at his feet, returning it to me before the eyes of my father but utterly unbeknown to him.'

Richard laughed. 'So I have heard, for Edward relished that small discovery, and mentioned something of it to me, though he did not say where exactly it was kept!'

'He was so kind to me, even though 'twas an unhappy time for us all.' I thought back upon my dance with the king.

'I still cannot believe you have it after all these years.' Richard's eyebrows raised, revealing his surprise.

'Of course I have it, 'twas a gift from my dearest friend, and one I treasure.'

Though he smiled, neither of us spoke for some time, surrounded by bees and birds and the beauty of a late spring day. Sat side-by-side, 'twas as though we had become strangers in these last moments. I forced myself not to register any disappointment for I had already received gifts far beyond my worth.

'Tell me, Anne,' Richard blurted out. 'Was I wrong to hold to the hope we might become more than old friends?'

Richard's expression had changed, becoming unexpectedly serious. His eyes were ablaze and I had to look away from their intensity, lest it unnerve me too much to speak. 'To . . . to become your wife is more than I have dared hope for. Such thoughts kept me going during the darkest of days, but I must say again how I am not worthy of you.'

'You were wed before God, Anne, and no doubt did your duty as was expected. I have no qualms with that, so be assured what came before matters not to me.'

'Are you certain?' I could barely form the words, so fiercely did my heart pound.

'Once I learned you were discovered in the church with Queen Margaret, and were whole and unharmed, I have never been more certain.'

'Whole I am not, oft times I feared madness would take me, not least after that despicable wedding took place . . .' I stopped, unable to discuss the matter any longer. My beloved wanted to keep me safe, to make me his wife and yet I could not shake the feeling his mind could still be changed.

Richard repeated his assurances as if privy to my thoughts and fears. 'Anne, hear what I am saying; the past matters not, indeed, some things are best left there. What matters now is the future.'

Such profound words and so easily spoken, but with long-reaching consequences. For a brief moment I wondered if he too, had something in his past he preferred I did not know about. I pushed the thought away. He was a man, and as such, would do what he would. 'Twas not my place to question him. I must think of myself.

'And . . . and what might that future hold from this moment on?' I stuttered. 'I am still in mourning and unable to wed anyone for some time to come.'

Richard gave a wry smile. 'This is what I came here to tell you before we became somewhat distracted. The king has ordered you be sent to Isobel and placed in her care.'

'Thanks be to God!' I clasped my hands. This was not an outcome I had expected, but a most welcome one, nonetheless.

'And you shall stay with her until, God willing, the day we wed.' He kissed the tip of my nose. 'If marriage to this particular duke pleases you enough, my Lady.'

All was now right in the world – at long, long last. Oh, I was blessed indeed; for The Lord in His Mercy had seen such gifts placed at my feet, I scarcely believed this bereaved and abandoned girl might ever receive such generosity.

But I must answer my beloved duke, lest he be gone from me. I smoothed my skirts and looked him in the eye, for unless I did so, it would not seem real.

'Richard, my dearest and oldest friend. Know that to become your wife would please me more than anything since the day you left Middleham Castle.'

# Chapter Sixteen – Out of Reach

*The City of London – Summer 1471*

'So this is where you sit each day.' Isobel's voice carried through the walled herb-garden behind the kitchen-range.

'It is, sister.'

'But there are far more comfortable seats in the courtyard . . .'

'There may be,' I replied, closing the book sent by my beloved Richard. 'But 'tis so lovely here, and no-one disturbs my peace.'

In the days since my arrival into the Clarence household, I had escaped into this small private space at every available moment. Not just because I could, but also because the past weeks had given me a deeper appreciation for the beauty of God's creations. Moreover, since George was absent most of the time, there was no-one to say I could not do so whenever I pleased. My brother-in-law spent much time at court, enjoying his new-found favour with King Edward and forwarding his career in whatever ways he could. In truth, I was not as unhappy as my sister over this, for we were able to pass many contented and uninterrupted hours in each other's company and revelled in our re-acquaintance. As I turned fifteen years of age, my birthday had, for once, been a joyous and pleasant occasion as I relished both company and freedom. The only thing lacking was the company of my beloved but he was needed beside the king – or so I was informed.

'This garden is charming,' Isobel looked around with the wonderment of a child. 'Perhaps I might join you for a moment.'

Clearly my sister did not venture this side of the great house often. Surprised Isobel had even considered sitting, I watched as she clutched at her fine silken skirts, holding them away from the rough planks of the seat. Such splinters were merciless upon fine cloth, as I had discovered to my cost but a few days past. But for now, I smiled. My sister, the grand duchess, did not relish being forced to use such an ill-made seat and I appreciated the effort made in joining me here.

'The sun is strong today, Anne.' Isobel busied herself rearranging my silk veil. 'Take care not to colour your complexion overmuch.'

A pale complexion was a desirable attribute for any high-born woman, for it displayed to all she did not need to toil out of doors, and, combined with soft manicured hands, proclaimed she was a lady in charge of a household and not one who must work for her keep.

Though acknowledging my sister's concern I did not fret overly for my complexion. I adored sitting in the gardens; bright flowers, birdsong and the heady fragrance of herbs was the only company I wanted if Richard could not be with me.

'Is George returned from court?' I enquired, needing only word of my beloved to complete this perfect world.

'He is.' Isobel sighed and for the first time since my arrival, I sensed all was not well in the Clarence household.

Recovered both in body and mind from the stillbirth, my sister was a perfect picture of grace and dignity befitting her position of duchess and sister-in-law to the king. The duke and duchess made a handsome couple, yet there was still an air of melancholy about Isobel at times, leaving me to wonder whether she had not quite banished the ghosts of the ship - or if something else caused her to fret.

'That letter in your hand,' I changed the conversation. 'Is it from George?'

Isobel frowned and for a moment I feared it was the wrong thing to say but she lifted the letter up to show beneath lay another, the seal still unbroken.

'For you,' she said. 'From Mama.'

'Another letter? Have you not informed her how George has spoken to the king about her situation?'

Isobel nodded. 'More times than I can count – but still her letters arrive. This does not recommend her to my husband or the king. She has not been idle, writing to every lady of good birth she can, including the king's sisters and his wife's mother.'

Considering Papa had executed two of the queen's menfolk without justified reason or fair trial, it seemed wholly inappropriate Mama should pen words to the Wydville matriarch. But perhaps from the cloister, things appeared differently.

'This behaviour does not help Mama's cause,' Isobel continued. 'For her industry has brought Edward's close attention upon her worth and situation – but not in the way she hoped.'

'Will he force her to wed, perhaps to a man he thinks deserving of such vast estates?' I could not keep my concerns inside, though Isobel scowled at such forthright speech.

'I know not,' she sighed. 'Though I suspect that was why Mama did what she did after Papa's death at Barnet. As a wealthy widow she would be seen as fair game – perhaps even from the king himself, for oft times she makes veiled comments how His Grace poses the greatest threat to her position. Her letters suggest she wants to be allowed to leave sanctuary of her own free will, to be safe wherever she wishes to go and, moreover, keep control of her fortune.'

'And is she not able to leave of her own will?' I had taken little interest in Mama's situation, still unable to see past her abandonment of me.

'From her letters, it almost sounds as though she is being kept there nowadays,' Isobel dropped her voice to little more than a whisper. 'And that the king is somehow involved.'

"Tis so unfair!' I cried.

Isobel took my hand. 'Nothing in this life is fair, sister, as you have already learned.'

'What can we do?'

'Very little.' Isobel pulled flower-heads from the bush of thyme beside her, collecting the tiny purple blooms in her lap. 'For her actions draw more than a king's interest.'

With such cryptic words, I could not help but be drawn in. 'Whatever do you mean?'

'As conversations have ensued around our father's estates and what shall be done with them, George is taking more than a healthy interest. He talks of little else, proclaiming as you are now in his care, he is entitled to both our shares of the inheritance.'

'But Mama is alive and well . . .'

Isobel shifted around on the seat, the little flowers scattering at her feet. 'She is indeed but it seems, as no-one answers her pleas for assistance, rumours abound Edward and his brothers conspire to steal everything from her.'

'Richard would never do such a thing!'

'Wouldn't he?' My sister's eyes looked deep into mine. 'Greed is one of the Seven Deadly Sins. Such sins we are taught to avoid but we are all mortal – and imperfect. Your duke might outwardly appear to be beyond reproach, Anne, but he is still a man and, as Our Father has taught us, inevitably given to temptation. Certainly, if it were not for Mama's fortune, he would have no interest in marrying you.'

Though Richard had spoken of the exact same matter, I could not believe he would do something so calculating and callous as to see my mother's worth be taken from her while she lived. Yet I knew only too well how wealth and power could corrupt a good man. Why should Richard be any different? In truth, I had no answers, only more questions.

'George says we may leave the city soon,' Isobel mused, plucking at the marjoram and rolling its green leaves between her fingers to release the sharp, heady scent. 'He does not wish to endure this incessant summer heat, and suggests we head west to avoid any plague that might follow.'

This was nothing unusual, our family had oft left a city residence before the height of the summer, but I was keen to remain in London, for a certain duke occupied my thoughts these days. Seated in my usual spot in the herb-garden, I sought to escape thoughts of Mama and the difficulties her wealth were causing us all after receiving yet another of her letters.

'I pray we do not leave too soon,' I murmured. ''Tis most comfortable and I have no yearning to be elsewhere.'

Isobel glared. 'Dickon is kept busy by the king. He has no time to attend you, Anne, if that is what your meaning beneath such innocent words.'

I sighed at her refusal to use his full name. 'But he promised to visit.'

My sister stared out into the day. 'Men are fickle creatures and oft selfish, especially those without wives to consider. I doubt he has given you a second thought since departing Coventry.'

Nothing could be further from the truth. My beloved had sworn to apply to the king for my hand in marriage and I had no reason to doubt that he, of all men upon this earth, would not keep his word.

'He sent this book for my entertainment and amusement but two days' ago. That hardly suggests he has forgotten me,' I snapped.

'What else has he sent you?' Isobel's manner had changed with the speed of spring weather. From convivial and relaxed, she was much discomforted, as though I had committed a grievous sin.

'A letter or two, and this book,' I replied, regretting revealing so much. 'That is all. In truth, I am disappointed with so little.'

'When did they arrive, and which of my household servants brought them to you?' My sister had transformed into a demon, her voice demanding, features brooding and dark. Something was gravely amiss.

'I . . . do not recall, but 'twas only a couple of brief notes enquiring after my health and to advise he was sending this . . .' Though unnerved by Isobel's swiftly-changing mood, I sought to placate her by offering out the slim volume.

'Get rid of it!' she hissed, pushing the book away. 'Burn or destroy it, but do not let George see you with this in your hands at any time!'

'Isobel, what is all this about? I do not understand.'

She gave a great sigh. 'In truth, neither do I but my husband has something upon his mind. It keeps him awake at night and distracts him every moment of the day. I have no doubt it is to do with you.'

'But I thought it pleased you both to think the king might agree we should wed.' sobel's tidings had shocked me. I clutched the volume to my chest. 'Indeed, you seemed delighted my future might be so secured.'

Isobel stared at her hands. 'That was before.'

'Before what?'

'Before George considered what would happen to our inheritance.'

It was as though I had been slapped across the cheek. 'The inheritance is to be divided between us. We have always known that.'

'In a perfect world, yes.' Isobel still did not look at me. 'As I am wed to George, he knows my share will be within his reach, but yours. . .'

'Will be in the hands of my husband — whosoever he might be.'

'Exactly.'

I drew a loud breath. 'But nothing is settled, the king still might not agree to marriage with Richard, especially given the extent of the lands and monies.'

Isobel scowled as she heard me use my beloved's full name. 'Edward may not want you to wed Dickon, but I have suspicions George does not want you to wed anyone.'

Once again, I took a sharp intake of breath. 'Though a widow, I am only fifteen years old. Surely he does not intend me to remain so for the rest of my days?'

Isobel finally looked up. In that single heartbeat, before she said a word, her eyes revealed the truth of this matter. 'As my younger sister, you have been discharged into my care. In truth, that means George's care, for he is my husband and all I have is his.'

'And so all I have will be his also.' 'Twas as though cold water poured down the back of my neck. I had lurched from one desperate situation right into another – except this one was swathed in a cloak of familial care and concern.

I whirled about, clasping hold of my sister's hands. 'For the love of The Virgin, can you not speak with him, help George to understand how much this marriage means to me? I did not agree to wed Richard because I have to, I agreed because I want to!'

Wrapping her arms about my waist, Isobel held me tight. 'I know, sweet sister, and after what has befallen you, I wish with all my heart this marriage comes to pass, but my husband is distracted beyond reason by our inheritance. At times, I am convinced he is going mad, for he barely resembles the man I wed in Calais, and is quite changed from the amiable boy we knew in childhood.'

George had never been amiable, but his character was not a subject for discussion at this time.

'What should I do, Isobel?'

'I do not know, Anne. Each time George returns from court, his fury deepens. He refuses to discuss the matter with me, saying I am prejudiced by it. Of course I am prejudiced, sister, for we are blood. Moreover, I have never begrudged you the share of our family's wealth and I never will, especially after all we have endured for them. My husband, however, thinks quite differently, and I fear there is nothing I can do to gainsay him. I have no proof but suspect he has instructed the servants that Dickon is to be refused entry should he arrive at the house. If that is the case, then any letters

278

you send or receive will surely be opened. Bear that in mind, sister, for though I shall do what I can, this duchess has little power to alter her husband's mind – or orders.'

The threat of a convent drew closer. Though Richard had assured me 'twas not to be my fate, perhaps others saw it as the perfect solution.

'Am I to be put away?' I whispered, clutching at Isobel.

'Not if I have anything to do with it.' She still held me close. 'But do not antagonise George when he returns. Do not mention marriage and most assuredly do not mention Dickon.'

'Your colour is much improved this day, Anne. Good food, a comfortable bed and new gowns have brought you back to life, I see.'

George stood so close, his figure shadowed the embroidery frame in my hand. I had retreated to the solar to enjoy an afternoon's stitching in the plentiful light of the great window but while lost in my thoughts, he had appeared from nowhere – as always.

'I am grateful for your kindness and continued generosity.' Inclining my head at his words, it was all I could do to keep the disdain from my voice. As George was now my guardian and, it appeared my gaoler, I had little choice but to remember my manners.

'And so you should be, little sister.' He grinned, sweeping the chestnut-coloured fringe from his brow. 'For if I had not offered you a home, the cloisters would provide your only freedom now.'

I swallowed. 'I doubt King Edward would have seen me walled up inside a convent; he will wed me off as soon as he is able.'

'No doubt he will,' George's tone became icy as his gaze fixed upon my face. 'But as you do not have to attend to such matters yet awhile, sweet sister, enjoy your freedom.'

Though I acknowledged his words with a smile, I said nothing else to my brother-in-law. His demeanour grew more menacing each time we met and, as upon this day, I dreaded the occasions he crept up upon me in a quiet corner of the house.

'It must have been distressing for you,' he said, fingering the corner of my embroidery.

I looked up, moving the frame to the side and out of his reach. 'What must?'

'Waking each morn and not knowing where your loyalties lay.'

Of all people on God's green earth, George dared to ask that particular question. I wanted to laugh in his face, remind him 'twas not I who sold out a brother for hopes of a crown. But I dared not. Instead, I gave another sweet smile, inclining my head in a lady-like manner.

"Twas indeed distressing, dear brother, as I am sure your good wife has told you. But The Lord saw to it I found strength to endure the worst and so here I am, safely returned to my family.'

George scowled. 'Indeed, here you are.'

The expression upon his face grew darker the more he watched, so I bowed my head and concentrated hard upon my stitches. The silence grew heavy yet I stitched on, giving what I hoped was a good impression of being unaware, as George stood above me, menacingly close.

280

"'Tis said such hardships can affect a person's mind.' He leaned down, daring to lift my veil to look upon my expression. 'And though they may seem well enough in body, an incurable melancholy soon takes over. I have heard such poor souls lose their senses, oft believing their lives are in peril.'

My head shot up at this comment and, though George tried hard not to react, a sly smile curved one corner of his mouth. 'Moreover, such sorry cases oft think 'tis their own families who wish them dead, seeing daggers in the night, poison at every mealtime and dangers everywhere they go. Soon they trust no-one. 'Tis a sorry state to find oneself in.'

I did not speak, did not react. I simply watched. In turn, George leant upon the wall, waiting, I suspected, for a chink to reveal itself in my armour. Cornered in the window-seat, the golden sun of late summer beaming through the glass, the world stood still as we stared at each other. At last, I looked down upon my stitching once more, knowing as a woman 'twas not my place to challenge any man, and for certes not a duke of the realm. Yet I swore to The Lord above, if I had been the boy my parents had so desired, I would have risen to whatever challenge he threw my way.

'Anne,' George's voice was low, but menacing. 'I am glad you have come to us.'

I forced another smile. 'I too am glad, brother; glad to be with my sister and glad the comfort of your home is at my disposal. I have nothing but gratitude for your generosity.'

It cost me dear to keep the tone of my voice amiable and calm but this falsehood was entirely necessary, for the light in George's eyes was not one sprung of the kindness he would have me suppose. He joined me on the window-seat, leaning back to open up the window.

'Perhaps you wish to remain here after your mourning is passed.' He gazed out into the day.

'If the king does not demand I attend the court, then I shall most surely do so.'

I drew some comfort from that open window, knowing should he do anything to hurt or compromise my person, one loud call would be heard by those outside. At least, I prayed that might be so.

George gave out a high, shrill laugh. 'Ah, sweet Annie, if you return to the court my dearest brother, the king, will have you wed within a heartbeat. And we cannot have that.'

'Whyever not?' It was necessary to play the innocent and, though increasingly fearful of this man, I must be brave and use whatever weapons lay at my disposal.

'You know why, Annie.'

I tilted my chin and looked directly at him. 'My Lord of Clarence, if I should wed a man known to you, the matter of my mother's inheritance might be reconciled, but if I wed an unknown, one outside of your influence, then you might lose all you had hoped to gain.'

Grabbing my arm, he pulled me forwards with such force I feared I should tumble from the seat. Suspended in his grasp, I could do nothing but look into those cold eyes.

'I will not lose,' he hissed, spittle spraying across my cheek. 'For I will not see you wed – to *any* man!'

As the words ceased, 'twas as though George knew he had stepped over a line he should not have. He released my arm, almost carefully guiding me back into the seat. Picking up my sewing, he placed it upon the cushion with care, as though it might have been damaged in the fall. His aggressiveness had vanished as swiftly as it had appeared, and he had resumed the demeanour of a courtly knight once more. We sat in silence for some moments before he rose and stepped away, striding out towards the doorway before turning to speak.

'Forgive my lack of manners, sister, I ought not to have behaved so. Yet this matter boils my blood like no other, for I will not see my wife cheated out of what is due to her.'

The inheritance was mine just as much as it was Isobel's, even without the fact Mama was still alive. George knew all this and more, but his venomous words implied he considered Richard's desire to wed me unfair and unnecessary. I did not understand why the king simply did not insist upon a fair divide – unless the king had ideas of his own over Mama's wealth.

'Let us pray a solution will be found,' my voice cracked and faltered as I spoke. 'For this delicate matter ought not to tear a family apart.'

He paused, thinking over my words. 'If you truly wish to keep a family together, then perhaps you should curtail any thoughts of marriage – especially marriage to my *brother*!'

'No!' the words shot from my mouth as I rose to my feet. 'You cannot stop us, you will *not*!'

Though far across the room, I felt the chill of George's gaze. Then, with determination that struck fear in my heart, he strode back to my side. I braced, but he did not touch me this time, leaning in so close, I could scarcely breathe.

'You shall do as bid, sister, for as your nearest male relative you are in my charge and as such must obey my will. If I choose to forbid this marriage, then I shall do so without question from you!'

Utterly in his shadow, I ought to have cowed in fear. But I did not, for Richard's words were still fresh in my mind, giving me the strength to face this adversary.

'I may be your charge but I am not your servant,' I spat. 'Do not speak to me thus. As for forbidding the marriage, if the king forbids we wed, then I shall accept it – but only if His Grace deigns to tell me to my face!'

Where I found such courage, I had not the faintest idea. I had tried and failed to convince my beloved father not to wed me, now I was forced to convince another to allow me to wed. The world was a cruel and contrary place at times.

For a heartbeat, George's expression changed to one of puzzlement. Then a wide grin crossed his face.

'Little Annie, be thankful you are not my servant, or else I should have you beaten for such insolence.'

'I will not give up Richard,' I braved another stab at this new and unexpected enemy. 'And shall pray for divine intervention if you and brothers are unable to come to an accord.'

Striding back towards the door, he gave a great laugh as though an idea had formed in his mind. 'Perhaps a little less-than-divine intervention might persuade you to heed my wishes, sweet sister.'

# Chapter Seventeen – Desperate Deeds

*The City of London – late summer 1471*

Each night before bed, indeed, before prayers, I spent much time combing out my hair. Seated at the dressing-table, oft already in my nightgown, I sent away the maid kindly provided by my sister, and enjoyed a few moments' solitude attending to my tresses. This had been my routine since a young girl, though Mama had oft needed to remind me to perform this task. Yet now, I found comfort in the rhythmic strokes of the comb, and satisfaction in the shining nut-brown tresses draped over my shoulders. I was no beauty like Isobel but, after attending to my hair in this manner each night, I held up the hand-mirror and looked upon my face, flushing as I imagined Richard awaiting me in our marriage bed.

Even through the unhappy weeks both before and after my marriage to Prince Edward, I had shamefully refused to desist in such imaginings. They had given me strength and, at times, hope, but moreover, they allowed me to cope with the dreadful reality of my life, for in my mind lay the world as I wished it. A world where my dearest friend was with me in every sense.

Despite enduring weeks of George's threats and persistent demands I give up all thought of marrying Richard, I never wavered for a moment. Richard had said he wished it to happen, had remembered me through the darkest times of his life. I had to trust he meant each word, had to trust he would find a way to reach me and take me as his wife.

'My Lady?'

An unfamiliar voice called through the outer chamber. My hand stilled, the comb falling onto the table as I recalled the door was not yet barred. Another of my nightly routines was to secure my chamber door before I settled into bed. Though the maids had objected loudly to such unladylike behaviour, I sensed Isobel's approval, for she demanded they cease complaining and do as bidden. Though we said naught of it between us, perhaps her gentle words in Amboise echoed through her mind also. I did not fear George's attentions in that way, for he seemed content enough with sister, but I feared a visitation in the dead of night, dragging me from bed and into the convent I so dreaded.

'Come,' I called, recalling it was one of Isobel's newer maids.

I slid the silvered boar beneath a kerchief upon the table. It was ready to fix inside my nightgown once all preparations for bed were complete, but I would wait till I discovered what the maid wanted first, for no-one, not even my sister knew of the pin's existence. Though her footsteps still sounded in the outer chamber, she cried out once more.

'You must come, Lady Anne, this instant!'

'Whatever is the matter?' I turned to see a face I barely recognized, even though she wore the colours of my sister's house.

The maid held out my dressing-gown and slippers, clearly scooped up as she had passed my bed. 'Your sister, my Lady, she is ailing.'

'But she was well enough just a short while ago, what can have happened?'

Isobel and I had parted company in the passageway between our chambers. George was at court and we had sat up late talking of the old days when life was good, and Papa still in the king's favour. In truth, 'twas a pleasant evening and I was saddened to think it had ended badly.

The maid assisted as I put on the dressing-gown. 'Her Grace returned downstairs recalling she had a message to relay but tripped upon a step. She is hurt and calling for you.'

'Who attends her?' I demanded, hopping to put on the slippers as we made for the outer door.

'The Steward and one of her ladies,' the maid said, holding the door open for me. 'But make haste for they are concerned over her injuries. . .'

Down we stepped and down again. Through passage and chamber and passage again.

'Where on earth was my sister bound?' I could not fathom why Isobel should need to travel so far across the house at this time of night.

'In here, my Lady, make haste now.' The maid stopped, her hand upon a door latch.

Something deep within me cried out to turn. It cried out to flee from this place but I did not listen. Filled with concern for Isobel, I walked into that room as a fly into a spider's web.

The room was bare, except for one poor chair and a three-legged stool. Upon the stool sat a candle, spitting out a feeble light.

'Sit, my lady,' the maid said. 'Someone will join you shortly.'

Before I had a chance to object, the door closed and I heard the distinctive sound of a key turning in the lock. There was no point beating my fists upon the door, no point screaming and shouting about unfair imprisonment; I knew in a heartbeat this entrapment had been meticulously planned for the sole purpose of prompting me to reconsider marriage to Richard. And so, wrapping the dressing-gown tighter around my body, I sat upon the chair and gathered my thoughts, waiting for my gaoler to return.

I did not have to wait long. Soon after, the door opened just enough to allow a shadowy figure to slip inside.

'Lady Anne.' Another unfamiliar voice came through the darkness, a man this time. Whoever stood before me, 'twas not George, nor was it any of the household servants I had encountered thus far. 'Do as I ask and all will be well. Your life is in no danger if you follow my instructions exactly.'

'How can all be well?' I retorted. 'I am alone in a locked chamber with a man I do not know and you ask me to believe my life is not in danger? Explain yourself, Sir!'

'You are to dress, my Lady. Here are the clothes you are to put on. If you need assistance with anything, knock upon the door and the maid will come.'

With that, he rapped to be allowed out. Though I wanted to run as I had once run as a child, the woman inside me knew I should not make the door before he slipped back through. Even if I had, there was not the strength in this petite form to gainsay the strength of a man, as I had already learned to my cost.

Rather than give way to maudlin thoughts, I attended to the clothing. On top of the pile lay a gown made from roughly-woven wool-cloth of an inferior quality and indistinguishable dark colour. Though stitched together well enough, I had only seen its like once before, many years ago in Middleham, when Fridha and I had first met. My friend of those days had been clad in a garment of similarly plain cloth and design. Beneath this uninviting gown lay a linen underdress and chemise, which to my delight, such as it was at that moment, proved to be my own. These garments I had sent to be laundered only the day before. Beneath, lay a pair of worn leather shoes, a pair of hand-knitted stockings that I knew simply by looking would irritate my legs, and a large, white linen kerchief.

In the feeble light I dressed, folding my nightgown and dressing-gown with great care upon the chair, placing the silk slippers atop. Only as I looked down upon that small pile, did I recall the silvered boar upon my dressing-table. Never had it been so far from my person since the day it was gifted and, if my suspicions were correct, I might not set eyes upon it again in this life. Hiccupping back a sob, I prayed The Lord would look down upon his lamb and see she was in dire need. Never before, in all the travails that beset my family, did I need a friend more than at this moment.

'Are you ready, my Lady?' the young maid had come back into the chamber without my realising.

'I am.' I stood tall, for, whatever my fate, I would not have them say I wept and wailed of it.

'Your kerchief.' The girl held out the linen piece.

All that remained to me in this bare and empty chamber was pride, so I tilted my chin and asked for the assistance I sorely needed. 'I know not how to tie this, would you be so kind as to show me?'

Wherever I was bound, whatever awaited me, I would be alone and so must fend for myself. Though the women-servants of all the fine houses I had ever lived in wore their hair covered in this manner, I had not seen how it was done. I knew the intricacies of a headdress and veil well enough, but not this. I must learn – and swiftly too.

'My Lady, your hair . . .'

The girl held out several leather strips towards me. With only my fingers, I swiftly combed through my tresses and plaited them as neatly as could be managed given the circumstances. The maid used some sort of wooden pins to fasten the plaits to the top of my head. She then secured the long edge of the kerchief around my head, tying it fast before twisting it to cover all my hair and part of my forehead. The loose end of the left-over twist was wound over and over to give the appearance of a plait, before being tucked tightly within to keep the entire headdress secure. After she had done, I felt around this strange garment, trying to sense exactly what went where, for I knew this would be a task I must perform for myself come morn.

The nameless maid stepped back to admire her work. She nodded before reaching into the shadows to bestow another gift. 'Twas a rough bag fashioned from a type of sackcloth, coarse but not as coarse as some I had seen. Inside lay a woollen cloak, cut from cloth similar in colour and quality to my drab gown. Beneath that, lay another pair of the dreadful stockings and an old, broken comb that appeared to be made of wood. But that was all. No psalter, no rosary. No other clothing.

'I must have more than this.' I held out the sack but the young maid had vanished.

'That is all she was instructed to provide,' came the man's voice from without. 'You have sufficient for your needs, Lady Anne. If all goes well, you will not be absent for long.'

Courage surged up within. 'Pray, where am I bound?'

'Nowhere you have been before, and God and your stubbornness willing, nowhere you will be again.'

Even though he stood outside the chamber, even though the room and passage were ill-lit, I knew he smiled. I knew he was enjoying this humiliation of a helpless and friendless widow, and I prayed one day I would be able to forgive his impudence.

'Wherever I am bound, I would have my rosary and psalter,' I demanded. 'You cannot deny me access to The Lord.'

The man laughed. 'Ah, little lady, he said you would make some such demand of me. Alas, you may not have either, for they would give you away in a heartbeat. However . . .'

He stepped into the small room and into its tiny pool of light. The man's hair and beard hinted of lighter, sandy tones, his eyes of a blue, yet I could not discern exactly what shade. It made no matter, for I would recall that lean, hungry look again should I need to, recall also the chill of his tone and arrogant manner.

'Fear not, you shall not be denied The Lord, for that is a grave sin itself – or so I am told.' He held something out. 'A rosary more befitting of your new situation.'

I snatched the rosary from him. Though I could not see it well, it, too, was of inferior quality. Carved from wood, the beads had not been fashioned by an especially skilled craftsman. Irregular in shape, they had seen many years' service to God but perhaps this was exactly what an impoverished widow might own.

'Come,' he said, extending an arm to escort me through the door. If the situation had not been so grave, I would have laughed, for though icy cold, his manners were delightful.

In the passageway, the mystery man still held one arm out to guide me. 'This way, my Lady, and, before it crosses your mind, calling out will avail you naught. The duke has sent for Lady Isobel, she makes her way upriver to Westminster as we speak. The household servants are all abed and, no doubt sound asleep, after the strong ale they were served this evening.'

'My sister travels at this time of night?' I gasped.

He smiled. 'The duke missed his wife, so summoned her to him. As any good woman ought, she obeyed his command.'

So I was utterly alone. Exactly as George had planned. He was at court, before eyes and ears and witnesses of the highest reputation. His wife, too, would attest how she said goodnight to her sister before being summoned away to attend her husband. Days could easily pass before my absence was noticed by anyone other than those paid to stay quiet. There was naught to be done but follow instruction.

Head held high, I stepped out beside my gaoler, destined I knew not where. Yet dressed in this manner, most likely a kitchen or scullery awaited. I sent a silent prayer to Our Lady of Heaven that she would watch over me from this night forth, and that somehow, my beloved Richard might learn I was gone.

I also prayed for an angel to deliver me from this evil.

The story of Anne will continue in:

# The Maid's

# Tale

# Book Two

# Johanne

# Author's Note

Anne Neville is often portrayed - both in fiction and non-fiction - as the ailing, bereft, and unwilling queen of Richard III. I too, have previously portrayed her as a mortally ill and grieving queen in my tale of fifteenth century England: *The King's Niece* and *The King's Wife*. Anne might well have fitted this description, especially after their only child, Edward, died in 1484, leaving the couple childless, the throne without an heir, and her health in rapid decline. But long before she became queen, indeed, before she married and became Duchess of Gloucester, the young Anne's life was the stuff of fiction.

Born in 1456, Anne arrived into a world of privilege and comfort. The younger daughter of the Earl and Countess of Warwick, Anne's bloodline could be traced back to King Edward III, through both her parents' ancestries. She was descended from two of King Edward's sons: Edmund Langley on her mother's side and John of Gaunt on her father's. Between, lay a vast array of noble names and titles, though it must be pointed out that the majority of noble families of England in the fifteenth century were related to some degree and, therefore, could also trace their heritage back to King Edward III. The family had its roots in pre-conquest aristocracy of Anglo-Saxon England, although the Norman name of Neville was not adopted until the twelfth century, when Robert, grandson of the curiously-named Dolfin, and a descendant of the Saxon Earl of Northumbria, Gospatric, married a Neville heiress and took her family name. The Neville line is believed to descend from a landless knight, Gilbert de Neuville (literally — Newtown), from Normandy, who accompanied William the Conqueror to England in 1066.

By the fourteenth century, the family were an established power in the north of England, the Neville family's principal seat being in Staindrop, County Durham, and their principle residence being Raby Castle. They went on to serve in wars against Scotland and during the Hundred Years' war with France, significantly increasing their house's standing. Anne's great-grandfather, Ralph Neville, was the 1$^{st}$ Earl of Westmorland, and supporter of his brother-in-law, Henry Bolingbroke, later King Henry IV. The earl was well-rewarded for his support. Ralph married twice. First to Margaret Stafford, with whom he had eight children and, later, to Joan Beaufort, daughter of John of Gaunt and his mistress, Katherine Swynford. Ralph and Joan had nine sons and five daughters, including Anne's grandfather, the Earl of Salisbury. With so many children to provide for, it was a matter of necessity to find spouses that would benefit the family, bringing lands and titles upon marriage. The eldest son of Ralph, Richard Neville, Anne's grandfather, married an heiress and held his Earldom of Salisbury in his wife's right. Later, Anne's father, another Richard Neville, the Earl of Warwick, was also married to an heiress and held the Warwick title in right of his wife, Anne Beauchamp. To demonstrate the complexity of extended family relationships at this time, Salisbury was also the elder brother of Cecily Neville, wife to Richard, Duke of York, and mother to King Edward IV, George, Duke of Clarence, and Richard, Duke of Gloucester, later King Richard III.

As a daughter of such a noble house, Anne's future would be mapped out for her: to be educated as befitting her position and to marry and bear children, hopefully one of which would be the required male-heir. She would be married to a man of rank and good birth, one who had been chosen for her. Most young couples had no say in their choice of spouse, with parents and often the king deciding, sometimes when the couple were small children, even infants. Marriage was an important business, not just a way to produce legitimate children. It was also used to improve and secure the family fortune, and as a way of securing settlements. Land agreements, trade agreements, peace treaties and any number of other arrangements were secured by a marriage throughout most social classes, but especially within the nobility. It is hardly surprising that chaos and disillusion cut a swathe through the noble families of England after Edward IV's irregular wedding to Elizabeth Woodville, the widowed daughter of a squire.

Anne's betrothal to Edward, Prince of Wales, seems to have been a deal-maker for her father, a card played when negotiating with the wily King Louis of France to support his cause. There is nothing to suggest Warwick had designs upon marrying his daughter to the prince at an earlier time, certainly his plans seemed to follow the line of replacing King Edward IV with his younger brother, and Warwick's son-in-law, George, Duke of Clarence. It can only be presumed that as time went by, the young duke did not show the promise Warwick had hoped and so he chose a different angle from which to aim at the throne of England.

To write about the young Anne Neville, is inevitably to write about her father, the Earl of Warwick. The two are inseparable, not because Anne exuded any influence upon her father's career and decisions, but because his actions had a direct – and at times, adverse – affect upon his daughter's life. Warwick is an elusive man, no letters or books or contemporary portraits have survived, and so we must view him through eyes of his contemporaries. This undoubtedly gives us a diluted impression of the man. That he was rich and influential is not in question. Nor is the fact he enjoyed wielding great power and, for the most part, wielded it well. The questions arise when we try to understand why he made some of the decisions he did. For many years he was Captain of Calais and an admiral, had fought and earned a reputation as accomplished soldier and seaman, supported and fought for the House of York, lost his father and brother at the Battle of Wakefield, and helped set the Yorkist king, Edward IV, upon the throne of England. Why he subsequently set off on such a controversial journey to thwart the young king he had fought so hard for has been debated by historian for years. Perhaps Warwick resented King Edward's lowly and rather unusual choice of wife, especially after he had worked hard towards arranging a marriage with French nobility and, in doing so, cultivated not only diplomatic ties with France, but a friendship of sorts with King Louis, The Spider King. Perhaps Warwick's resentment originated closer to home; seeing the privileges bestowed upon a family (the Woodville family – or Wydville to use an earlier spelling) who had bettered themselves at the expense of the older, more established families of the land, became more than he could stand. Or perhaps, Richard Neville saw his power ebbing away as the king grew in confidence, rewarding the queen's father and brothers with positions beside the throne, as well as marrying off the heirs and heiresses of the land to his wife's numerous siblings. Whatever his reasons, resentment ate away at Warwick, pushing him to take greater risks and more unusual decisions to keep hold of power as time went by. This

297

obduracy resulted in his death in 1471, while facing in battle the man he had set upon the throne. The earl's desire to see his family upon the throne came to fruition some years later when his youngest daughter was crowned as Richard III's queen, though the Neville family never regained the power and influence once wielded by Warwick's hand.

The conversations and inferences of the story are all mine, but wherever possible I have tried to keep to the timeline of events during Anne's younger years as close to actual events as I can. However, it has also been necessary to be selective with many of these events. This period in English history was a time of complex political turmoil, in England as well as in France, Burgundy, and Brittany. As a child and, moreover, as a girl, Anne would not have been privy to her father's movements during many of these events and certainly not aware of the reasons behind his decisions. No child is ever fully aware of their parents' thoughts, and I have tried to reflect this, though some detail of wider events has been needed to keep the reader informed.

With the exception of the seamstress's assistant, Fridha, Anne's friend at Middleham Castle, all the characters I have written about actually lived. Eagle-eyed readers will note Fridha has also appeared in my other novels of this time. Alys Winterbourne is a name of my invention, but a lady of similar bravery and determination was reputedly sent by King Edward IV, sailing across the Channel to reach Isobel Neville. It is possible her messages had some influence on the reuniting of George, Duke of Clarence with his brother, the king. Though her true identity is unknown, there are several suggestions as to who this mysterious lady really was.

Isobel Neville, or the Duchess of Clarence as she was at the time, is recorded as having given birth aboard ship in the waters before Calais, and under fire from cannon after fleeing England, as I have described. The child did not survive and Isobel was lucky to do so. There is some dispute as to whether she was delivered of a stillborn son or daughter, and so I have chosen to be deliberately contrary over the sex of the child, especially as it suits the countess's counter-argument with her husband.

The tale young Anne hears as they sail the River Thames under London Bridge, is also true and recorded in a number of chronicles, including that of the famous John Stow. In 1428, John Mowbray, the 2nd Duke of Norfolk, leapt onto the starlings (wide supports built into the river bed) of London Bridge as his boat was dashed to pieces. He and a few others were then rescued by ropes lowered from buildings on the bridge above. 'Shooting the Bridge' was a dangerous undertaking for many centuries, and countless lives were lost over time as Watermen failed to negotiate the treacherous waters between the starlings. Interestingly, John Mowbray's wife was Katherine Neville, daughter of Ralph Neville, 1st Earl of Westmorland, and Anne Neville's great-aunt.

The finely-painted playing cards I depict both Anne and Isobel admiring are real and still exist, and are kept in the Metropolitan Museum, New York. Though not owned by the Neville family, the cards are mid-fifteenth century in origin, so contemporary with this period. They can be viewed online and are stunning in their colour and detail.

The jewel I describe Anne sewing into her mother's cloak is deliberately intended to be The Middleham Jewel. Though no-one is certain who owned this magnificent piece, unearthed near Middleham Castle in 1985, the Countess of Warwick is one possible contender. I enjoyed imagining how it might have become lost so many centuries ago. There is plenty of information about the jewel available online, while the actual item is displayed in the Yorkshire Museum, York, England.

John Vanne was elected abbot of Cerne Abbey in 1458, dying at some point during the tumultuous year of 1471. Other than his name, position, and the fact he died in that year, little is known of him. Because of this, I felt at liberty to portray him as an old man, at the end of his days, and kind to Anne, at a time when she must have felt alone and frightened.

The letters written by Anne's mother, Countess Ann, when in sanctuary in Beaulieu Abbey, are also documented. Only one of these letters is known to survive; addressed to the House of Commons. The letter is detailed in a fascinating book (by another fascinating woman, Mary Anne Everett Green; Letters of Royal and Illustrious Ladies of Great Britain, from the commencement of the Twelfth Century to the close of the reign of Queen Mary, first published in 1846). Though the letter is written with all due reverence, Countess Ann implies she is at great risk and, by her own admittance, states she has written to the queen, the king's mother, the king's eldest daughter, the king's sisters, the queen's mother and other noble ladies of the realm. She assures the king of her continued loyalty, requesting she be allowed to keep her property and administer it as she would. In the letter, she hints of 'sinister information', but says no more. Does she know something is afoot, does the king know something? We can only speculate, but Countess Ann was certainly concerned her sanctuary had been turned into imprisonment, and feared that it could be violated at any time, removing her with force. Sadly, this was not unusual behaviour with regard to heiresses. The king was already married, so could not take the countess's wealth by forcing her to marry him, but what he later did to the countess (and noted in the next book) is a dark stain upon King Edward's character, revealing how ruthless he could be when he chose, but also how vulnerable were women of wealth when they had no male relatives to speak up for them or, as in this case, when those relatives-by-marriage were already preoccupied fighting over the lady's property.

One issue when writing of medieval England is the endless repetition of names. This lack of originality is not the historical fiction-writer's friend, and there are simply too many named Edward, Richard and Anne living at this time (along with Elizabeth, Katherine and Margaret, to name a few). I have, wherever possible, tried to make clear who is who as the story progresses. One particular issue in this story is that three of the women have the name Ann. For simplicity's sake, I have kept the 'e' on Anne Neville's name as she is the main character, dropping it from those of her mother and cousin.

Many historians are of the opinion the marriage between Anne Neville and Richard, Duke of Gloucester, was not a love-match, especially as Anne was probably the best choice of bride for Richard at the time. As I have noted in the story, Richard would not have considered marrying Anne if not for her wealth and status. Yet it is hard not to believe the arrangement might have pleased them both. The romantic in me wants to believe how, after years of turmoil and uncertainty, both welcomed marriage to someone familiar, someone who understood the trials the other

301

had faced during their formative years. Certainly, there was no scandal attached to Richard, or illegitimate children born after he married Anne, suggesting, if nothing else, he was faithful to his wife.

Having accompanied the young Anne along this turbulent journey, I have grown inordinately fond of her. It is easy to view the difficulties she faced as simply 'par for the course' for a medieval woman, but I have often had to remind myself that Anne was only in her early teens when experiencing her most traumatic and difficult times. Social pressures aside, most of today's teenagers have little of this nature to negotiate as they grow up, apart from paying attention to their education, exam revision and parental nagging to spend less time on whatever device they are almost-permanently attached to. Medieval attitudes and expectations were very different to those of today, even those of children, and so it is almost impossible for us to see into the medieval mind, much less understand it. We cannot comprehend the apparent detachment with which children were married off to unknown partners (and often sent far away into their spouses' households to grow up), at ages that might horrify us today. Nor do we have any way of knowing what psychological effects the events she endured might have had upon Anne, but being forced to flee from the life she had known, marry a complete stranger she had been taught to despise, and to lose both her parents (albeit in different circumstances) must have affected her deeply, all before she reached the age of fifteen.

After the Battle of Tewkesbury, when the Lancastrian threat was finally defeated, Anne might have hoped for a quieter life. Though sent into her sister's care, Anne still had one more adventure – or perhaps *misadventure* – to endure before her life settled for a few years. What happens to Anne in the weeks after disappearing from the Duke of Clarence's household, is the subject of my next book: The Maid's Tale, Part Two – Johanne.

# About the Author

British born and bred, as a young girl I loved the comfort of being immersed in a good book and surrounded by characters I knew as well as any friend. I wanted very much to write and though I began to do so, life often got in the way. Only after a life-changing move did I earnestly put pen to paper and begin noting down the scenes running through my head as I went about my day.

I especially enjoy musing about the impossible becoming the possible, where incredible events happen to ordinary people. History often encompasses both these aspects and my deepest interest lies in the later Fifteenth Century, especially King Richard III and anything connected with The House of York. I have been a member of the Richard III Society for more than twenty years and my interest in this intriguing man has not waned over the years. After moving overseas, I was delighted to find a society close to my new home and am actively involved with all they do.

I am also fascinated with the Dark Ages and the early Saxon Kingdoms of England. The dark and distant history of such turbulent times is not only fascinating but holds a wealth of riches for the fiction writer.

Now living in New Zealand's lower North Island with my family, I write every minute of the day when not needed elsewhere. When not writing or being needed, I can be found tending to my very own lemon tree in readiness for the gin.

Made in the USA
Charleston, SC
14 December 2016